DEPLORABLE TRAGEDY:

A FAMILY'S MYSTERY ANSWERED

Phyllis —
Hope you like it —
thanks, Rick

DEPLORABLE TRAGEDY:

A FAMILY'S MYSTERY ANSWERED

Alix Crawford Carney

ISBN 978-1-7355513-0-2

To Anna, for without her, our family would not exist.

OH! YE TONGUES THAT GATHER AND SPREAD THE VENOM OF SUSPICION, THAT KINDLE AND FAN THE FLAMES OF JEALOUSY, THAT ENOENDER THE SPIRIT OF MARTIAL DISCORD, BE YE NOW SATISFIED AND SILENT IN THE PRESENCE OF THE WRECK YE HAVE DONE SO MUCH TO CREATE!

E H— April 29, 1898—Pascagoula, Mississippi

"Sometimes the unrelenting but unspoken pressure of community, family, and circumstance can wear like carborundum until there is nothing left. Things unravel."

Unknown

Contents

1—MITCHELL—1886

"So, Hazen, today's the day," said Charles at the breakfast table, looking up briefly from the *Bangor Daily Whig and Courier*, the only newspaper allowed in the house. "I hope you'll be happy," he grumbled. "At a school, teaching the future men of the state of Maine."

"I hope so too, Charles," replied Mitchell, ignoring the sarcasm and the deliberate choice to use Hazen, his detested first name. He was reminded once again of how easily Charles had supplanted his father, Watson Plummer. Mitchell was thirteen when his father, the president of Bangor Savings Bank, had suffered a mortal heart attack as he was addressing the board of directors. Charles Pond Wiggin was next in line as the head of the bank and, as it turned out, as his mother's next husband. It was a seamless transition. Except in looks, Charles was a duplicate of his father, including how he treated Mitchell.

Hazen Mitchell Plummer was the youngest of the three Plummer sons. He had just graduated from Gorham State Teachers College outside of Portland, Maine, and today, September 5, he was to start his life as a teacher at Lincoln Academy, a boys' boarding school located in Newcastle.

Charles continued. "I'm still not sure why you went into teaching. If you had chosen a regular college, like your brothers, you could have had a position waiting for you at the bank. Though, considering your grades, Gorham probably was the best choice." He gave a small chuckle. "Well I guess we do all need teachers, don't we? Considering what I had to go through to get you into Gorham, you've surprised us all."

Abruptly, he ended his end of any conversation to lean into his just served breakfast of eggs (fried, soft and runny) bacon, potatoes and thick toast, heavily buttered with preserves.

Mitchell nodded. "Yes Charles, we do at that. And thanks to Gorham, I feel well prepared to start at Lincoln." Unsaid was his longing to get away from his family and the family business of banking. He had deliberately chosen (not settled for, as Charles insinuated) a teachers' college. Not so much because of a yearning to teach, though, he did think it would suit him. But because Gorham offered him direct entry into a different career.

Charles was right about his below average grades in prep school, but college had served Mitchell well. Perhaps it was the milieu, or maturity or the difference between a teacher and a professor but he thrived. Especially in his last year when he proved adept at student teaching which resulted in his hiring by Lincoln Academy. He enjoyed the setting of academia and the peacefulness and beauty of a campus; the structure and the sense of fellowship all enticed him. Sometimes in daydreams, he saw himself, older, having advanced to dean, strolling his campus, wearing a tweed jacket and smoking a pipe, chatting with his students and his faculty.

His mother, Alice, rustled into the dining room, the maid silently following with her cup of coffee. "Mitchell, darling. Are you all packed and ready? James will have the carriage out front by ten to drop you off at the station. He can't wait to see you off as he must get back to take me to the garden club. I had so wanted to ride with you on the train and see you settled into your rooms, but Charles said no," Alice said, glancing at her husband with some distaste.

3

"It's all right, Mother. I'll be fine. I am twenty after all."

Charles nearly choked. "Good Lord, Alice. He's right. You can't mollycoddle him forever. And think how it would look, your son—a Plummer, no less—arriving for his first job with his mother along to tuck him in. It would be grist for the gossip mill for sure. Newcastle is practically next door."

Charles stared hard at Mitchell. "I hope you know what you're doing, son. I really do. Whatever you do, remember your place. You are a Plummer, as your mother reminds me so frequently. The third and youngest son from a well-known banking family, one which I have been happy to join—a very, successful banking family as you well know. It is important to uphold that image, Hazen. I trust you will do just that. Even if you did opt for another field." He stood, rattled the paper closed, leaned over to extend his hand for a perfunctory handshake and left the room.

For once Mitchell agreed with Charles. He knew how it would look, although a part of him would have liked to have had his mother there. She, too, treated him impatiently but less insultingly so.

4

"Oh, dear," Alice said as she finished her coffee and toast. "Well, he is right. Appearances are important." She looked at her son. He was the best looking of her three boys, all of whom were tall and slim. Her mind, as always when she looked at them, secretly thanked her first husband, whose build they had inherited, not—thank goodness—Charles's portly physique. Thomas and Harry, her other two sons favored their father with dark-brown hair and eyes. Mitchell was lighter skinned and blond, like her, with her blue eyes behind his glasses. Though, the resemblance ended there. He had none of his parents' nor his brothers' inclinations or ambitions. He was an enigma to them.

"You do look very handsome today, Mitchell. Make sure you fix your tie. And that forelock of yours needs to be pushed back. It's too casual." She stood up, surprised at the sudden lump in her throat and the tear in her eye. "I must go." She leaned over and kissed his forehead, lifting away the wayward hair with a finger. "You will do just fine at Lincoln Academy. I think teaching will be a good fit for you." Then she was off in a bustle of long skirts, her perfume lingering behind.

Mitchell sat at the table a little longer wondering what life would have been like if he had grown up in a different family. Maybe of teachers. Or even the original occupations of his English ancestors—plumbers with a *b*. Would things be different? He knew he could never live up to his family's expectations. Gorham was just a teachers' college. But it had resulted in a job, freeing him from thinking of himself as his parents' disappointment. And what better way to begin one's independent life than to be a teacher with room and board provided?

He nodded, smiling at the butterfly flitting in his stomach. James waited outside with the carriage, the train waited at the station, and Lincoln Academy awaited in Newcastle.

2—LINCOLN ACADEMY—1886

Except for the imposing main building—two story, red brick, with a tall bell tower —there was little to distinguish the school and outbuildings from the neighboring farms dotting the wide countryside of rolling hills. Lincoln was a self-sufficient campus, with its own stables, livestock and gardens. It used its ruralness to make itself stand out from the other schools in the state by including agriculture and animal husbandry in its curriculum.

From the time Mitchell was twelve, his student life had been spent in dormitories—his high school years at Kents Hill in Augusta and four at Gorham. Lincoln Academy was just another campus, which gave him a comfortable feeling of *déjà vu*, and helped to ease his transition from student to teacher. Thanks to Gorham's good preparation, he'd had little nervousness, though the sheer delight at being on his own probably aided in his easy adaptation.

In addition to freshman English, he taught music history, only because he could play the piano, not because of his (scant) knowledge of music, and coached archery, a sudden add on. Without the constraints of family, he was reinventing himself daily, including becoming more social. He had become friendly with another teacher, John Mahoney. This was John's second year at Lincoln and remembering well how it felt to be the new teacher, he had taken Mitchell under his wing. Mitchell, testing his newfound sociability, had invited John to join him after classes on a Friday at his apartment.

Except for the head of school and some of the senior educators who lived in houses off campus, most of the teachers' quarters were in the dormitories. In most cases, two dorm rooms were converted into an apartment, sometimes more rooms depending on if the teacher was married and had children. This gave each teacher privacy but allowed for an adult's influence in each building; in *loco parentis*—literally to take the place of the parents. As a new teacher, Mitchell knew his chances of good quarters were slim, but because of the archery coach's sudden illness, Mitchell had been assigned that apartment.

Mitchell knew better than to boast about his rooms. "I know I lucked out," he said abashedly as he showed John around. He had a living room and a bedroom, normal for most apartments. But this one also had another small room with just enough space for a desk and a cot. "My study," he grandly called it. "I sent home for the good chair and the rug and the framed prints in the living room. I think it looks a proper scholar's dwelling now," he said proudly. He had surprised himself at how much he had enjoyed the decorating.

John nodded. "I'll say. I am envious. It's not fair; I should have had seniority."

Mitchell wasn't sure if John was joking. "I know, I was surprised too." He took out two bottles of beer. "I kept them outside as you suggested. They're not icy cold, but cool at least. It's warm enough to go outside. This is the best part of the apartment," he said trying not to get carried away. "This small courtyard. Have a seat," he said, pointing at the two cast off garden chairs. "I've been very content these past few evenings watching the leaves change.

"I must admit this teaching life is a bit of all right, isn't it? I thought I'd be really nervous standing in front of a class and trying to get the first words out. It has only been a couple of weeks, but so far, most of the boys seem all right. I have a couple that might turn in to troublemakers and three that are really smart; I'll have to work to stay ahead of them."

"I'm teaching sophomores," said John. "So I'll get them next year. If they are really bad, don't tell me their names. I like to stay objective for at least the first week." He laughed. "But you're right, Mitchell. It is a good life. I told you, didn't I? One really has no worries, what with room and board paid for. I only wish it paid more. And an apartment off campus. Now that would be more my style." He winked at Mitchell. "I could lead a...well, let's just say a more social life than what one has on a boys' school campus. Then again, maybe not, we're so far out in the country here."

Mitchell laughed nervously. Sometimes, John made him uncomfortable with his not-so-subtle remarks. He was Irish and had their good humor and gift of storytelling, including many off color jokes. He was from Augusta, which even though it was the state capital, was considered rough and tumble compared to Bangor, or so thought Mitchell's family. John's father was vice president of a company that made cotton textiles. John had a nonchalance about him which Mitchell envied, though, he did not particularly like his apparent comfort with the seedier sides of society.

"Well, maybe. I guess in a year or two I could be itching to get away. But this suits me fine right now," said Mitchell.

"I thought you told me you weren't athletic," said John. "But you're coaching baseball, you're teaching archery—though, I guess that's the least you could do for inheriting these rooms," said John. "I'm sorry. That was rude. And you ride, you play a mean game of tennis, and someone said you sailed too? My god, man. You seem pretty athletic to me."

Mitchell gave a small laugh. "I'm not really a sailor. Gorham offered sailing and I took it one year but didn't stick with it. And I did go out in my uncle's boat. He always needed crew when he raced. In comparison to my brothers, I am certainly not athletic. At least not in the desired types of sports the men in my family preferred. I did them in school of course. We all had to. But I didn't enjoy them, especially the rough team sports. I do enjoy the outdoors and pushing myself, though. I'm not a total sissy.

"Plus, all those sports are individual sports, challenges with me or against one opponent. If there is going to be sweat, I prefer it to be my own, not mingled with that of other boys. I did take up baseball my last year in college. Catcher. I like the communication, between myself and the pitcher, silently trying to outfox the batter."

John said, "Well, I ride too of course, as do we all. And I can play an adequate game of tennis, but that's about it for me. And I get what you're saying about the sweatiness. I don't like it either, though I do enjoy going to football games. You know, cheering and fellowship and all that, along with liberal amounts of beer," raising his glass.

Mitchell went on. "Actually, my best sport was wing shooting, using clay targets. We three brothers grew up competing in shooting matches at the Bangor Gun Club, which I usually won. That was the only sport I ever bested them in."

Maine was still not far removed from its frontier days, and most men of means had gun collections, while those of poorer status had at least one firearm. "Our father gave each of us boys a Smith & Wesson .38 caliber revolver when we reached the age of thirteen. Later, Charles, at his

12

first Christmas after marrying my mother, gave each of us a Winchester M97 shotgun."

Mitchell continued. "I cooled on it while I was still in college. An older schoolmate after he had graduated, committed suicide by shooting himself. He was of Russian descent and he would tell us the tales his grandfather had told him about the Caucasian War. In particular, a game the Russian officers played— a revolver was emptied of all but one bullet, the cylinder spun, the gun put to its owner's head, and discharged. If nothing happened, it was passed on to the next soldier and so on. You get the picture."

Mitchell looked increasingly uncomfortable. "How this boy relished telling the story. He would conjure up a thick Russian accent and with great drama demonstrate by using an empty revolver. Of course, my imagination always went directly to what I would see if the boy accidently put a live bullet in the gun. It just nauseated me, although I always listened when he told the story. Then, when I heard about his death, I couldn't help but think that's the way he must have done it. There was no way to know; there were no witnesses. What would make a person do that? A young man no less.

Would it make more sense if he had been an adult?" Mitchell shuddered. "Anyway, that's why I don't do shooting any more. Just a little too unnerving for me."

The next day, after coaching his archery team, Mitchell walked into Newcastle. Only two miles away, it was one of his shorter walks. He enjoyed ambling around this new countryside. Newcastle sat on the bank of the Damariscotta River. It was a mudhole compared to Bangor, but Mitchell liked its simplicity and its warmth. He had become friendly with the owner of the town's general store, and with the proprietor of the Publick House, where he was presently sitting.

Rose, the owner's wife, came over with a chilled beer. A round, motherly woman, she had taken a fond interest in Mitchell. "Now, here you go, dearie. Nice and cold, just the way you like it. How about something to eat before you head back? I can make you a nice ham sandwich. Or better yet, how about some shepherd's pie?" She glanced over her shoulder to the girl standing in the kitchen doorway. "Jenny made it, and it'll be comin' out of the oven in ten minutes."

"Thanks, Rose. Just the beer. Another day I'll take you up on it."

"All right then. But you're missin' somethin' delicious."

3—CHRISTMAS EVE—1886

December arrived quickly, surprising Mitchell. He felt as if he had just arrived at Lincoln, and next thing he knew, he was on the train home to Bangor for the Christmas holidays. He felt different— matured, successful. Certainly not the rube who had arrived at Lincoln three and a half months before. Gainful employment makes time move quickly, he thought. Well, that and being away from his parents.

Christmas Eve at the Plummer-Wiggin house was always just family. At the time they were all in the drawing room having drinks and chatting. The young children were upstairs in the nursery with their nannies having their own small party. Mitchell could still remember those nights when he was little and upstairs, fighting the drowsiness, the hum of adult voices and laughter lulling him to sleep. Then the excitement of being woken by the sounds of sleigh bells and allowed to run downstairs to find Santa standing in front of the fireplace, dusting soot from his suit. To this day he still remembered how he had felt the night he had learned that Santa Claus was his father in costume.

It was Charles now, who continued that tradition, usurping even that duty of Watson's.

A banker's social life was intense during the holiday season and a time for his mother to shine, which she did intensely. Mitchell participated reluctantly; his brothers, also bankers, proudly shined with her.

Thomas, the oldest, lived in Bangor with his wife, Louise, and their four children. Thomas had worked in the bank with their stepfather, but recently he had become president of the newly opened second branch of the Bangor Savings Bank built on the western outskirts of Bangor. As the eldest, Thomas still carried strong, close memories of his father, which had led to some conflict between himself and Charles. Working in the same building had become increasingly difficult and the move satisfied them both.

The second Plummer brother, Harry, was the head teller at the Kennebec Savings Bank in Augusta. Their stepsister and the baby of the family, Marion Wiggin, was only three years old and upstairs with the other little children.

Harry approached Mitchell. "I heard John Mahoney is teaching at Lincoln. Is that right?"

Mitchell smiled affectionally at his favorite brother. "Yes, John's been great helping me to navigate my way through this year. He has become a good friend. Do you know him?"

"Only to say hello. His father is on our board at Kennebec Savings, and I met John a few times when he's been in with his father."

"Funny you should mention him," said Mitchell. "He told me he was going to be here in Bangor day after tomorrow visiting his cousins, the Stetsons—they own Stetson's General Store."

Harry smiled. "Stetson? One of the sons, Edward, went to Harvard with me. He went on to law school there, I believe. That means John will be here for Boxing Day. You should invite him to the party."

"I hadn't even thought of that. Good idea," said Mitchell, reminded again of his social ineptitude.

"Dinner is ready," said Alice. Taking her husband's arm, she led the family into the dining room. Alice had spent weeks supervising Maureen and Beulah, the housekeeper and cook, preparing for this night. The windows, which had been washed inside and out, sparkled with the reflected

18

light from the candles in the chandelier, the candelabras and the sconces. Every piece of silver and each crystal glass glimmered. The white linen tablecloth was set with the Plummer family china. Red and gold, it complemented the burgundy draperies and the gold tassel tiebacks.

Everyone moved around the table looking for their place cards. Mitchell was pleased to see he was between Caleb, his young nephew finally old enough to dine with the adults, and Mary Potter, a cousin on his father's side. Mary attended Mount Holyoke College, and as her family was abroad for the season, Alice had invited her to spend the break in Bangor. She and Mitchell had always gotten along well, both a bit removed from their families.

"Mother," said Harry. "I told Mitchell he should bring his friend, John Mahoney, to the Boxing Day party. He's a friend from Lincoln and will be visiting his cousins, the Stetsons. His father is on our board."

"It's about time you brought a friend around, Mitchell. I was just at Stetson's the other day for some linens for the holidays; they carry a nice assortment. There is a nice young lady working there now who was very helpful. It looks like they are adding on. Didn't one of the boys go to Harvard with you two? He's a lawyer now, isn't he?" Alice asked.

Thomas spoke up. "That was Edward. It's his brother George who runs the store, and he was my first customer when we opened the new branch," said Thomas. "He applied and received a loan for that expansion. I'm glad they're doing well. Keeps the engines of commerce purring along, right Charles?"

There was a pause in the conversation as they started to dine. It was a long enough pause that Caleb, the youngest (and as such should have known to keep quiet), spoke. "I know what we can talk about," he piped up. "What about that man, Tom Stevens? He rode around the world on a bicycle—a Penny Farthing. Well, of course he had to take ships for the oceans, and I think he took some trains too. It took him two years. He started in California, went east to New York, and finally ended up in Yokohama," Caleb said. "That's in Japan," he proudly added.

"Exercising your admission to the adults' table kind of early, aren't you Caleb?" admonished Alice.

"Oh, I don't know, Mother," said Mitchell, smiling down at Caleb. "My students were sure excited about that trip. So was I."

"Well, I think it's total foolishness," said Charles. "You'd think he would do a real job. A total waste of time and a brain. Who in their right mind would do that? It's absurd."

"Charles don't upset yourself now," Alice said, leaning back to let her plate be removed by a maid. "Thank you. Tell Maureen she can bring in the dessert in a while."

"Yes, ma'am."

"I heard they're finally going to tear down the old Stillwell place. About time, don't you think?" asked Harry. "It burned down in the '72 fire. What took them so long?"

"Oh, you know," said his stepfather. "The usual political stuff. It certainly is far out; I will give you that. But the main railroad tracks have always gone by it, and now the lumber companies are putting up depots there, turning it into a lumber transfer point. Both Morse's Mills and Bangor Lumber have already started. They are using small rail lines to transport the cut timber from their sawmills to the depot. Then they hitch those cars to

21

the larger trains and from there to anywhere in the country. Much faster and cheaper than the rivers and log rolling."

He looked around the table self-importantly. "Lumber is what your father and I hitched our wagons to when we opened Bangor Savings Bank. We had the vision and we helped make Bangor into the boom city it is. They don't call it the *Queen City of the East* for nothing."

With an inner groan, Mitchell took a large sip of his wine. Good God, he thought. Every year he says the same exact thing. It's mind boggling. How can Thomas and Harry listen so raptly?

As if to spite Mitchell, Thomas picked up from Charles. "And it will bring in even more businesses. Those depots were why I pushed for our second branch so close to that edge of town. Everyone wonders why so far out but, mark my words. You'll see. In another five years, West Bangor will be a new downtown. And, Louise, my dear, I will build you a grand house, and you will be living in the middle of *the* place to be in Bangor, Maine," he said, looking at his wife affectionately.

"Ma'am?" Maureen stood at the door.

"Yes, Maureen, you can turn down the lights."

There was a feeling of expectancy at the table, especially from Caleb. "Snap dragons? Are we doing snap dragons?" he asked, barely able to sit still, looking at Mitchell beside him.

With the lights down, Maureen and Beulah each came bearing silver flaming trays. Their contents had been doused in warmed brandy and set aflame, giving the room an eerie, flickering, blue glow. The tray of snap dragons was placed in front of Caleb, his eyes agog; the other, a Christmas pudding was placed in front of Alice.

Mitchell told Caleb what to do. "The blue flames are from the brandy and are not that hot. You reach in—through the *flames of the dragon*—and pick out a raisin or an almond and *snap* your mouth shut around it. It's good luck to eat them. Then you pass it to the person on your right, and it goes around to everyone else."

Later that night, after the sleigh bells had announced Santa Claus's arrival, Mitchell stood against a wall watching as Caleb and the younger children stood in line to see Santa. Mitchell saw Caleb's face suddenly change. Mitchell remembered that look. It had been on his own face when he recognized his father in the red suit. Caleb nervously sneaked looks around the room. Mitchell smiled sympathetically when their eyes met. Caleb was leaving his childhood.

4—BOXING DAY—1886

The day after Christmas, Mitchell rode over to Stetson's to leave an invitation for John to come to the party later that night. It was cold but sunny, and Mitchell took the long way around the outskirts of Bangor. Laddie, his horse, tossed his head and pranced in the fresh, cold air, each enjoying the other's company. Passing Thomas's new bank, he couldn't help but wonder if his brother really knew what he was talking about. But the men in his family had proven themselves talented financially, a lack he felt acutely when he was with them.

Stetson's store was in the middle of town. He tied Laddie out front and walked into the store, the bells over the door ringing. A young woman came over to him.

"May I help you?"

"Yes. I wanted to leave a message for John Mahoney. He told me he would be staying with the Stetsons. He and I teach at the same school." He gave her the note. "Sorry, it's a little wrinkled, but I don't think John will care."

"Oh, yes. He's due in on the one o'clock train. I'll be happy to give it to him. What did you say your name was?" she asked.

"I didn't, sorry. Mitchell. Mitchell Plummer."

"Any relation to Thomas Plummer, the banker?" she asked with interest.

"Yes, he's my brother," he nodded. "Whole family is in banking. Except for me," he said almost apologizing. "I'm the teacher."

"Oh, but teaching is wonderful. Even bankers need to be taught," she said, laughing.

Mitchell wanted to make her laugh again. She was pretty, in a simple way—short and slightly plump and pleasing to his eyes. Her light-red hair was pulled back in a soft bun from which loose tendrils fell along her face and neck. She had china skin and clear blue eyes that looked straight into his.

As he turned to leave, the back door opened, and a middle-aged man entered.

"Uncle George, this is Mitchell Plummer, Thomas Plummer's brother. He works with John and wanted to leave him a message."

"Mitchell, nice to meet you. Thomas has been a great help to us. What's this about John?"

"I have an invitation for him for tonight. We're having a Boxing Day party, and I thought he might want to come."

"Well, I'm sure he would. We will make sure he gets the message. But it will have to be after supper. My sister-in-law is making a meal in his honor. He'll be able to leave after that."

"Certainly. I'll send the carriage over around seven, if that's all right. Sorry it's such short notice," Mitchell said turning for the door. "Mr. Stetson and...?"

"I'm sorry. My name is May. May Lobdell."

"Thank you, May. Thank you both for your time," Mitchell said, backing out the front door, hoping she wouldn't see the flush on his face.

Mitchell kept thinking about May on the ride home. She was flirting with him; he was sure. It made him feel special but foolishly so. Flirtatious encounters didn't often happen with him. He hoped it wasn't because of his name; he hoped her interest might be solely in him.

Back at home the family was setting up for the party. As it was Boxing Day, the staff had been given the day off to visit with family and friends. Each had been sent off with a box, which was wrapped and filled with gifts, food, and a cash bonus. As upright and stern as Mitchell's father had been, he believed his employees should be compensated well. Alice felt so too, making sure Charles continued the generosity, which he did reluctantly. Before leaving, Beulah had prepared a buffet of leftovers along with eggnog and mulled cider.

The party was a casual family affair with a few close friends and neighbors. When John arrived, Mitchell introduced him to the family. After chatting a bit with the relatives, they headed to the buffet.

"How was your trip?" asked Mitchell.

"The trip was fine. Spent most of it sleeping off Christmas. I don't know about your family, but we tend to go overboard at this time of year. Too much Irish whiskey and people dropping in, but it's always fun."

"No, we're definitely more staid. Very traditional," said Mitchell. "And dinner with your family here? The Stetsons?"

"Good. The Stetsons are my cousin Edith's in-laws, and when she married Edward, May—her younger sister—came with her. Edith cooked up a feast. I don't get up here often, so it's a special occasion. Edith and May and their mother, Aunt Agnes, lived with my parents for several years and my mother became very close to her nieces. I had to fill them in on everything going on in Augusta, though, some of it I just made up. I see everyone so little now."

John, with a slight smile on his face, looked at Mitchell. "By the way, apparently you made quite the impression on May. She kept asking about you. Whatever did you say to her?"

"She did?" Mitchell said, feeling a flush creep up his neck. "I didn't say much."

"If she knew you were a Plummer, you wouldn't have had to say a word. May works in the store, which is still in the family and run by Edward's brother, George. He thinks May is a wonder in the shop. She's unmarried and older than me. Probably getting a bit desperate, if you know what I mean. She has had a few fellows that came around, usually older and of ill repute. One that nearly ruined her, or so said my mother. Edith and Edward have always had to chase them away, but soon they'll have to pay someone to marry her."

"Oh, I think that's going a little too far, John. Someone will claim her soon." Mitchell was reminded of how John's observations often went too far. Mitchell himself had found her quite fetching. Though he was disappointed to find out, that just as he'd thought, she'd flirted with him because of his name.

"Hit a nerve, did I? Sorry. She is nice, and I hope she does find someone good for her," said John. "Enough talk about boring families. I'm here through tomorrow. What could we do?"

"How about we go for a ride tomorrow. I'll take you around Bangor."

5—AN EVENT—1887

After the holidays, Mitchell was happy to be back at Lincoln, the routine and normalcy suiting him. He felt far more comfortable speaking in front of a class of young men than socializing at parties in Bangor. The boys liked him, often coming to his classroom late in the day for help or just to talk.

"You know, Mitchell, I'd be careful about having your students come to your room after classes. Some people might read something into it, if you get my drift," John said. They were out on Mitchell's patio, taking advantage of an unseasonably warm February evening.

"No, John, I'm not sure I do get your drift. Enlighten me." Mitchell did get the drift, and it bothered him. "And who are *some people*? As far as I can tell, you're the only one who's thinking along those lines."

"Oh, come on, Mitchell. Don't be such a prude. I'm only saying that someone might think you were a little too close to them. After all, these are young impressionable boys, and we are older single men. It's not unheard of, you know. I'm just watching out for your better interests, that's all."

31

"All right, I guess. Does that mean I should thank you? I never like it when you try to lord it over me with your experience."

It did bother Mitchell, and it did hit close to home. All his life he had felt different, and not just the obvious differences between himself and the other men in his family. When he was younger, he had had infatuations on a few of his teachers, just as John had pointed out about their students. There had been one teacher at Kents, who tried to take Mitchell into a closet, scaring him nearly to death. His stepfather found out somehow and confronted Mitchell, telling him he'd had the headmaster dismiss the teacher. Even though it was the teacher who was terminated, Mitchell always thought it was him who Charles felt should have been punished.

Relationships, intimacy, and anything to do with romance confused him. Sometimes he was attracted to men his age. Not to boys, he thought, thankfully. And some women attracted him, though, rarely. He thought he could enjoy being married and having children. A normal, safe life. What he knew for sure was that he did not want to ever be considered that teacher who preyed on young boys.

After that conversation, Mitchell found himself uncomfortable around his students. He was no longer at ease with them. When they came to him to talk or ask for help, he felt he had to watch himself. He made excuses as to why he couldn't be available to them. Most appeared not to even notice. But one student, Nathan—a favorite of Mitchell's—seemed saddened and would look at him reproachfully.

Returning to his classroom one afternoon he found Nathan sitting at a desk, alone and staring. "Nathan, what's going on?" asked Mitchell. "You've not been yourself lately."

"Nothing, really, Mr. Plummer," the boy sighed. "Mostly, I miss coming to your room after school. It was fun, and the other boys liked it too. I think anyway. They didn't tease me as much when you were around."

"Well, Nathan, I like you too. You're a nice boy and smart. And you don't have to miss me; you're still in my class every day. But I've got things I must do after classes, just as you do. Is there something I can help you with right now?"

"No, not really," said Nathan. "But I like you, and I miss you."

Mitchell was torn. Perhaps what John had said was true. Could Nathan have a fancy for him? But he was also feeling guilty about leaving the boy alone. "What do you say I walk you back to your dorm, OK?"

Two weeks later, Nathan left school. There was no explanation. A few days later, Mitchell was called to the office of Mr. Stone, the headmaster.

"Mitchell, thanks for coming in," Mr. Stone said. "I called you here because I need to ask you a few questions about Nathan. As you know, he left here suddenly. I know he wasn't particularly happy here; some boys just never fully adjust. But there were some unsettling letters he sent home to his parents, one referring to you."

Mitchell flinched inside. Oh no. Maybe John was right.

"It's not uncommon for young boys to form a...how shall I say this? An unusual attachment to their teachers? And it seems that Nathan was very fond of you. In his letters home, he had written often of how he felt about you. And he made it sound as if you reciprocated those feelings. I'm not

34

accusing you of anything, mind you, but his parents are a bit upset. I am sure it's just a young man's affection for an older male figure. He did mention that you had walked him back to his room a few times. Is that true?"

"I did walk him back. Once. And to the dorm, not to his room," said Mitchell. "Often he and the other boys would come to my classroom in the afternoons. But it became difficult for me to attend to my other duties, and I cut it back. Nathan was particularly upset. He came by one afternoon a couple of weeks ago and told me how he missed our afternoon meetings. He looked so forlorn, I felt badly for him and walked him back to the dorm."

"Well, I figured it was something like that. I guess we can never be too careful about appearances now, can we?" asked Mr. Stone as he stood up. "I'm glad we had this little talk, Mitchell. We have been very happy with your work here at Lincoln. This is just an example of boys being boys. In this case, a forlorn boy."

Mitchell walked slowly back across the campus to his apartment. He felt he had just had a stay of execution. He felt terrible about poor Nathan, just a boy who liked his teacher; one who didn't quite square with his classmates, right? But part of the reason Mitchell liked Nathan was because he reminded him of himself, another person who didn't always fit in.

6—SPRING BREAK—1887

Mitchell elected to stay on campus over the spring break. It gave him a good reason to not go home. There were four boys who could not go home for various reasons, which was not unusual, as transportation was difficult and costly. Mitchell, with a skeleton crew in the kitchen and on the grounds, would mind the campus and the boys. He looked forward to it and had planned various activities and field trips. At the last minute, five more boys had to stay back, requiring another teacher to remain on campus. John volunteered.

"I've got nothing to do at home either, just like you. This will be a vacation for us," said John. It was Friday afternoon. They had ridden into Newcastle and were sitting outside the Publick House, enjoying the beers Rose had just brought them. The next day, Saturday, the rest of the students would leave.

"You'll stay for dinner?" she asked them. "Jenny's made a beef stew. Just waitin' for two healthy men to dig into it."

John smiled at Rose. "If your charming daughter made such a meal, we would love to have dinner in your establishment. In a bit. We're just enjoying this wonderful weather on your patio."

"Ahh, ain't it now? I think spring is finally here. My crocuses and daffodils are opened, and I'll be puttin' in my flowers and vegetables soon," said Rose as she turned and bustled back through the door.

"Lord, John. You are such a rake. You'll flirt with anyone."

"Well, why not? It makes them happy; it makes me happy. What's not to like?" He laughed. "It's not like I'm going to act on any of it. Little Jenny has nothing to worry about with me. Even though Rose would probably faint with happiness if either of us took a liking to her precious daughter, who is quite fetching. But not for me."

"No, not for me either," said Mitchell. "Now May, maybe. Your cousin."

"Hah! I knew you liked her. And yes, she is available and lovely. But remember what I told you. She's not as pure as she looks. At least that's what I've heard. I couldn't know for sure, obviously." He gave Mitchell a sly grin. "It might just be all smoke and no fire."

The next day, John came to Mitchell's apartment with a sheepish look on his face. "Mitchell, old friend. Do you think you could help me out? One of the custodians has agreed to repaint my apartment. You know how I hate the color. It's brown, for God's sake. And it's extra money for him. Anyway, I thought I could sleep in your study for the few days it will take."

"Sure, I don't see why not, though, it is just a cubicle. You'll be jammed in there. You could have your own quarters if you took over one of the empty rooms in the dorm."

"I could, I guess. But I'd feel uncomfortable staying in someone else's room without their permission. Especially a student's room. Who knows what could be growing in there, or what I'd be sleeping on." John shuddered. "Your cubicle sounds just fine."

"I didn't think anything made you uncomfortable," Mitchell said, looking at him with amusement. "But sure. It's all right."

"Thanks. I really appreciate it. Plus, you have the patio."

The campus and its few inhabitants settled into a routine. Casual late breakfasts followed by

39

activities: tennis, archery, cross-country runs, and long walks. Mitchell put together some baseball games. Lunches were often taken as picnics outside. The staff were busy doing repairs and housekeeping duties. Mitchell and John volunteered themselves and the boys to help, especially in the kitchen. Despite creating more work for the cook, she enjoyed the company. Cooking was something none of them were familiar with. "Consider it a part of your education," she said. "About time you boys find out what real work is."

In the evenings they played board games, charades, chess, bridge...Two of the boys were budding thespians and corralled the others into putting on performances. There were nights spent singing along with Mitchell at the piano. All were in their rooms by ten, usually.

"It really is like a vacation, isn't it?" asked John. They were outside on the patio after the boys had gone to their rooms, having a smoke and a beer. "I feel like I'm at camp."

Mitchell laughed. "I know. One I actually like. I don't know about you, but going off to summer camp was a torture I hoped to never relive."

"I'm surprised, Mitch. I'd have thought you'd have loved to get away from your stepfather."

"I did. That was the only good thing." Mitchell paused. "No one has ever called me Mitch before," he said, affectionally.

"Does it bother you? I won't use it if it bothers you."

"No. It's just different. I've never been close enough to anyone for them to use a *nice* nickname for me. For Mitchell, anyway. They used plenty for the dreaded Hazen—Hazy, Hasty, hazard..."

There were two students who needed extra attention—Jason and Ashley. Jason was the son of an owner of the Boston Fruit Company, who along with his wife was in the West Indies tending to business, thus Jason's stay on campus. Ashley was from New York City, and his father, who was with the state department, was posted to London with the family. Jason was a bully, and his target was usually Ashley; two boys dealing with loneliness in their own lonely ways.

"Anyway, it's been another day of calm. No taunts from Jason, no breakdowns from Ashley," said Mitchell. "I've become fond of Ashley. He reminds me of myself. Always the odd boy out. He's a good egg, despite Jason's tormenting."

John chuckled. "Believe it or not, I sort of have a soft spot for Jason, the little twit. I don't think he's really mean. And Ashley is a crybaby. He makes it too easy for Jason to pick on him."

They were outside, smoking and having a beer. John had ridden to town that day and brought back some bottles from Rose at the Publick House.

"I like to drink beer, especially on vacation. She told me to bring the empty bottles back, and she'll sell me more. How come you're smoking a cigarette and not your pipe?"

"I don't know. Just felt like it. It's easier, though there is something to be said about the pipe ritual. The smell of the tobacco, putting it in the bowl, tamping it down...I'll probably switch between them."

Over the past days, they had become closer, telling stories of their upbringings. Mitchell told John how he could never live up to his family's expectations. He had become comfortable enough with John to tell him how he had always felt different from his classmates and how they had teased him.

John had similar stories of feeling different but seemed less bothered by it. "I guess I've developed a shell. You need tough skin if you're Irish. I've been called names all my life. Mick, Paddy, Mucker...Hell, someone even called me a Bridget." He laughed. "How's that for my masculine persona? I've heard them all. But I do know what you mean about feeling different. It's a sort of shadow of yourself, hiding inside."

In fact, John had become so comfortable to Mitchell, he wondered if there might be something between them. John hid so well behind his bluster, with his off-color jokes and innuendo about women, that there was no way to know how he really felt. Mitchell was certainly not going to risk their friendship trying to find out. John was his first true friend.

The next night around ten, after the boys were in the dorm, John was coming back from his room after getting some clean clothes and another book. The painting of his apartment had been started but was nowhere near finished. He heard a

43

strange sound. Crying? Laughing? Growling? It was hard to tell.

"Hello? Anyone there?" He looked around and listened, but there was nothing.

"Strange thing on my way back, Mitch," John said. "I couldn't figure it out. At first, I thought it might be some of the boys sneaking around. But I think it must have been an owl with a mouse, maybe? Or a fox?"

The last Saturday, before the staff and students returned on Sunday, had been a day of chores and cleanup for everyone. John's apartment was done, and he had moved his things back in. The students made the last night's dinner by themselves, inviting the cook and the other employees to be their guests. After a rousing game of charades, all had turned in.

Mitchell and John, on the patio as usual, toasted themselves with their last beers from Rose. "I'm going to miss this," said Mitchell, leaning over and touching John's hand. Their chairs were side by side, looking out over the lawn. The night was cool, the sky dark with each star vividly shining.

"Me too, Mitch. Thanks for letting me stay with you. It was fun. It's been a long time since I've spent so much time with someone," he said, turning in his chair to look at his friend.

A noticeable rustling in the bushes made them look around. "Maybe it's that fox or whatever I heard the other day," said John. He got up to look. As he got closer to the shrubs, there was a sudden movement, and two boys jumped out and ran away.

"Jason, get back here," yelled John. "You too, Ashley." They continued running, Jason dragging Ashely by the arm.

"Well, I'm not going to chase them back to the dorm. Hopefully we won't have to deal with them again. Everyone else gets back tomorrow." John took a swig of his beer. "Do you think that's what I heard the other night? The two of them sneaking around? I bet it was, the little bastards. I should have gone after them."

"I don't know, John. Do you think they were spying on us? Whatever for?" asked Mitchell. "That probably was them the other night. Maybe we should be prepared for them to go to Stone."

"Maybe," said John. "Though, whatever for? We'll just have to see."

Mitchell worried through the night. Should he go to Mr. Stone immediately and tell him exactly what happened? But maybe Jason won't say anything. He wondered if he would lose his job. For drinking some beers? He didn't think so. Most of the teachers kept alcohol in their quarters.

At eleven thirty, there was a knock at the door. Mitchell opened it to find John, Mr. Stone, and his secretary, Hayes, standing there. Mr. Stone shouldered his way in, the other two following, Hayes shutting the door behind them. John nodded grimly to Mitchell.

"Sit down, Plummer. Both of you," said Mr. Stone. "I assume you know why I'm here. I am going to do all the talking right now. Do not interrupt me. You'll get your chance to talk when I'm done."

"Yes sir," they both said.

"We're meeting here, in this den of iniquity, where fewer people may hear what I'm going to say. Hayes is here as my witness. Hopefully, we can contain the repercussions from this unholy mess you both have created." Mr. Stone paused. His face was red, and he was almost panting with rage as he paced in the small room.

"Mr. Stone?" John asked. *"Den of iniquity? Unholy mess?* What are you talking about?"

"Mahoney. Plummer. Not another word until I say you can speak," said Mr. Stone. "A student, Jason Tillman, has accused you both of misconduct, saying that the two of you carried on an abnormal relationship. That it had been going on the whole year but became plainly obvious this past break. That you were drinking beer, touching each other, and gazing into each other's eyes outside on that very patio. That is not just abnormal. It is deviant—utterly, totally deviant. Never mind that it is a gross dereliction of professional ethics. Good God, Plummer!"

He broke off, out of breath, staring at Mitchell with outrage. "How could you do this? Tillman said you let Mahoney stay with you in your apartment. That you were cohabitating! Doing whatever it is people like you do! And at Lincoln Academy. I don't know if the school will ever recover its reputation. Because no matter how hard I try to keep it quiet, it will get out. Things like this get out. They slither out like serpents from the pit.

47

"As if that isn't bad enough, he presented even more horrifying information. He said Ashley Burke, one of our more delicate boys...Jason said that you *touched* Ashley. Touched him! On a private part of his body. Ashley bravely come forward and confirmed the accusation. God, Plummer, you are vile. You are both vile, but you especially."

He sat down for a moment in an attempt to regain his composure then jumped up and looked at the chair with disgust, as if it was somehow contaminated. "Appallingly, for me, I feel partly to blame, Plummer. This is not the first time I've had to deal with this issue with you. I should have terminated you when that situation with Nathan happened, but I took your side. I even complimented you on the job you were doing here. God forgive me." This time he did sit down. He could not stand another minute, or he would faint. "Mahoney, you go first. Try to explain yourself."

"We're friends, Mr. Stone. That's all we are. And we do things together, the way friends do. In hindsight, I could see an impressionable young man might think we were *too* close. Especially when I moved in with Mitchell. But my rooms were being painted, and he has an extra room, and I thought it was better than taking a student's room, invading that student's privacy."

John went on to explain the events leading up to the accusations, but he knew it was useless. It was obvious Mr. Stone was having none of it. His mind was made up, and no amount of explanation was going to change it.

"Plummer, do you have anything to add to Mahoney's story?" Mr. Stone asked. He was standing now and in an obvious hurry to leave.

"No, sir. Just that both boys are lying. I would never have done the things they have accused me of. Never. I am innocent and moral and honest, as is John. He has described everything as it happened. I have nothing more to add."

Mr. Stone dusted off his suit. "Good. I do not think I could stand to hear any more. You both are terminated as of this moment. Hayes here has twenty dollars for you each, in case you don't have enough money on you to buy a ticket. Mahoney, you will follow Hayes back to your rooms and pack immediately. Plummer, you will do the same. You will stay in your rooms with no contact with anyone. Anyone! Is that clear? Hayes will get you both later, after lights out, and have you brought to the station in the carriage."

Pausing at the door, Mr. Stone turned back, staring at the two men with contempt. "I hope I never see either of you again, ever. Nor the likes of you and your pederasty. Do not leave your rooms, do not speak to anyone, do not meet with each other until you are in the carriage on your way from here. Be gone with you both." He wrenched the door open. "If anyone asks, say it was because of staff cutbacks. It's what I am going to say." He left, storming out with John and Hayes behind him.

Mitchell's mind was whirling. This was way worse than drinking. When his family found out, he would be doomed. What could he do? He would be ostracized. Even Harry—his favorite brother, the one who always took his side when Charles was coming down on him—even Harry would be disgusted with him. *Pederasty.* If anyone in his family even *thinks* he was guilty of that sin, he might as well be dead. Certainly, Charles would wish that; he was already suspicious. What if he had to kill himself? How does one go about doing that? Is this how it happened to his friend? Was he ostracized from his family and suicide was his only choice? He shuddered at his thoughts.

8—AFTERMATH—1887

Mitchell and John, along with their luggage, had been unceremoniously dumped at the Newcastle station at midnight. It would not open until seven.

Mitchell paced the length of the tracks in front of him. "God, John, how am I going to explain this? What can I possibly say? And Charles, that fat pig. In his eyes I will be lower than a cockroach. John, how can you just sit there, like it's just another day? Night? Whatever it is."

John slouched against the wall, looking casual as usual. "Mitchell, relax. It's going to be all right."

"Damn it, John! This is the greatest disaster to happen to either of us. And you have a solution already? Just what is your so-easy answer to this mess?"

"Nothing. We will do nothing. Because nothing will leak from Lincoln Academy, that great bastion of learning. Stone will make sure of it."

"But what about the students? They must know. Ashley may not say anything, he's so timid. But Jason's probably bragged about it all over the place. How he caught us. How we were doing...what? We were not doing anything.

52

Boasting how he got us fired. What about the other boys who stayed on campus? What did they know? Or think they knew?" Mitchell asked. He had stopped pacing, though, curious to know what John might say.

"When Hayes walked me back to my room, he told me. Hayes felt bad for us and said we were being set up. Why do you think it took so long for Stone to talk to us? He was talking to the boys. There was a letter in Stone's office lying on the floor, and it was the first thing Stone saw when he entered. It wasn't signed, but he figured it was Jason. Stone took him in first and lit into him and made him give up Ashley. Hayes said Jason walked in there like the cock of the walk and crept out thirty minutes later in tears, his face beet red. Stone did go easier on poor Ashley but basically told him he knew he was lying, and that Jason had set him up. When he talked with the other boys, it was obvious that they knew nothing." John looked up at Mitchell. "Do you see where I'm going with this?"

Mitchell sat down. "Maybe. Stone does not believe any of us and really could care less what the truth is. We are dispensable; the boys are not. If he expels the boys, their families will get involved, and

Lincoln Academy is ruined. As is Stone. All he cares about is his reputation."

"Correct. So, now we do our part, and everyone comes out relatively unscathed," said John. "Stone said he was going to say it was because of cutbacks. We'll say the same. It's easy, doesn't require a lot of explaining, and it will match his story. If, God forbid, it needs to."

By the time the sun came up, their plans were set. John was going back to Augusta, hopefully to work at Edwards Manufacturing, the company his father worked for. "I'll be employed in the cotton textile market, Mitch. *Textiles*. Can't you just see me?" He laughed.

"I can," said Mitchell, almost smiling. "Probably no different from me. I guess I'll be working at the bank with dear old Charles. *Banking*. Can't you just see me? At least you and your father get along."

"Hell, Mitch. We'll adapt. That's all we can do. And when you consider the alternative, it's damn good," John said.

"I hope we can still be friends, John." Mitchell sighed. "I consider you my best friend. Augusta and Bangor aren't that far away."

Mitchell arrived in Bangor in the afternoon. He had left his luggage at the station and walked home, arriving moments after his mother. She was still taking off her gloves when he walked through the front door.

"Goodness, Mitchell. You startled me. What in the world are you doing here?" asked Alice. "Is everything all right?"

"Yes, Mother. Well, mostly. But I am no longer working at Lincoln Academy. They needed to cut back on their teaching staff, and I was the first to be let go. Along with John."

"Oh, dear. Mitchell, I am so sorry. You look tired," Alice said, leaning in to give him a kiss. She called for Maureen. "Where are your bags?"

"I left them at the station. I walked here. I thought James could pick them up later."

"Of course. Maureen, bring us some tea in the drawing room. And a few finger sandwiches for Mitchell. Oh, and tell James to drive to the station and pick up Mitchell's bags. He can do it on his way when he picks up Mr. Wiggin."

"Yes, ma'am. Welcome home, Mr. Mitchell," said Maureen.

"Thank you," said Mitchell. She was probably running off to tell the rest of the staff. He'd best get used to that feeling.

And now he was having to go through the whole thing again with Charles. His stepfather was definitely not taking it as well as Alice had. They were in the drawing room before dinner—the doors closed—having a drink, a needed fortification for them both.

"God damn it, Hazen. You didn't even keep the job for a year," said a furious Charles.

So, it's back to Hazen again, thought Mitchell. He had almost forgotten that was his name.

"And what do you mean that they are cutting back on staff? There is more to this, I know it. What did you do?" Charles eased his pacing to take a long gulp of his sherry and stared hard at Mitchell. "I always knew you would do something. Your father felt you had a *deficiency* in your nature. He never told me any details, but since I married into this family, I've agreed. I just hope to God it was not a deviant act. Don't think I've forgotten about that thing at Kents."

"Charles, what are you saying? That I somehow was at fault for that revolting man taking me into a closet?" Mitchell was aghast. Charles's disgust in him was confirmed. "You know that's not true."

"All right, Hazen. I did go too far. I apologize. But it is only out of concern," Charles said. "Concern for your mother. And your family name."

"I already told you, Charles, twice. This is exactly what Mr. Stone said: 'We are cutting back on staff.' He said it to me and John both. He told us late yesterday evening, so I do not know if any other teachers were terminated. We were the last hired, therefore, we were the first to be let go," Mitchell said. "That's it."

"John Mahoney, a damn Mick. I could tell just by looking at him he was a bad influence on you."

"Oh, stop. He's a friend. And being Irish has nothing to do with what happened." Mitchell took a deep breath and stared at Charles. It was now or never. "And Charles, please stop calling me Hazen. I hate that name. I use Mitchell, and you know it."

Charles was not mollified. "I will get to the bottom of this, you can be sure. Either you are lying, or that Mr. Stone has some serious explaining to do when I talk to him. And I will talk to him, *Hazen*."

"If you feel you must, though, I think you'll be wasting your time." Mitchell sighed, surprised at how calm he was. There was no way Stone was going to tell him the truth.

"I'll be the decider of that," Charles huffed, slamming his glass on the table and stomping out of the room.

9—JUST BUSINESS—1887

Charles, as Mitchell had predicted, did not let it go. He posted a letter demanding to meet with Stone, stating he could be at the school the following week. Stone wrote back saying he would be in Bangor on the coming Thursday on business and could meet with him at the bank.

"Come in, Stone," said Charles at his desk, purposely not standing and barely disguising the hostility in his voice. "Sorry I kept you waiting so long. A problem had arisen with one of my employees. I'm sure you can understand how these problems must be handled quickly. Before they get out of hand."

"Oh, yes, Mr. Wiggin, I do understand. I trust all turned out well?" Stone asked blandly, taking a seat, uninvited, in the chair in front of the desk. "So, tell me what you wanted so urgently to talk to me about. I was just in Augusta yesterday with Mr. Sean Mahoney. Would I be correct in assuming it might be something to do with his and your stepson's dismissals from Lincoln?"

"Obviously," said Charles, surprised at how quickly Stone had broached the subject and slightly miffed that he had talked with John's father first.

"Well, yes, I figured that was what it was about. I can understand your concern. And perhaps I was not totally honest with your stepson and young Mahoney."

"Ah, so there is more. And, how, exactly, were you not honest with them? There's always a reason for an unceremonious exit," said Charles.

"I told them we were having to make cuts in staff, which is the truth but not the whole truth. It was not because of financial problems. No, sir. Lincoln Academy is very secure financially. So secure, the board has decided it is time to expand. Competition is fierce in this business, and there are many private schools here in Maine—Foxcroft, Gould, Kents..."

"Get on with it, Stone. What does all this have to do with my stepson?"

"As I was saying, we're the fourth oldest school in Maine and we mean to maintain our place amongst them. The board of trustees, of which Mr. Mahoney—the elder—has just joined, are all esteemed gentlemen of business as are you."

Stone settled into the chair more comfortably. "The board has finally agreed with me on the need for improvements to our school. This will obviously require some belt tightening in how we spend our dollars, thus the *unceremonious*, as you put it, discharge of your stepson and Mahoney. They were our newest hires, and it was only fair to our other educators that they be the first to go. This is the reason I gave to them and will continue to give to anyone who asks."

Stone shifted slightly in his chair and continued smoothly. "There may have been another reason, which I will not divulge to anyone. Even to you. I'm sure you can agree that is for the best," said Stone, looking Charles in the eye. "I hope you realize appearances are everything in this kind of situation and, as such, should be no reflection on either yourself or on Mr. Mahoney, the elder. I told him exactly the same thing I've just told you when I was in Augusta yesterday."

Stone took a deep breath. "The board has begun interviewing architects and builders, but nothing can begin in earnest until we have the financing we need. That, Mr. Wiggin, was the main reason I was coming here to speak with you. When I received your letter, I thought what perfect timing. I was planning to meet with the banks here in Bangor, and you were first on my list. At the same time, I could speak with you about your stepson. His dismissal was the cost of maintaining our school's reputation. It was business. Nothing more, nothing less, Mr. Wiggin. You understand, right? Business."

Charles stared at Stone. Then he took a deep breath and with a small smile, held out his hand. "I understand perfectly, Mr. Stone. I think Bangor Savings Bank can meet your needs. Let me introduce you to our loan manager. He will be happy to help you."

10—BANKING—1887

That Friday, Mitchell began his first day in banking. He was aware of the irony—working in the business he had always disliked. But his stepfather had made it clear he had no choice. He also made it clear he had spoken with Stone who, he said, while staring sternly at Mitchell, had cleared up his questions. After breakfast James had driven Mitchell and Charles in the carriage to the bank. It was an unpleasant ride for Mitchell; he would walk from now on.

Before the bank opened, Charles gathered everyone in the lobby.

"I want to introduce my youngest stepson, Hazen Plummer. He will be working with you all. He may be part of my family, but he is to get no special treatment. Treat him just as you did Mr. Plummer's other sons. He will start out as every other employee has, attached to one of you, observing and learning each job. His wages will be the same as any new hire and will increase at the same rate as did yours," Charles said. "I thank you all in advance. I'm sure Hazen will thank you also, as he learns the banking business from the bottom up." Charles went over and opened the doors. "It is

63

just another day of business for us all. Make it a good one."

Mitchell smiled awkwardly at everyone, feeling as he had when he was a young boy coming into the bank with his father—everyone smiling at him, patting him on his head, saying how much he'd grown. At least now, no one could do that to him anymore.

He was assigned to an older cashier, a Mr. Michael Gurnsey. "I remember you when you were just a wee tyke," he said. "I trained Thomas and Harry, and I'm happy to train you too. Just follow me like a shadow. You'll get the hang of it soon enough."

"Thank you, Mr. Gurnsey," said Mitchell, trying to get the picture of a cow out of his head. Mr. Gurnsey was anything but cow like. He was tall, skinny, and stooped with spectacles low on his nose, white fluffy hair, and a white handlebar mustache. He looked old, but Mitchell felt he was probably younger than either of his fathers.

"You can call me Michael, when it's just us, if you want. I always feel as if I should be chewing on my cud when I hear my last name," Mr. Gurnsey said, cackling at his own joke.

"Thanks, though, I'll probably stick with the formality," said Mitchell. "At least until I feel more comfortable. And you by the way can use Mitchell, not Hazen, as my first name. I prefer it, though, I don't think my stepfather will ever use it."

Thus, began his new life. And remarkably, he found it agreeable. His fellow workers were more than helpful. He missed the give-and-take he had had with his students and fellow teachers, but there was a reserved formality at the bank that made it possible for him to remain detached, which he wanted. His dreams of becoming a college dean faded. He missed his apartment. Mostly, he missed John.

Sometimes he allowed himself to wonder what might have happened between them that night at Lincoln if they had not been interrupted. He wondered about poor Nathan and Ashley. He avoided thoughts of Jason. He honestly thought he could be capable of murder if he ever saw that detestable, vicious boy again.

Mitchell and John corresponded often, giving humorous accounts of their new lives. John traveled frequently, which suited him. He was pushing for a trip to Bangor, but so far, no luck. As the new man, he got the long trips no one else wanted. He went often to Buffalo, Cincinnati, and Albany, touting the miracles of cotton textiles. Anonymous travel to large cities suited him, allowing him to experience the seedier aspects of life he had always seemed attracted to, or so he had alluded to in his letters.

Within weeks, Mitchell was manning a window on his own. His discomfort with anything mathematical was fading. Banking, at least at a teller's window, was not calculus. All he had to do was count money, smile, and socialize briefly. Of course, having the name *Plummer* on his nameplate probably didn't hurt either.

"Plummer, is it? Hazen? What kind of name is that?" a familiar voice asked.

"John, well, I'll be! What a nice surprise. What are you doing here? Oh, pardon my manners. Can I help you? We at Bangor Savings Bank are here to serve all your banking needs," Mitchell said, laughing.

"I finally managed to wrangle a business trip here from the boss, dear old dad. The regular person who has Bangor is ill. I just arrived and decided before I did anything, I'd come here to see if you really look the part of a banker. Not bad, by the way. You look bankerly without being stuffy. I've missed you, old man," said John.

"Don't *old* me," said Mitchell. "We both know who's the older, and it's not me." He looked beyond John. "I'm the only cashier right now, and there's a few behind you. I get off at five. Can we meet someplace later?"

"Sure. I'm staying at the Penobscot Exchange Hotel over by the station. I'll go ahead, check in, and meet you at the bar later."

An hour later, they were sitting in the hotel lobby, cigarettes and drinks in hand, toasting each other. "Boy, I've missed this," said John. "Almost as good as the Publick House, eh Mitch? No Jenny or Rose, but not bad."

"I know. I've missed it too. We certainly had some good times. Fill me in on everything going on with yourself. Well, not everything," he said, smiling slightly. "Some things you can keep private."

"Still the prude, I see," said John.

They fell to talking as if no time had passed since their last meeting, commenting on how their lives had ended up with no serious repercussions. Despite their initial worries of working with their fathers in businesses they thought unsuitable to themselves, they were both not only excelling but enjoying the work.

"Who would have guessed?" asked John. "When I got home, I thought my father would harass me about why Lincoln let me go so abruptly. Even though I told you not to worry; that there was no way Stone would let anything get out. Well, I'll be honest with you. I was worried. But a few questions, some coldness, then a few days later it was as if nothing had happened."

Mitchell nodded. "Yes, same with me. Although Charles did torture me with the same questions over and over. I just kept to our story. Then he started in on Stone. 'How could he do this to my stepson? I know there must be more to the story.' I thought he would never stop. Then he told me he had set up a meeting with Stone, which made me really nervous. After they met, he stopped talking about it. Just like with your father, nothing. It was as if the curtain had gone down on a bad play. You were right, John. You hit it right on the nail."

They toasted each other, but not jubilantly. They had been humbled by the experience and the slimly avoided disaster.

"So, John, why are you staying here, at the hotel and not with...?"

"The Stetsons?" interrupted John. "I knew you'd bring them up. I'm surprised it took you this long. It's business I'm here for, so I get the business lodgings, which is fine with me."

"No, John, I was just wondering, that's all," said Mitchell, hoping the flush he felt creeping up his face was not too obvious.

"I know you'll never come out with it. I've been invited for dinner tomorrow night, and I took it upon myself to ask if I could bring a friend. None other than Mitchell Plummer. Edith and Edward were more than gracious in saying yes. The lovely May, I am sure, will be welcoming too. As far as I know, she's still unspoken for."

"Lord, John! You haven't changed a bit," Mitchell said, unable to keep from laughing.

The next morning at work, Mitchell found himself thinking about May. He remembered how she had looked up at him in the store last December. The way her hair had come loose on the sides and framed her face. Her laugh. How she had said teaching was a good profession and that bankers needed teachers too. Well, now he's both, he thought, wryly smiling at himself.

During the lunch break, he went to Forrest's Florists. He was unsure of what to get; he had never bought flowers in his life. Watching the women behind the counter arrange the blooms into various arrangements, he realized he had no idea where the ever-present flowers in his parents' house even came from, never mind how or by whom they were arranged.

"I must admit I'm a bit out of my element," said Mitchell to the man behind the counter.

The man, Mr. Forrest himself, smiled and said, "Not to worry, sir. Most men are. Tell me what you need them for. A celebration? A dinner? A gift? For a young woman, perhaps?"

"A dinner. I think small. A family dinner. And yes, a young woman," Mitchell said, blushing yet again.

"I know exactly what you need. We will make you the perfect arrangement. The parents will like it, the woman will like it, and you'll be the hero," exclaimed Mr. Forrest, all smiles. "It will be ready at four. We close at five."

At five, Mitchell and John were walking to the Stetsons' home. "Mitchell, you didn't have to bring flowers. Do you need a hand with them?" He was trying not to laugh at Mitchell struggling with his burden on this hot spring evening.

"I'm fine, John," Mitchell said curtly. The precious arrangement was heavy, large, and totally inappropriate in his eyes, but what could he do? Maybe he could just hide behind it the whole night.

Edward Stetson answered the door. "John, my man. Great to see you again. And, Mr.

Plummer, nice to meet you. Thank you for coming. Can I help you with those flowers?"

John laughed and said, "He's carried them the whole way here, Edward. You may as well just let him carry them on into the house."

"Edith, look what Mr. Plummer brought. Can you make a spot for them?"

"Oh, my goodness, Mr. Plummer. You shouldn't have. Here, follow me into the dining room. You can put them there on the buffet. There's more room on it."

Mitchell, sweating from the effort and his embarrassment, gladly placed the vase of flowers on top. "Thank you, Mrs. Stetson. It's a bit bigger than I thought it would be," said Mitchell, as they walked back to the parlor. "Thank you for having me to dinner."

"Oh, we love to have company. And please, call me Edith, and my husband's name is Edward. And this is George, my brother-in-law, who I think you met last winter in the shop."

"There you are, May," said Edward. "You remember Mr. Plummer? You met him in the store last year."

"Mr. Plummer, how nice to see you again," said May, blushing slightly as she smiled at him.

"And for me too," Mitchell said, happy to know he wasn't the only one blushing. "And, please, everyone, call me Mitchell."

"I think we can go to our seats," said Edith, as she offered her arm. "Mitchell, will you come with me?" They walked into the dining room, where she stood at an end of the table. She offered him the seat to her left. "John, you sit down there on Edward's left. And May, you sit on my right, opposite Mitchell. And George you're over there across from John."

Dinner was comfortable for Mitchell. Not as formal or fancy as at his home but relaxed. Edith got up occasionally to help her cook prepare and serve. Conversation initially consisted of John regaling the table as to why he and Mitchell were no longer at Lincoln. It was a humorous tale, with clever anecdotes as only John could tell it, never hinting at the true reason for their departures. Mitchell interjected occasionally, but it was John's moment, and Mitchell let him go on. It gave him a chance to glance surreptitiously at May.

Conversation drifted into family history. Edith and May were originally from Connecticut but had moved with their mother to Augusta, after their father died, to live with their mother's sister, Lucy and her family.

Edith continued talking. "After Papa died, Mama just wasn't the same. And she was sickly." She nodded to John fondly. "Lucky for all of us John's parents, Aunt Lucy and Uncle Sean, graciously invited us to move in with them. Our brothers were older than us and stayed behind in Hartford. Mama died three years later. When I met Edward, who was visiting a friend in Augusta, he had just finished law school and was interviewing with law firms in the state. He went with the Higgins law firm here in Bangor, where he was from. One thing led to another, we married, and May moved with me here, to this house, that he had grown up in.

"May was sixteen when we married." At this, she and May rolled their eyes at each other. "And I was only twenty-two, a bit young to be raising a teenager. She gave us a run for our money, I don't mind telling you. But we managed. Now she's practically running the store in addition to being our son Clarence's favorite aunt. She's prepared us for when he becomes a teenager."

George said, "She's great in the store. It's thriving, thanks to her. So much so that I'm thinking of branching out and opening a new one on the western edge of Bangor because of the new rail depot that's being built out there. That whole area is going to boom. They're starting to call it the *Little City in Itself*. Really. Don't laugh."

"I know," said Mitchell. "My brother, Thomas, opened his new branch out there."

Mitchell immediately connected with Edith. Not only was she easy to talk to, he felt an underlayer of true kindness. When she spoke with him, she focused fully on him, making eye contact and gracing him with her attention. At first, he thought it might be because of his name, but she made everyone feel special. His initial embarrassment vanished quickly, and he found himself easily talking with her. Even the excessive flower arrangement began to look good.

Also comfortable to him was May. Sitting opposite her, he was able to sneak looks at her. She caught him looking and smiled, not at all embarrassed, though he was. She was attired simply in a royal blue dress with a contrasting pale-aqua collar, the colors accentuating her blue eyes. Her hair was swept up on her head, the loose tendrils around her face just as he remembered.

After dinner Edith went to the kitchen to help Selma, the cook, prepare the dessert. John was talking with George and Edward at the other end of the table. May leaned across the table to speak directly with Mitchell. "I was so glad John suggested you come for dinner. I didn't know you had moved back to Bangor and had left teaching. Though, I guess there was no reason I would know. I should feel badly about that nasty headmaster letting you two go so abruptly, but I don't. Sometimes, things happen for a reason. Or so they say. I hope to see you again."

Later, when Mitchell got home, he laid in bed thinking about May and her family. He liked them. Edith, with her warmth, seemed very levelheaded. Edward, who became a little bombastic, especially after a few glasses of wine, would need that in his wife. He seemed a gentleman happy with his family and his chosen profession. And George appeared a decent fellow also. Mitchell had to smile at himself. How *he* could presume to know anything about a family or what a couple needed for a marriage was laughable.

May, in real life, attracted him even more than she had in his thoughts. She didn't have the same calm steadiness as her sister. May also charmed but in an unpredictable and bold fashion. He found her alluring and impetuous, as evidenced by when she leaned over and spoke so intimately to him. It was exactly what he could never do. He envied people who were spontaneous and did what they wanted, like John. And she had that wonderful laugh that lit up her face—no polite, simpering giggle from her. At the same time, he felt there was a fragility about her, a crack in her porcelain, belied by that bold laugh.

12—MAY—1887

That same night, May also was lying in her bed, thinking similar thoughts of Mitchell. She had found him attractive when she met him in the store last December. He was around her age; in fact, she suspected she might be a few years older. It was unusual for her to be attracted to men her age, but she could not allow herself to think of him as a possible beau. All that was over for her now...

***

May was seven when her father died, and even at that young age, she had helped her mother and Edith in his care. After his death, their mother declined rapidly, sped along by the move to Augusta. May found school difficult. She missed more days than not, preferring to stay home with her mother. After her death, May fell into a prolonged sorrow, missing so much school she needed to repeat the class the next year. She'd never had many friends in the past, but that year, one of the girls, smart and motherly, took her under her wing.

Dora was May's first true friend. She too had suffered losses and moves and helped May navigate the educational and social landscape. They, along with three other girls were always organizing something: a cookie sale, a lemonade stand in the summer, a hot chocolate stand in the winter, animal shows featuring their pets in various costumes doing silly tricks. In time they became more civic minded, adding clothing and food drives to benefit the poor.

When Edith and Edward married, May had to start anew in Bangor. She felt lost without Dora and school became another chore to get through. She did the least she could to get through school, spending most of her time at home, writing to Dora and reading magazines.

After she graduated, she went to work in Stetson's. Some boys tried to court her. After all she was pretty and flirtatious (depending on her mood) but to her, young men were unsure of themselves and unworldly. As time went on, there were some eligible suitors, young men her age, but she became dissatisfied with them after a short time. It was older men that attracted her; they were more sophisticated. Her family tried to keep a close eye on her, but she made it difficult. Despite their vigilance, she would still sneak out for occasional flirtatious walks in the park without a chaperone. To her it was a kind of game.

Until she met Ivan Festair, a salesman for a dry goods supplier out of New York City. May was twenty when Ivan first came into the store and she was immediately smitten. By now, Edith's and Edward's major concern was spinsterhood and they had relaxed their strict attempts at protecting her.

Ivan asked Edward if he could court May, hinting at an engagement. He was accepted, grudgingly, by her family. Ivan always stayed at the Penobscot Exchange Hotel, conveniently located by the train station and his clients. May and Ivan often sat in the lobby, where they chatted and watched the goings-on. Frequently, they dined in the adjacent restaurant. They became a familiar sight to the staff and clients. What was scandalous, a single young woman, unchaperoned, meeting a single older man, had become almost usual. The lobby was a maelstrom of activity—people milling about talking, laughing, demanding help, bellboys pushing carts overflowing with luggage. Few people noticed the couple in the corner.

The relationship may have started as one of May's flirtatious games, but she had become infatuated with Ivan. They sneaked kisses and touches, often initiated by her. She was shocked at the feelings she apparently aroused in him with just a touch. She was even more excited at the sensations his touches aroused in her.

After about four months, Ivan suggested she come to his room. They planned it together, shivers running down her neck from his whispers in her ear, as she daringly placing her hand on his thigh. He would leave the lobby first. No one would notice her, just another guest, when she went upstairs. May did not hesitate, despite the warnings running through her head. Those feelings she'd had from just a kiss...Was that all? What happens between a man and a woman when they were alone? Her sister had hinted at things, so had her few friends. Why shouldn't she know too?

Kisses and touches worked their way up to sexual relations. It was just one more step in Ivan's slow, calculating seduction of May. Just one more similar affair with similar women in similar towns, all hungry for the attentions of a suave older man.

Not surprisingly, their trysts had not gone unnoticed by the hotel staff, who talked amongst themselves. "That salesman from New York?...The one who always leaves a big tip...My cousin in Portland says he has a girlfriend there too...He's just a little too charming for my tastes...She works at Stetsons, you know...Have you noticed they're fighting a lot now?...I wonder if her family knows..."

Word had gotten to the hotel manager, a Mr. Stevens, who had been waiting for the right moment to speak to the man. Regrettably, he had waited too long. After a loud argument, Mr. Stevens knocked on the door of Ivan's room. He waited an appropriate time before entering the room to find them both dressed and seated, the bed sheets roughly returned to some normalcy.

Mr. Stevens addressed May by her full name and told her to go home. After May ran out of the room, he told Mr. Festair to pack up and leave the hotel at once and never return. But Mr. Stevens felt he owed Edward an explanation. After all, they were fellow professionals in town. And if she were his daughter, he would want to know (wouldn't he?), thanking his lucky stars he'd only had boys.

He waited until nearly closing time before he entered Higgins and Stetson's. Mr. Stevens told Edward a sanitized version of the sordid affair, apologizing profusely, stating he had had no knowledge of this affair; that he himself had just found out today. He described the measures he had taken to ensure that the offensive Mr. Festair would never step foot in his establishment again. He reassured Edward that no one else knew of this indiscretion and that he, personally, would make sure that no one would ever become aware.

Edward locked up his office and walked slowly back to his house, a different man than he had been twenty minutes before. He found Edith sitting at the kitchen table looking upset. She told him how May had come home, crying, running past her, up the stairs and refusing to talk. Edith assumed it was just another of May's moods. Sometimes she was like a child in the attention she required, especially when in the extremes of those moods, either euphorically high or despondently low.

Edward told Edith everything Mr. Stevens had told him. As scandalous as the events were, they at least knew what had happened. They blamed Ivan, then May, then themselves. They should have known better. They should have watched her more carefully. They should have noticed her moods were changing. How often did these meetings happen? Was she really in his room? A hotel room, good Lord! Could they? What if she's...?

The Stetsons were Catholic, and Edward, though not a prude by any means, was mindful of the grave sin of fornication outside of marriage. Edith had converted when she married. The Presbyterian Church she and May had been raised in, and that May still attended sporadically, was just as unforgiving. The weight of the two religions would come down heavily on May and the Stetsons.

Upstairs, May, as was typical of her emotional storms and despite the whirl of thoughts going through her head, found her mood lifting. She was drowsy, as if coming out of a fog, and hungry. Not uncharacteristically, she found her feelings for Ivan fading, her thoughts more coherent. If it was over with Ivan, so be it; he's too old anyway. She could hear Edith and Edward talking. After checking herself in the mirror she went downstairs for dinner.

May's moods had been weathered like storms over the years and she and her family had adopted ways to deal with the turmoil. She would apologize, they would shake their heads, ask some questions, accept her apology and all went on about their business until the next inevitable disturbance.

But when she entered the kitchen hoping for dinner, May knew immediately that this time was different. Edith was openly crying while Edward held her hand and sat stonily beside her. Neither made eye contact with May.

"What's the problem?" she asked. "Edith, I'm sorry I ran past you with no explanation. Ivan and I argued about something stupid, I must admit. But he made me so angry I just couldn't talk about it." They continued to sit in icy silence. "What is wrong? Don't you care about what happened? He treated me terribly. In fact, I'm thinking I'll break it off with him." That should please them; they never liked him anyway.

Edith was the first to speak, having stopped her crying and regaining some of her usual control. "Mary 'May' Agnes Lobdell, you are lying. Stop it right now. We know everything."

"Edith, what are you saying? Why are you saying I'm lying? I told you what happened. You should be upset at Ivan. He was a cad. He lied to me," May said angrily. A small voice in her head wondered, what exactly did Edith mean by *everything*?

"May, sit down," Edward said, uncomfortable but firm. This was his sister-in-law, and he was going to have to talk with her about subjects that would ordinarily be taboo between two nonmarried adults of the opposite sex. "A Mr. Stevens, the manager at the Penobscot Exchange Hotel, came to see me this afternoon. Would you be aware of that name? Would you know what he said to me? And what I had to tell your sister?"

May looked at Edith, hoping for understanding. There was none. She looked down at the table, waiting for the axe to finish falling. Edward related the story. May tried to deny it, but she knew it was useless. She was doomed. She had become the *fallen woman*. Could she live such a life? Isn't this when the heroine must kill herself? How does one go about doing that?

For a while the three sat in stunned silence, each nursing their own terrible scenarios. Finally, Edith stood. "Well, it's done. Let us eat some dinner. It's only a stew, and we can eat it here in the kitchen. When you stormed home, I knew it was going to be a bad evening, so I asked Selma to leave early and take Clarence with her to spend the night. I didn't want him to hear shouting, and I certainly did not want Selma hearing about this and spreading it to her friends. Though I'm sure the chambermaids at the Penobscot have already spread it around town like confetti."

May made as if to leave the table. "Do not think of leaving this table, young lady," Edith ordered. "You are not to leave this table. You will not run away, as usual, from the problem. By the end of tonight, we will have worked out something to deal with whatever happens. All because of your impulsive, irresponsible behavior," Edith said, taking charge.

Edith and May left for Augusta the next day on the early morning train to stay with Aunt Lucy and Uncle Sean. Not knowing how much of the story was known in Bangor, they felt it was best to leave immediately. If people were going to gossip and point fingers, which of course they would, it would be better if May was gone, removing the target of their outrage. Edward stayed behind for Clarence and his legal work and to help in the store. The store would probably suffer most from the scandal, but both Edward and George felt sure it would be short-lived. May, the object of their anger, would not be available, and Stetson's really was the best store in Bangor.

The crucial, obvious reason they wanted May safely away from town was the specter of pregnancy. No one had to verbalize what their lives would be like if she were. They would all be ruined. While in Augusta, Edith would surreptitiously seek out possible places for May to stay if she was pregnant. There were places like that in every city, even in Bangor. Maternity Homes they were called, where secrecy was guaranteed for the mother during her confinement and for the adoption of her baby.

Edith had sent a telegraph to her aunt and uncle from the station before they left. They couldn't wait for a reply, and Edith could only hope they would be accepted into their house. Uncle Sean was Catholic, and Edith did not know how he would react to having May in his house when he found out what she had done. There was a risk he might refuse to take them in, but it was less risk than staying in Bangor and dealing with angry outbursts from the more self-righteous townsfolk. They all had to put their faith in the belief that peoples' memories of events would be short-lived. This would blow over, especially if May was not there in town as a reminder. The plan was for Edith to return to Bangor in two weeks. May would stay for two months, until the end of March. By then they would know if she was pregnant. Or not.

She was not. But May did not return from Augusta until June. Her aunt and uncle had been more than kind to her, and they needed her help. They had two toddlers, change-of-life babies, Aunt Lucy said ruefully. Twins, a boy and a girl, now two years old. Their nurse had left to care for her dying mother. Until she could return, May offered to stay and help with the children, which Lucy accepted gratefully.

Dora, now married with three children, still lived in Augusta. The two women took walks with the babies and reconnected with each other. May became keenly aware of how much she missed her dear friend. Having such a friend in Bangor might have prevented the foolishness with Ivan. Perhaps May was finally beginning to recognize what her moods could make her do.

Self-reflection was not something May she had made a practice of, but now she had time to do

89

nothing but think. May was sympathetic to the risk her aunt and uncle took when they allowed her to stay with them. She knew these moods that came upon her were grave flaws in her character. They emboldened her to do things suddenly and without thinking of the consequences.

While in Augusta, she had thought of Ivan often, now mostly with embarrassment. It was hard for her to believe she had been complicit in his seduction of her. More than complicit if she was totally honest with herself— something else she was not accustomed to doing. All she had wanted was the excitement he offered. Now look at her. *Disgraced.*

What did she want when she returned to Bangor? Did this mean she could never have a normal life as a wife and mother? She had always assumed that would be her future. What else was there for a woman? But now she was stained with this scandal. No one would want her. Despite her episodes, she did have some of her sister's pragmatism. The disgrace would fade in time, she was sure. But would her sins follow her forever? Maybe they would lend her an air of mystery. She might end up an old maid, she thought, but one with a hint of scandal.

When she returned home from Augusta, she was resistant at first to leaving the house despite Edith's urgings. Boredom won out and she ventured out for minutes, then longer. Initially, there were coldness and stares from some people on the street, but her sister was by her side and stared them down. It occurred in the store as well, but George's presence and Edward's when he was there discouraged any rude comments. By the end of a month, she was back working at the store full time. She had become that woman with a hint of scandal...

***

Still in her bed the night of the dinner at her home, May forced herself to stop brooding about her past and allowed thoughts of Mitchell to enter her head. When she had first met him, that December of 1886, her life was back to normal, but certainly no men came courting her. When Mitchell came into her store, she thought he was an attractive young man, just a friend of her cousin John's. She flirted with him, the way she did with most men. She flirted with women, too, in a different way of course. It was just part of her nature, even after her fall from grace. She enjoyed bantering and laughing with people.

During tonight's dinner, she knew he was attracted to her and she to him. Was it possible that he did not know about her past? The Plummers were of a different class. Maybe they couldn't be bothered with the goings-on in other parts of town. Mitchell didn't strike her as the type who would enter into that kind of gossip; he seemed self-effacing, timid almost.

She was twenty-four now. Between her age and the sins of her past, her future was ordained, and there was nothing she could do about it. She had worked hard at accepting her fate as an unmarried woman (she never used the word *spinster*). Thinking of Mitchell could only lead to despair. She would not let herself go there again.

13—A COURTSHIP—1887

May continued to play a significant part in Mitchell's thoughts. Generally, he had had very little interest in women. He had escorted some to dinners and debutante balls, as was expected of a son in a prominent family. For him, those events were something to get through. A few girls were interesting enough to see a second or third time, even one that he saw for a few months. But none truly captured his attention.

So, it was surprising, especially to himself, when, shortly after the dinner at the Stetsons' Mitchell found himself paying a visit to Edward in his office, ostensibly to discuss a legal matter. As he had hoped, it was only Edward in the office.

"Why, hello, Mitchell. How nice to see you again," Edward said, welcoming him warmly. "Sit down, please. How can I help you?"

"It's a pleasure to see you also. I know I said I was here for legal advice," Mitchell said. He took a deep breath. "I'm really here for another reason."

"Yes?"

"Mr. Stetson, as you seem to be the man of house, I should like to ask your permission to see May." He sped on. "I find her a lovely woman, and I

93

would like to know her better. Perhaps I could call on her from time to time at your home?"

He stopped the rush of words. The chapters he had read in *Manners for Men*, suggested what to say in this situation. But they sounded foolish now that he had uttered them. He sat there, his face red, waiting for a reply, his fate in Edward's hands—a man only slightly older than himself. Does every man have to go through this torture to see a woman?

"Mitchell, I think that would be very nice. And just because you had to ask my permission does not mean you must call me Mr. Stetson. Not at all. Please call me Edward. I will need to check with her sister, too, of course, but I see no reason why not. And I think May would be more than pleased," said Edward, thinking here was one more time he found himself in a position of maturity he was not prepared for, due to his sister-in-law. Well, if this works out, Mitchell will be responsible for her, not him.

Mitchell and May began their courtship. A real courtship this time, not a sham of one, May dared to hope. She liked Mitchell and thought they could form a lasting affection. But she worried about their differences in class. Would his parents accept her? She worried about their age difference. She was three years older. Would that bother him? What if he found out about her past?

Edith and Edward could not believe their luck. They approved highly of Mitchell—who wouldn't? A wealthy young man wooing May was more than they had ever dreamed for her, even before the Ivan fiasco. But they, too, had their reservations and worried she would lose interest and break his heart. They wondered how Mitchell would react to one of her episodes. Would the Plummers approve of her? Had the gossip reached Mitchell and his family?

A routine began. Mitchell would call on May at her home, and they would go for a walk. Through the town, to the park, with a rest on a bench, and then the return trip. They were usually accompanied by Edith. Sometimes Selma, the cook, saved her marketing so she could escort them. There were still some contemptuous looks from those with spiteful intent, but Edith stared them down; Selma dreamed of kicking them. More often, they were stopped for friendly exchanges with friends and neighbors.

Their courtship progressed to meetings in the house under the semi watchful eyes of Edith as she attended to her household duties. The courting couple found themselves in the pleasant situation of enjoying each other's company. Mitchell was timid, as May had guessed, but kindly and humorous and safe. There was none of the passion she had had with Ivan, but that was fine. Maybe, she thought, it should be something that grows with time and knowledge of each other.

Mitchell always tried to get May to laugh her wonderful laugh. She slipped into his thoughts frequently, brightening his days. She seemed a little scatterbrained sometimes, and there was that hint of fragility, but he liked her company. He dared to think about marriage and children. He had always assumed he'd be the bachelor uncle like Harry. He worried about the vague feelings he had felt towards John, but maybe they were gone. Maybe the love of a good woman would make them disappear.

One afternoon they were sitting in Miss Sarah's Tea Room, a new establishment in town.

"Thank you, Mitchell, for suggesting a walk. It was lovely today, wasn't it Edith?" asked May.

"Yes, it was. And Mitchell, thank you, too, for the tea. I can't remember the last time I've had such a spread. I've been wanting to get in here."

"So have I," said May. "Not just for the tea, but to see the other wares they sell. A professional evaluation of the competition, so to speak. They do sell some of the same items, but we can exist in the same town."

"You're very welcome, Edith. It was my pleasure. And May, I am always happy to offer friendly business espionage," said Mitchell. "It was my mother who suggested this place. She said it was perfect for a stop after a stroll."

The comment did not go unnoticed. Both women felt a small quickening in their chests; so, his mother knows.

Mitchell and May's times alone increased. The cook went on errands. Edith took a leap of faith and helped in the store for longer hours. She worried her flighty sister might let emotions carry her away. As awful as Ivan was, she suspected he had not acted alone in his seduction. May, she was sure, had led him on. Edith was careful to stay just long enough at the store. She still remembered her courtship with Edward and how they stole touches and kisses. Every couple does, she thought, smiling.

Mitchell and May were no different. For Mitchell it was newly exciting. This was his first intimate relationship. Other than John, he had never been close enough to anyone to share his feelings with. He told May how he had never wanted to be a banker, how he had loved teaching. But those events that John had related so humorously at dinner? They were not humorous at all and had put an end to his dream of teaching. He told her that he had always been a disappointment to his parents. How he wished for children, with a wife he loved and in a kinder, warmer home than the one he was raised in.

For May, it was much the same. She may have been scandalously involved with Ivan, but she had never spoken of her dreams to him. She hinted to Mitchell about a relationship with an older man that had ended badly, and that some people still spoke disparagingly of her. How if it had not been for her family, she didn't know if she could have coped. That sometimes she had moods that came on her and led her to do foolish things or took her to dark places. She also dreamed of children with a husband she loved. She hoped her marriage could be like her sister's with Edward. Like Mitchell, she had few friends, and none close enough to tell secrets to. Only Dora, and there was no way she would ever tell her about Ivan. She had written to her about Mitchell.

They both enjoyed the increasing physical intimacies. Within the constraints of a formal courtship, it was surprising how much the two of them could push the limits of touch. Does every couple do this? Mitchell wondered. For him it was new and thrilling to know they could bring such pleasurable feelings to each other. He felt the total novice, which he was. Oddly, he found it provocative that May was the practiced one. For May, it brought back those feelings she had had with Ivan with none of the sordidness. She found his innocence and kindness appealing and enjoyed being the demure guide.

14—AN ENGAGEMENT—1887

Though Mitchell was living at home, he and his parents had little to do with each other. Alice and Charles had a busy social life; Mitchell's was noticeably quieter. Now, he often ate dinner with the Stetsons, their warm home a welcome change from the coldness of his parent's house.

Mitchell had spoken cursorily of May to his parents during their infrequent dinners together, the three of them at one end of the dining table, large enough for sixteen. Initially, he had only given the barest of information to them. Her name was May, and she worked at Stetson's. He said only that she was a friend he found pleasant to be around. The word courtship did not pass his lips.

A month later, he told them he was courting May, that he felt more than just a friendship towards her. Alice and Charles reacted with smiles and subdued congratulations, saying they were looking forward to meeting her. "Soon," said Mitchell, hoping he was hiding his anxiety. He had nightmares of how May might be received by them.

His parents had often wondered if Mitchell would ever marry. Alice had assumed he was just a slow starter in the games of romance, though, she had begun to adjust to the fact that Mitchell might just stay single forever, as it seemed to be with Harry. Charles was still convinced that there was something intrinsically wrong with Mitchell. Watson, Mitchell's own father, had hinted at such, and Charles had not forgotten Mr. Stone's veiled accusations.

As behooves a family of their standing, Charles and Alice had done their own snooping of May and the Stetsons, and hired a detective, a Mr. English, from a well-known firm in Boston. In his report to them, it was confirmed that Edward was an attorney of good repute, a partner in the law firm of Higgins and Stetson. Stetson's, the family store run by his brother, George, was solid financially. They all were well respected within their social circle. The Stetsons were Catholic, but May was not. She was Presbyterian and went to church sporadically. The Plummers, though Episcopalian and regular attendees, were not overly concerned about that. Neither felt that anything in the Stetson family was an obstacle, and if *they* didn't think so, well then no one else in their circle would think so either.

However, Mr. English's report on May, herself, had more than a hint of scandal about her. "She *is* a scandal," Alice moaned. There was the relationship with the salesman, commonly known about in town. They had been seen together unchaperoned, dining in hotels and at other establishments. There were rumors. Then there was her sudden departure with her sister to Augusta to visit her relatives. "Likely story," Alice harrumphed. She remembered hearing something about it back when it happened a few years ago. But it was of no importance to her—then. She was mollified however, when, on further reading, the detective confirmed that May had indeed been helping her aunt and uncle by caring for their small children.

Further, the report continued, Mr. English was unable to confirm if there had been any intimacy of a sexual sort between May and the man in question. Since her return from Augusta, she had assumed her previous position in Stetson's General Store. In fact, it was remarked by many how she had improved the quality of Stetson's dry goods, especially the clothing lines, the household niceties and the magazines and books. She was even offering classes in decorating to young women.

Not included in Mr. English's report was the statement from the Penobscot Exchange Hotel manager, Mr. Stevens, detailing his confrontation with May and Ivan in the hotel room. And statements from the hotel's chambermaids were omitted also. Nor did he mention anything about the maternity homes May's sister had contacted in Augusta. In the process of his investigation, Mr. English had also become aware of the accusations leveled at Mitchell, resulting in his termination from Lincoln Academy, but as they were unsubstantiated, they were omitted also.

While performing his investigation, Mr. English had not only observed both May and Mitchell, he had also met each of them under false pretenses. Part of what made him a good detective was establishing contact with the people he was investigating in addition to the party that engaged him. Occasionally, he allowed himself the license of disregarding information. In this case, the chance to play Cupid overtook him. He had found May charming and Mitchell earnest and could not help but appreciate how they both had risen above their supposed transgressions.

Alice and Charles both came to the same conclusion: if Mitchell continued courting May and it led to a proposition of marriage, they would not object. Charles continued to fear that Mitchell's possible *proclivities* could become known if he continued as a bachelor. Having him safely married to any woman was the solution.

Mitchell had been courting May for two months. His mother had met May once, two weeks ago, when Mitchell had invited her to join them for afternoon tea at Miss Sarah's Tea Room. Both he and May were nervous, but their worries were for naught. Alice was gracious and, if not exactly warm, amiable. All three left the meeting feeling comfortable with their performances in this age-old rite of passage. He and May were sure they wanted to marry. Now, the time had come for Mitchell to introduce May to Charles also.

The four of them were sitting in the Wiggins' dining room, enjoying dinner—Mitchell and May attempting to. Each was hardly able to eat. Mitchell was worried his parents would be coldly polite. Or worse, his stepfather might say something rude about him in front of May.

May was sure they would not like her. That they would think her too low in station for their son. Maybe they knew of her disgrace. She was afraid her dress was not good enough, even though it was the loveliest and most expensive dress that Stetson's carried.

She had survived the meeting with his mother, but it was his stepfather that filled her with dread. Everything Mitchell had told her about him reinforced that feeling. She could usually flirt her way through most uncomfortable situations with men. But that might not be exactly the best thing to do in this case, she thought sardonically.

The intimidating array of silver and china at her place did not send her into a panic, thanks to Edith insisting they read *The Lady's Guide to Perfect Gentility* together. They had done several dress rehearsals over the past week, Edward shaking his head in amusement and enjoying the three and four-course meals.

"May how are things going in the store now that the addition has been finished?" asked Alice.

"Well, Mrs. Wiggin," said May, gently placing one of her two forks on the edge of her gold-rimmed plate. "Very well. Thank you for asking." There was a long pause. May felt she could slide slowly down her chair and die under the table. Would anyone but Mitchell even notice?

"May, dear, don't be so reticent," said Mitchell, placing his hand encouragingly over hers. "Tell them the rest. How your brother-in-law let you organize it. How, in fact, he's given you the responsibility of the dry goods."

"Well, yes. I have done some of the work," she said modestly. She continued, warming to the subject. "Now the store is laid out with all the dry goods in one section, the new section. That's the part George said I will run. And he's going to let me help him organize the other parts too. He said it's obvious the place needed a woman's touch, so to speak," she said, finishing in a rush.

"That sounds nice," said Alice. "But isn't that a lot of responsibility for a young woman?"

"Mother, what do you mean?" asked Mitchell. "May has the time, and she loves working in the store. She has a real talent in organization, and the store needs it. A lot I might add. And she is an excellent salesperson. I think she's perfect for the job," he finished, smiling fondly at May, who warmed to his praise.

"I agree," said Charles, surprising everyone at the table. "If the need is there, and she has the time and the talents, why not? I know she's a young woman. Obviously. And a lovely girl you are, my dear," he said, smiling at May. "But, it's not unheard of for some women to work, especially if it's in a family establishment."

"Thank you, Mr. Wiggin," said May, giving him one of her winning smiles. Maybe he's not so bad after all. No different than any other man. From now on, she'd pretend he was just another customer in the store.

"May, Mitchell, of course I did not mean anything by what I said," said Alice, looking at them both and purposely not including Charles. She would deal with him later. Why, he was almost flirting with May. And did she actually wink at him?

In September, the Stetsons invited the Plummers to their home to meet and to formally announce the engagement of May and Mitchell. Edith was overcome. These people were wealthy beyond anything she knew. Their names were in the paper every week, hosting some banquet or ball or charity event. Right now, she was the one who needed charity.

How would they entertain them? A dinner? Gracious, no. She could not handle a dinner. Maybe afternoon tea. Yes, that would be better. But what to serve? What to serve it on? Their china had belonged to Edward's parents and it was chipped and old. Her table linens were worn and thin. Edward was doing well and earning more money than ever before but not enough for new place settings of china and crystal and good linens. She managed to work herself into a state.

At first, Edward thought it was humorous, though, he knew better than to let his wife know that. Then he became concerned. He had never seen her like this. She was his rock; she was the rock to them all. He called a family conference.

"Edith, dear," he opened with. "I'm sorry I haven't been of much help to you in this gathering we're going to host. We're all here to help, and together we will decide what to do."

He, George, and May all nodded sympathetically at Edith, which did not make her feel better. Now she was embarrassed by all their attention, which further fed her feelings of insecurity. What was happening to her?

"First, let's get one thing clear," Edward continued. "The Plummers and Wiggins are people just like us. We have never knelt to anyone, and we certainly are not about to start now. Being an attorney is nothing to sneeze at, and I went to Harvard with Harry Plummer. Sure, they are highborn, and we obviously are not. We all know this, as do they, so let's not pretend to be something we're not. We will entertain them the same way we entertain everyone else at our gatherings. But...there are ways we could do it a bit more grandly," he said, with a conspiring smile to his brother. "George said we can *borrow* some china and linens from the store."

"Edward! George!" said May. "What clever men you both are." She turned to her sister. "Don't worry, Edith. I felt the same way when I went there for dinner. But with your help, I made it through, and now it's my turn to help you. They are forbidding, but if I could do it, you can too."

"As my father used to tell me when I first started at Harvard Law School, feeling completely out of my element, 'Remember, son, even the Queen of England has to use the commode, just like us common folk,'" Edward said, abashed, but feeling the moment needed some levity. He had never before used coarse language in front of his family.

"Edward, your language." Edith admonished her husband, suppressing her smile. Bless him, she thought, bringing some humor to the situation. "It's fine, Edward. Sort of like a splash of ice water in my face," said Edith. "I needed that."

Preparations for the affair began. May, Edith, and Selma dusted and polished the house beyond its usual state of cleanliness. Edward washed the windows in and out. Mitchell offered to take Edith to Forrest's Florist, but with her usual confidence returned, she declined. There were plenty of fall blooms in her garden, and flower arranging was one of her joys. May helped Edith pick out a new dress from the store's ever-expanding inventory. Selma made her finest scones and tea sandwiches, looking forward to serving them on the borrowed china.

It was not the most convivial of events. But the engagement was announced, and a date in

October was chosen for the wedding. Edward and Charles went for a walk after the tea, during which Charles offered to help financially.

Edward and Edith had prepared for this, having discussed what they assumed the Wiggins would want for their son's wedding. It was well beyond their means, yet they understood that Mitchell, given the Wiggins' standing in the community, deserved a large celebration.

Edward kindly refused Charles's offer but suggested a way that could let all parties involved be comfortable. The Stetsons, as was customary for the family of the bride, would be responsible for the wedding itself, say four in the afternoon? They would have it in their home, also traditional. May's minister had offered to share the officiating if the Wiggins wanted their own minister there. It would be small, just the two immediate families.

Immediately after the ceremony, they would host a small reception at their home, similar to today's tea. Edward knew that they, the Wiggins, would want—and could afford—a more elegant affair befitting a man of Mitchell's stature. Therefore, perhaps they could host a second reception. Say, a wedding dinner? Later that

111

evening. Done as lavishly as they wanted, he did not verbalize.

Charles happily agreed. He and Alice had discussed the same issue, with his wife convinced it would be a shabby affair. How could she possibly invite any of *their people*? Charles had felt something could be worked out, especially man-to-man, at which Alice had sniffed. Hah, he thought, as he and Edward shook hands.

15—A WEDDING—1887

The day of the wedding, October 12, the Stetsons' home was a crowded whirl of activity. Aunt Lucy and Uncle Sean had come from Augusta and were staying in the spare bedroom. Dora too, was part of the activities; she and Edith would be May's attendants. Dora and her husband were staying at the hotel for the weekend. "After all these years. A first honeymoon," she giggled to May.

Preparations that had been worked on during the week were finalized. Despite the wedding being a small affair, they still needed seating for eighteen. Extra tables and chairs were scattered between the dining room and the parlor. The five tables were draped with white linen tablecloths, four of them set for guests. The fifth table was set aside as the cake table, along with champagne glasses for the toast, the champagne having been generously provided by the Wiggins from their wine cellar.

Edith was finishing up the floral centerpieces using yellow pansies and violas, contrasted with lavender asters and white alyssum (sweet Alice), all from her garden. The napkins were a pale gold, the same fabric from which May had sewn parts of her wedding dress. Between borrowing from friends and the store, each table had a complete tea set with china, glasses, and cutlery—but, each table was set with a different pattern. Edith had raised her eyebrows at this break in tradition but May convinced her it was a modern new look, as was the color and design of her dress. She had devoured articles from *Peterson's*, *Godey's*, *Harper's Bazar Weekly* and other women's magazines, all now carried by Stetson's.

Selma, the cook, was adding Edith's flowers as decoration to the cake. It, along with a smaller second cake, had been baked the day before. As was traditional, the cakes were a rich, dark fruitcake covered in almond paste with a hard white-sugar icing—so hard that May would need a special knife to cut it; Alice donated the knife she had used when she married Mitchell's father. The second cake, the small cake, had already been cut into little squares. May and Dora were putting them into boxes tied with yellow ribbons. These would be given to the guests as they left. Selma's daughter was tending to an array of finger sandwiches and scones.

At noon, the family with Dora and her husband, gathered for lunch, after which the women would go upstairs to rest then prepare for the wedding, which was set for four. This would be May's last meal in Edward and Edith's home. Once wed, May would be living with Mitchell at the Wiggins' home.

"Edith, I remember moving here when you and Edward married. But it never occurred to me that it might have been difficult for you moving into someone else's house. Was it? Mrs. Wiggin wants to have me right there so she can teach me how to be a *lady of society*. I'm all right with that but...I'm really nervous about how I'll fit in there."

"No, May, it wasn't at all difficult. The Stetsons welcomed me with open arms, and you too. They were elderly, and this house was far too large for them. I could help them here, and it was close to the store, so I could help George also. Edward's and my backgrounds weren't that different, which made it easier." She gave a sympathetic smile to May. "I think it is going to be much harder for you. You will be the outsider and must learn all the intricacies and customs that go along with that way of life. I don't want to speak ill of your future mother-in-law, but I don't think Mrs. Wiggin will make it easy for you." Everyone at the table nodded and rolled their eyes.

Having difficulty speaking around the lump in his throat, George said, "May, just treat them like they're customers in the store. You've got a special way about you; you charm all who come into the store."

"May, remember what I said about the queen," Edward said.

"Edward don't go any farther," said May, laughing and joined by an agreeing chorus. "I remember it well. I've already thought it on occasion, and I'm sure I will again."

The women went upstairs to rest and then dress for the affair while the men remained downstairs, commandeering chairs and the sofa to rest upon.

In sharp contrast to the goings-on in the bride's and the Wiggins' households, the groom had little to do on this day. All his duties, only four, had been performed earlier in the month: find someone to perform the ceremony, find a suitable home for himself and his bride, buy the wedding ring and arrange the wedding tour.

Edward had arranged for the pastor, and their home had been taken care of by Alice and Charles. Mitchell was unsure how that was going to work out, but for now it would be fine. He had to buy the wedding ring but May wanted to help choose it and together they had gone to the jewelers. According to tradition, the bride was not to know about the ring. The groom was supposed to wait for her sister to sneak him one of the bride's rings to ensure the wedding band would be sized correctly. Edith had offered but Edgar told her not to bother; that he and May had already chosen one. And, lastly, he was to make the arrangements for the wedding tour, which he and May had also enjoyably done together. They were leaving the next day by train for Rhode Island to stay the week in the Atlantic House in Newport, on Narragansett Bay.

John, as the groomsman, also had duties on this momentous day. He had to ensure that the ring, wrapped in silver tissue paper was in Mitchell's waistcoat pocket. Most importantly, he was to present the toast—in this case two toasts. One at the Stetsons' and a second later at the Wiggins', though being the natural born storyteller

117

he was, it was something he was looking forward to. He had taken into consideration the different social circles, personalizing each tribute accordingly.

Mitchell had arrived at the Penobscot Exchange Hotel earlier, where he and John had dressed into their formal attire of cutaway coat, trousers, and waistcoat. Much may have been occurring at the Stetson's, but Mitchell and John were now obliviously seated in the hotel bar with drinks.

John held up his glass to Mitchell. "I'll give you your own toast now. Here's to you and to your new life with May. I hope you have a long and prosperous life together."

"Thank you, John. I hope so too. I don't see why not. We love each other, and we make each other happy. We think we make each other better."

Harry, dressed in his formal attire, rushed into the room and ordered a double scotch. "Thank goodness you're both still here. One more minute with Mother and I don't know what I would have done. She was more overbearing than usual."

At three, the women began to prepare themselves. Edith, as the matron of honor, had the official job of dressing May, which she shared with Dora. May, unable to sleep, had already bathed before the others arose. They tended to each other's hair, May's swept up and tendrilled the way Mitchell liked it.

May had seen a version of her gown in *Harpers*. Once again, the store had proved itself invaluable. Fabric companies routinely sent samples of their new products, one of which was an off-white, almost gold satin. She ordered eight yards, using most for the dress and the remaining fabric for the table napkins.

She had made the pattern and the dress herself. The gown was classic in design with modern touches. Short cap sleeves and a fitted bodice with a deep V-neck inlayed with a contrasting, white, satin insert, all tapered down to a tight waist and into a long flowing skirt with a small bustle in the back. The waist was cinched with a sash in the same white satin as the bodice insert and tied in a bow with the ends draped down the length of the skirt. It was simple yet formal enough for both affairs. The biggest expense was ordering the matching slippers from Lord and Taylor in New York City.

Edith placed the dress over May's head, not disturbing a hair. Only after the dress was on and sashed, did she then put on the floor-length white lace veil. It had a border of the same gold fabric with lilac flowers appliqued along the edges and was attached to a flowered wreath headpiece made by Edith, using the lilac asters and the sweet Alice.

"Oh, May," said Edith, her eyes filling with tears. "You look beautiful—my little sister all grown up. I know I doubted you when you first suggested some of your newfangled design ideas. But you were right. Your dress, your veil, all the colors, and the decorating downstairs are perfect. Modern and different, just as you wanted. Like you."

"Edith, you made the wreath with your flowers. We created it together," said May, sniffling.

Downstairs, the men were standing around uncomfortably in their suits, thankful it was October and cool. The minister came just as Mitchell, John and Harry arrived. Thomas and Louise with Charlotte and Caleb, their two older children, came in their carriage. And shortly after, Alice, Charles, and Marion arrived. Marion was the flower girl, her dress a matching version of May's.

At five years old, she was thrilled to be part of the marriage—of May, the beautiful princess, to Mitchell, the handsome prince.

During the ceremony there were some tears from Edith and Alice, probably for different reasons, but uniting them for the moment. Edward also found himself dabbing his eyes. His responsibilities for May were over, but he would miss her. Charles thanked his lucky stars he could give up worrying about his stepson.

After the vows, everyone was seated, and champagne was served. John gave his toast, and as usual with John, it was lengthy, warm, and humorous, his gift of the Irish gab taking him through to a rousing, clapping finish. Everyone complimented May on her dress and its color. The ceremony and the tea were satisfying to all, rewarding the women for all their hard work.

"May and Edith, you are so clever to use the china in such an unusual and novel way. And having the napkins match your gown. I would never have thought of that in a million years," Alice said sincerely. The sisters proudly smiled at each other, accepting the compliment.

The groom's family left to finalize their preparations and welcome their guests. The rest of the wedding party returned to their seats, the men happily coatless with ties loosened, the women putting their feet up and sipping on champagne, a rare indulgence.

An hour later, Mitchell and May were sitting on the sofa in the parlor. Alone, finally. They were waiting for the carriage to come back from taking the others to the reception.

"Mrs. Plummer," said Mitchell, smiling affectionately at his wife and kissing her full on the mouth. "Mrs. Mitchell Plummer. How does that sound?"

"Well, Mr. Mitchell Plummer, I think it sounds just lovely. What I really like is that we can sit alone together, side by side on a sofa, unchaperoned. We can even let our shoulders touch," she said, moving closer until their upper bodies were in contact. "Even more if we wanted to. But this skirt won't let us." She giggled, letting her head rest on his shoulder, feeling euphoric.

Mitchell put his arm around her. "Soon enough, my dear. Soon enough. Though I suggest we taper off the champagne. We still must get through this next event. John said he made arrangements to have a bottle on ice in our room for later." Mitchell looked at her meaningfully. "Don't ask me how. He said he asked James to take care of it."

"Mitchell, I so want to be a good wife to you. I want us to be happy. I know we won't be blissful like this all the time. That's impossible. But content and loving to each other. And kind to each other, like Edith and Edward. And we'll have children who will look like the two of us. Four? Five?"

"Oh, May. You are so dear. I want us to be happy too," Mitchell said. "You and your family have made me the happiest I've ever been. I have no doubt you will be a good wife to me. I only hope I can be as good a husband to you."

There was a knock on the door, and James, the Wiggins' faithful driver and apparent romantic collaborator, entered the room.

"Mr. and Mrs. Plummer. Please allow me the honor of driving you to your reception," he said, smiling, his eyes twinkling at May. James had been won over by her early in the courtship. "And, Mrs. Plummer, to your new home."

16—A PREGNANCY—1888

May shifted uncomfortably in bed, trying not to wake Mitchell, though, it seemed he could sleep through anything. At eight months pregnant and always uncomfortable, her sleep was difficult. She gave up on this night and trudged into their sitting room, opening the drapes to a distinct lightening of the sky. Good, Beulah and Maureen will already be up and working. She pulled on the cord to the bell in the kitchen. Maureen would arrive shortly with some tea and toast. Maybe even a scone or a muffin, she hoped. Though the whole house knew she was supposed to be watching her weight.

***

The past year had been one of great adaptation for May. After their wedding trip, they had settled into their rooms in the large Wiggin home—*mansion* to May. Alice had remodeled the old nursery, which took up almost half of the second floor, into an apartment for them. Though lovely quarters, the new couple considered them temporary, until they had a proper house of their own.

Unsaid was that the Wiggins wanted to make sure that these young Plummers were successful, or at least on the road to success.

Mitchell continued at the bank. It had not gone unnoticed by Charles that the third Plummer son appeared to be an able banker, as were his brothers. Charles was more than pleasantly surprised, but he still had his reservations. And Alice was concerned that May adapt well to her dramatically different social conditions before they invested in a home for them.

An early pregnancy had not figured into anyone's plans. Alice particularly was put out. Typical, she thought, of a woman already under the cloud of questionable morals. No one could say it was a *Boston marriage*; there had been a respectable amount of time since the wedding— barely. Fertility is good, but some decorum is better.

After returning from their wedding trip, normal life had begun for the newlyweds. Mitchell had returned to work, and May had returned to— what? Could she just go back to the store? She wanted to, but she was not sure what her mother-in-law expected from her. She didn't even know where she could go within the house, intimidated by the manor's size and its mistress' demeanor. May initially hid in her room, coming down only for meals with Mitchell at her side. Alice did not allow that to go on for long.

On the third day, after Mitchell and Charles had left for work, she kept May at the breakfast table. It was a one-sided conversation with Alice telling her what was expected of her as a wife of a Plummer and a lady of Bangor society. She laid it out for her unemotionally. May mutely nodded, feeling like a small child having been caught doing something wrong.

At the end of her monologue, Alice said to May, "I know I sound mean, but I like to get to the point, and I really do have your best interests in mind; not just yours but Mitchell's too. And your family's. If you shine in this transition, we will all bask in that light." She smiled warmly, for her.

"May, I know what you went through. You are strong and you had a good family behind you to help. Now you have us too, and I will help you prepare for your introduction to society. It's not that hard. It's almost like a game, but there are rules. Some are silly but necessary if you want to survive in Bangor society—and I do want you to succeed. I meant it when I complimented you at your wedding. You have a talent. Use it."

"No," May said, understanding now that they *did know* about her past. "You weren't mean. And I am glad you talked to me. I was just too shy to come to you and ask. Tell me whatever you think I need to help me adapt. But if it's all right, I'd like to have mornings to work in the store. You can fill up my afternoons." They smiled at each other, a small crack in the wall between them.

May's new routine consisted of working in the store on most mornings, and the afternoons were filled with various activities and events scheduled by Alice. Initially, the activities had been in the house, just the two of them, basically how to run a house. How to work with the servants, which servant did what and where. How to talk with the servants in a way that conveyed orders, without being condescending. How to plan meals with the cook. How to decorate for events—the flowers, the settings, the colors.

Alice was the first woman May knew who read often and for enjoyment, not necessarily for edification. Alice told her she was welcome to read any book in their library, but May soon wanted more varied books. She began going to the Bangor Mechanic Association Public Library, which had started out with seven books in a footlocker at the Mechanics Hall and now carried twenty thousand plus volumes. Alice suggested that May start by reading *Little Women*. Used to reading short magazine articles, May initially found it difficult to stay focused. But as she became more practiced, the stories of the four March sisters began to captivate her.

Alice introduced May to the arts—literature, music, painting. May's first foray into public, using her enhanced manners and newfound information, had been at Alice's garden club. Then a luncheon for the new hospital building fund. May quickly picked up on Alice's instructions and cues. It *was* a kind of game.

Pregnancy, having occurred so soon after marriage, brought mixed feelings to both May and Mitchell. And a disappointment to Alice, who believed it was much too early.

Mitchell, of course, was thrilled and secretly proud of himself. Being able to sire a child was just one of his many insecurities. But he felt too young, only twenty-two. How would he support his family? Where would they live? He did not want to live in his parents' house forever. His worst worry was that something might go wrong with May or the baby.

May, too, had conflicting thoughts. She was thrilled and proud she had been able to conceive so easily and give Mitchell a child (and abundantly grateful that she had not become pregnant by Ivan). She worried about the whole process and whether she could deliver a healthy baby. She was fearful of her moods. It had been a long time since she'd had an episode. Being busy and married seemed to be good for her. But she had heard about women who had *nervous troubles* with pregnancy.

Edith tried to calm May's fears. "Every woman goes through a little letdown afterward. It's only natural, and it won't last. You'll be too busy and too in love with your baby." Edith had said this nonchalantly, despite a niggling worry about May's mood shifts in the past. We'll find out soon enough, she said to herself.

Preferably, May would have liked to have had a year or so to get settled with her husband and continue learning about her place in society, at which Alice reassured her she was doing very well. Most, May would miss working in the store, where her reputation as a decorating and entertaining

129

maven was growing by the day. George had even made and hung a sign, "May's Fashion and Designing" over her section of the store.

She had stopped working in the store in her seventh month after Alice told her well-bred women did not go out in society at this late stage. May had not needed convincing; she felt frightfully unseemly, swollen, and exhausted. During her confinement, Alice insisted May keep up with her studies, reading articles about society goings-on in the Bangor papers and her books. May's favorite book was *True Politeness, A Handbook of Etiquette for Ladies*, by An American Lady. She wondered about this author who did not identify herself. She also read the magazines she ordered for the store—*Ladies' Home Journal* and *Harpers*.

Alice had encouraged May to keep up with her recreational reading, the two often having tea together to discuss the book. May had just started *Jane Eyre*, which was her favorite book thus far. Alice told her she would be ready to join her book club if she could get through *Wuthering Heights*, with understanding and enjoyment.

"In truth, though, it may not be enjoyable. It is more difficult to read, my dear, with many more characters exhibiting terrible behaviors; and all so very melancholy. Too much for my tastes, but it would be a good test for you, and you might like it."

***

May startled when Maureen came with her coffee, having become lost in her musings. No scone, but toast with Beulah's lovely blackberry jam. "It's the last, ma'am," said Maureen. "Beulah said she would make some apple butter for you for tomorrow."

"Thank you, Maureen. You both are so sweet to me."

As with James, May had charmed her way into their hearts as well. Alice had to remind May often of the differences in station. "You must not get too close to them. After all they are servants, and there is a distinct separation of class. It will not do for them to get airs and think they are your friends. I cannot stress to you how serious it is that you remember this. Especially, as you are still learning how to be a young matron. There are rules."

Young matron had a ring to it that grated on May's nerves, but she did understand Alice's concerns. And she appreciated her mother-in-law's assistance in navigating this social maze she had married into.

A disheveled-looking Mitchell came into the room. "What time did you get up this morning, my dear? I do worry you're not getting enough sleep. And I feel badly that I sleep through your discomforts. I should be there for you. I don't even know when you're tossing and turning or when you get up."

"It's fine, Mitchell. One of us needs to get a whole night's sleep. I can nap during the day. When I'm not daydreaming about this little muffin in the oven," May said. She had learned the expression from Maureen but only dared say it inside their private rooms; Alice would say it was too common. She took his hand and laid it on her belly. "I wonder what it's going to be. What it's going to look like. Act like."

"I know," said Mitchell. "I do the same at the bank. I'll be daydreaming then suddenly hear a polite cough, sometimes not so polite, and there is someone standing at my window. Of course, most of them know about your condition, so they just laugh knowingly. We are certainly not the only couple who has gone through this." He leaned over to give her a quick kiss. It still amazed him he had this luxury of intimacy with her, that he could kiss her, caress her, and love her when he wanted. "I'm going to get ready for work," he said.

Alice had bought May some wrappers. Robe like, they had extra material that could be wrapped around her and sashed. Alice allowed that May could wear them at home. "That's what they are. Wraps to wear at home before dressing for the day. I am not so old I don't remember how cumbersome it was to dress when one is pregnant. And it's fine if you wear it to breakfast. Charles always leaves by eight, so you can come down after that."

If she could have, she would have worn them day and night. But principle dictated not. Certainly not for young matrons in Alice's household. Dressing was more than cumbersome. It was exhausting, and she needed Maureen's help, especially with the maternity corset. Even loosely tied, it was a two-person chore. Once it was on and positioned correctly, it was actually comfortable. Longer than a regular corset, it allowed her belly to feel supported. The seams in her largest dresses had been let out twice, and the way she felt now, she was sure they would have to be let out once more.

After breakfast, on her way back to her room, she checked the birthing room just to reassure herself that all was ready. Fittingly enough, it was Mitchell's old bedroom. His bed was still there, now feminized and plumped up with pillows for her to lie on before and after delivery. The birthing bed took up the middle of the room. A special bed—lightweight, portable, and high—it allowed the midwife or the doctor to get close without having to bend and reach across the breadth of a regular bed. It was, Alice told her proudly, the same bed in which her mother had delivered her, and the same one she had used for her boys and Marion. It was the most intimate information Alice had ever shared with May. When she told her sister about the conversation, Edith nearly cried.

"Oh, dear," said Edith. "I have neglected my parenting, well, sisterly duties. And to think I have neglected them to the extent that *she's* the one who is teaching you. I used Edward's family's birthing bed, the one he was born on. It had been in their family for years. Once you told me Alice had prepared a room for you, I didn't see the need to offer it. But I can answer all your questions—the ones you can't ask her."

"That's what I really need, Edith. And you will be there with me, right? Alice told me you would be there. That you two had discussed it."

"Of course, May. I told you that already. I think you have pregnancy brain. We've all suffered from that. And we all felt the same as you," said Edith.

"Maybe you told me already, but tell me, again, what's going to happen. Everything."

"Well, you know you'll be going through a number of hours of labor, with the pains becoming increasingly more painful and closer together. But you can get up and walk around, or sit, or lie down. We'll help you. At a certain time, Dr. Clark will come and decide what stage you're in. Eventually you'll get up on the birthing table, slide down on your back, and put your feet on the blocks. And then you'll push and push. For a long time, I'm afraid."

"Oh, Edith! In front of a man? With my legs spread wide apart? I'll be mortified."

Edith laughed. "Not for long you won't. I have heard that some doctors prefer the mother be on her side with her legs pulled up to her chest. Personally, I think that's foolishness. The midwives don't do that. It's because doctors are men, and if you're on your side, they don't have to make eye contact with you. All that purity stuff. And I don't understand how you could really push that way anyway. Luckily, Dr. Clark isn't one of those. He wanted me on my back with my feet resting on the blocks when I delivered Clarence."

Edith laughed again. "Yes, you will be embarrassed, and you won't care a whit. There isn't a thing you can do about it. You may even curse. Every woman goes through the same thing. Look at Queen Victoria..." She broke off when May interrupted her.

"I thought you were going to say she..." May was giggling hysterically. It was all just too much.

"Well, yes. She does go like us. That's true too. But no, I was going to say she went through nine births. Nine! And I'd bet you she swore too. She used chloroform for the last two. You can have that, too, to help you. I didn't, but you can. Most woman do now, at least the ones who can afford doctors."

Edith continued. "And more foolishness. You know what one of the reasons was for the birthing bed? In addition to the design, which really did make birthing easier, it was to use a separate bed than the one the baby was conceived on. To remove the sexual overtones associated with birth. Bah! How else did you get there?"

"I don't know if I can do all this," said May.

"Oh, yes, you can. You have no alternative." Edith leaned over and gave May a hug. "Welcome to the club. And you know what other foolishment they say? Having a baby gives a woman her rights. When a girl gives birth, she becomes a woman. I'm not exactly sure what all that means. As far as I'm concerned, it still comes down to your luck in choosing a husband. He's the one who has all the rights. Luckily, it looks like you and I made the right choices."

Pregnancy has a way of not following its own schedule. May was due the last week in November, but in the early hours of the fifteenth, her water broke. She was more than ready.

Alice called Dr. Clark to let him know. He would arrive later, when May's labor had progressed. The Wiggins were one of the few families in Bangor with a telephone. Still considered newfangled to most, only the wealthy could afford them. But more and more businesses, police stations, hospitals and especially doctors all were going to this new, improved communication device. Charles had just had the telephone installed two weeks earlier at Alice's insistence.

The Stetsons did not have a telephone, so James was sent to notify Edith. In the meantime, May had put on a shift and petticoat, and Maureen was braiding her hair and tying the braids up on her head. "You don't want your hair all tangled and matted, ma'am. Believe me. I know."

By ten, May was in active labor—pacing the floor, sitting, squatting, and sometimes lying down in between contractions. Maureen brought liquids for May. "You need to keep your strength for the

138

last part of the labor, ma'am. Keep sipping water. It's good for your kidneys, and it helps make your milk come in faster. And the chamomile tea will settle your stomach and relax you." Relax? May thought, managing a small laugh. Edith and Maureen kept her spirits up and told her how to breathe. Alice came in and out, never staying for long, which suited them all.

Edith, as the most recent woman to have gone through labor, did the coaching. "You've got to breathe. That is the most important thing. I'm just telling you what I did. But it really helps. It makes your mind focus on the breathing and not the pain. Take slow, deep breaths. That's it. Now when you get a big contraction, do a big sigh, and let all the air out. Try breathing through your nose sometimes instead of your mouth. You might want to change the breathing, make it fast and shallow. You can even pant when it gets really bad. Do whatever helps."

Mitchell came in for short periods, holding May's hand and feeling guilty. He wanted to share some of her pain. It was his fault she was going through this. He had to be there for her, but at the same time, he knew he was superfluous—utterly and completely useless.

Alice came in to announce that Dr. Clark had called and was on his way. Good, thought May. Maybe we can get on with this. Knowing she would have to get on the table and show her privates was now just a mere speck of a thought.

When Dr. Clark arrived, she did exactly what he said. She raised her skirts above her hips and buttocks and placed her feet on the blocks, and he examined her. Put his fingers inside her. Good God! Somehow, she had just thought he'd sit down there and catch it. He stood up and, without looking her in the eyes but taking in the rest of the women, said, "She's almost there. Maybe a half hour more. It's just a matter of waiting."

"Waiting!" cried May. "And why are you talking to them? I'm the one you just put your hand into. And I'm not a she. Talk to me!"

"I'm sorry, my dear. May, right? Most of my clients do not want to have anything to do with me, except to demand I speed things up. You're a breath of fresh air," said Dr. Clark, looking at May with a smile.

"I sure don't feel fresh," panted May. "And feel free to speed things up."

Alice looked put out at May's behavior. But Edith smiled. This was her May.

At 12:10, May delivered a healthy, perfect, ten-toed and fingered baby girl. She lay on that hard table waiting for the afterbirth, with her baby on her chest, feeling victorious.

Later, after Edith had washed May and put a clean shift on her, they walked over to the bed—the marvelous, soft, comfortable, cool bed. May fell into it. Maureen brought her the baby, now cleanly perfect in the infant shift that each of Alice's babies had worn when they were born.

Edith helped May get started with nursing. "I know, it feels funny. Some babies take a while to figure it out, but it looks like this one is going to have no troubles. Look at her."

May felt triumphant, again. Maureen finished cleaning up the room then left while Mitchell came in to sit with his wife and daughter.

"Oh, May. I am just so proud of you. I wanted to share your pain, but I guess it's something that only women can really know. Look at what you've produced. She's beautiful. The most beautiful baby in the world." Mitchell was crying but trying not to. "I can't help it."

"I know," said May with tears in her eyes also. "It's amazing, the joy I feel just looking at her."

She unwrapped the baby, and the two of them oohed and aahed over their child. "What are we going to name her?" asked Mitchell. This conversation about names had been going on for nine months. They had it down to six girl names but couldn't agree on which one.

"Just before I stopped working in the store, this lovely lady came in looking for linens. She wasn't from here. Boston, I think. And she had the most adorable daughter. Frances. I've been thinking of that name ever since, and the moment I saw this little one, I thought of her as Frances. I know it wasn't one of the names. Can we keep Bennoch for her middle name? Mama's maiden name."

Mitchell interrupted her. "Dearest, I love the name. Maybe the reason we couldn't go with one of those other names was because we didn't know her. You're right. She *is* Frances."

18—DESPONDENCY—1888

The small Plummer family tried to settle into a routine. The family cradle was brought into Mitchell's old bedroom, now the nursery, the birthing table having been folded up and stored back in the attic. The first week, May stayed in the nursery with Frances. Alice and Edith took turns helping May during the daytime, and Maureen helped her at night.

"You're lucky, ma'am," said Maureen on the second night. "Your milk came in quick, and this little doll nurses so easily. Some, oh my goodness, some take forever to figure it out. My second was like that, and he had the colic too. That's the one I had to stay away from work for two months. I thought Mrs. Wiggin would fire me for sure. But no. She told me your Mr. Mitchell was the same way. She even paid my wages while I was out. That sure shocked me, I don't mind telling you. But I'm eternally grateful to her. Not many employers will do that."

May's feelings of triumphant victory had faded, leaving awkward incompetence in its stead. And her modesty, which had vanished so completely during childbirth, had returned. If there were others in the room, she was uncomfortable when nursing. Having to listen to Maureen talk incessantly about others' experiences with birthing and nursing and infants disturbed her even more.

On another night Maureen said, "You know what they used to say? The mother must not get up until the ninth day. But look at you. Each day you're doing more and more. Sure enough, women in my family never stayed in bed. Not even two days, never mind nine."

"And, in two more weeks, when you're done recovering, you'll go to church and show off this beauty. *Churching.* That's what we call it, and it's always a big day."

During the long periods alone with her baby, May stared at Frances, the enormity of her responsibility lying heavily on her mind. She was unsure of what to do with her own baby. Edith and Maureen picked Frances up so competently, expertly changing her, cooing and laughing at her, fondling her. The only time May felt able as a mother was when she was nursing—Maureen was right about that. These feelings of inadequacy unnerved her. Worrisome thoughts darted through her head, like bats in the dusk. They didn't settle; they flitted, leaving unease in their wake.

As soon as Mitchell arrived home, he would run upstairs and ask May what Frances had done that day. He held Frances in his lap, going through the same process of getting to know her, just as May had. She felt small pangs of jealousy watching them together and firmly tried to squash those feelings, as they made her ashamed.

At the end of the first week, May moved back into their bedroom. Both Alice and Edith told her it was time. May agreed, thinking it might help the strange thoughts she was having if she was with her husband and not with Frances every minute. Mitchell was pleased to have her back beside him in bed. "I sleep better with you near me," he said, patting her thigh affectionally.

At first the move seemed to help. It was nice to be with her husband again, falling into their familiar patterns of sleeping side by side. She slept a deep and long slumber that first night, uninterrupted by Frances's small squeaks and noises. She had left the doors open to their room and the nursery. But the next day her worrying increased. It can't be right to leave an infant alone so long, could it? She must always be with her baby. Isn't that what a good mother should do? What if something happened to Frances when she wasn't there?

She moved back to the nursery after two nights. "I'm the mother, and I'm the only person who truly understands Frances. She needs me," she told a concerned Mitchell. Secretly—all her thoughts now were secret—she didn't want Frances to develop an attachment to Mitchell. Only to her. But he's her father, her mind said. Well, she needs her mother said her other mind.

Determined to be the perfect mother, May reread her books, *Maidenhood and Motherhood* and *Mother's Book*. They had become her bibles. She took all the suggestions to heart. Literally.

The new mother should be left alone and get adequate rest and sleep.

Babies are empty vessels, their hearts ready to receive impressions.

It is critical they not experience the evils of the world.

They should never be spectators of anger or any real passion.

A mother's influence should not interfere with the influence of the angels.

The new mother should govern her own feelings.

If possible, the new mother should take the entire care of her own child.

She must not get up until the ninth day.

The rigorous attention needed to accept these responsibilities further eroded May's self-confidence. She frostily declined Alice's offer of a nurse, assuming her mother-in-law's offer was because she thought May unable to care for her own baby. She refused visitors except Mitchell or Edith and for short periods of time only. The only person to see her on a regular basis was Maureen who brought her meals and tried to clean the increasingly messy, stale room.

"Ma'am. You need to stop this worrying. All you're doing is stirring the pot. Babies need some time to themselves. You know, a little growing room, so to speak."

May was overcome with her rigid adherence to her literary advisements. She felt she was running in place and that, if she stopped, she would fall off the edge of the world and die, taking her baby with her. Her love for Frances had become so ferocious that it made her terrified of her own self. By the end of the third week, she was in danger of *not governing her own feelings* and finally asked for her sister.

Edith had been watching May's downward spiral with great anxiety. She knew that eventually May would reach out for her help. It was her pattern; at least it had been so in the past. But this time there was another small being involved. Edith ached for mother and child, but if she tried to intervene too early, it could set May off into a longer period of melancholy.

It was all Edith could do to keep from breaking down when she entered the nursery. "Oh, my dear May. You must never wait this long to call for me. Especially now with a little one."

She bustled about, not looking at May. Her lovely sister, holding the tightly swaddled Frances, was in a rocking chair, still in her night shift. Her beautiful strawberry hair hung lank and dull along her face and shoulders and onto Frances's face, blessedly asleep and unaware.

May stared dully back at Edith. In a flat voice, she said, "I'm sorry, Edith. I can't do it. I'm not good enough to be her mother. I tried everything, but I'm a failure. I'm a bad mother and a bad wife. I should just die."

"Stop it, May!" Edith snapped loudly back at her. "Right now, you absolutely are all of those things. And probably more. But we will tackle this the same way we always tackle your spells. You will come out of this just as you always do."

"First of all, you need to bathe. While you do that, Maureen will air and clean this room, and I will clean and dress Frances. You do trust me to care for her, don't you?" Edith asked sarcastically, against her better nature. "You're going to have to give up some of your control and let others help you."

"Edith, you always know what to do with me. I love you for that. But this is so much worse than any of my other episodes. I have never felt so terrified. This certainly can't be just the depression everyone told me about."

"No, dear, I don't think so either. If I ever told you that, I am sorry. This is more than just the blues. I've heard of some women who become afflicted with a great despondency. With your history, we should have known you might react this way. It's all right, May. It's just how you are. You, we, all of us need to be prepared for this again. Mark my words, because you will have another baby, maybe more."

"God, Edith! I can't do this again, can I?"

"Yes, you can. But having gone through this once already, you can use this experience and anticipate your mood changes. I'm going to have Alice call Dr. Clark to send over a tonic. It will help you get some much-needed sleep. You can't do anything without rest. Only then can you start to work on getting back to your regular self. The one who told Dr. Clark how to do his business," Edith said, smiling. "That's the brave, wonderful sister I know and love."

After a hot bath, May dressed into a clean shift. "This is the last time you wear one of these during the daytime. From now on it will be regular day dressing with your hair pulled up," said Edith. "And starting today, you will sleep with your husband in your marriage bed. It is your place and your duty. Poor Mitchell has been tortured by your decline. I will stay with the baby the first few nights to help you and Frances adjust to normal life."

Maureen came into the sitting room bearing a tray with two bowls of soup, crusty bread and butter, and tea. She beamed at May as she placed the tray on the table. "Oh, ma'am. You look so pretty, and already I see some color in your cheeks. Nothing like some motherly love from your sister."

Like what I must give to Frances, May thought. She almost jumped up to go back to the nursery, but Edith put a hand on her arm, having anticipated just such a move.

"No, May. She does not need you every second. That is not what mothering is all about. It's loving them, but from their first day, it's always about letting them go. You'll learn."

19—TENSION—1889

"Mitchell," May said. "I've been thinking."

Mitchell looked up from the newspaper. They were in the dining room on an April Saturday morning, luxuriating in having the whole house to themselves. Well, Marion, Mitchell's stepsister and her nurse were still there, but Marion adored May and doted on Frances.

Alice and Charles had left the day before for a visit with Harry, now living in Asheville, North Carolina. He had been offered the job of president at the Bank of Asheville, which despite the huge distance he had accepted. Asheville's economy was on an upsurge due to its businesses in lumbering, textiles, furniture, and tobacco. The city offered Harry far more varied banking opportunities than staid Augusta.

"What about, my dear?" responded Mitchell, smiling. "Maybe something about the delight of being in this house alone?"

"As a matter of fact, yes. But don't you agree it's time we get our own place? Frances is almost five months old now, and it is a bit crowded upstairs."

"I know. I agree with you. I have been saving, and I'm making enough to support us. I've been planning on talking to Charles about it, but I just haven't gotten around to it yet. I'll do it when they get back."

He started to pick up the paper again then changed his mind. "May, you've been fantastic about all this. I am so impressed with how you rallied from your low spirits after Frances's birth. It was such an awful time for us all, and I was so frightened. I admit I've been remiss in not moving forward with our lives."

"I know, Mitchell. And I understand your hesitations. I had them too. But I feel so much better, like my old self. And everyone else has been more than understanding. I appreciate them all, but..."

Mitchell interrupted her. "I know what you're going to say: my mother. Don't think I haven't noticed. It has always been my father and my stepfather who have been difficult, at least for me. It is surprising so see Mother act so cold to you. I don't understand. But it certainly is another big reason for us to move into our own place."

"Thank you, dear, for being so sympathetic. It is hard. I don't understand it either. Maybe she can't accept weakness in anyone. She was so helpful to me in navigating my way into Bangor social activities. And when I was pregnant, and even during the birth. But when I began my slide into despondency—I don't know what else to call it—she became different. It's spread to include Frances too. She rarely holds her or plays with her. And I can tell it pains her to take me to any of her clubs or events. Thank goodness I'm back at the store for a few hours each day, or I'd go mad." She gave a little grimace. "I already did, sort of. I can't use that word jokingly."

"It is time, May. It is time. You're right," said Mitchell.

"On a totally different subject, I hope you haven't forgotten that Dora and her husband are coming tonight for the weekend," said May. "I can't wait to see them. And then John is coming next week. I love being able to invite our own guests. Beulah has been a rock. Between you and me, I think she likes cooking for us. Tonight, she's making her wonderful chicken fricassee and her bread pudding for dessert. All my favorite foods.

Well, why not? It's my party. She said she'll help me host our first dinner party when we get our own place."

The two weeks went by in a happy whirl, making their adjustment to residing back upstairs in their small quarters even more difficult. Having been away for two weeks made it equally difficult for the Wiggins.

"Alice," said Charles, a few weeks after returning home. "I just don't understand this sudden dislike you seem to have of May. You were the one who said she was adapting admirably to her change in social status. You took her to your clubs. It all started when the baby was born. When she had the vapors, or whatever it was she had."

"Charles," said Alice. "Why do I have to explain myself? It just is. She has adapted well and impressively risen to her social obligations." Maybe a little too well, she thought. "The other day one of the women in my book club came up to me and said what a darling daughter-in-law I had. That May had volunteered to help her with her work on establishing a Bangor symphony. I didn't know she even liked music," Alice finished huffily.

"I think that sounds admirable," said Charles. "We need to foster more artistic groups. It is what great cities do. Look at Boston and New York."

"I know that, Charles. I'm not an idiot. Do you always have to defend her? And another thing. She's back to working at the store again. You'd think she wouldn't want to risk her hard-earned social status, which by the way she wouldn't have without me. There are still many people, me included, who think women shouldn't work outside the home. She refuses my offer of a nurse. She takes the baby with her, keeps her in a cradle at the store, exposing her to who knows what. And then at my meetings, all I hear about is how talented she is with her ideas on decorating and fashion. Please!"

"Alice, my dear. If I didn't know better, I'd say you sounded jealous," said Charles, with a nervous smile. It was always a risk when he tried to humor her.

"Really? Me? You must be joking," Alice said. "But she has become tiresome to me. I don't dislike her, but I don't like her either. And it's not just me; I think she feels the same about me. It's just the way it is, and I can't explain it, so don't ask me again."

They were in the library with the door closed. She had been pacing the floor while talking but stopped and stared at her husband. "And, it is time they moved out and got their own place. Gracious, Charles. Thomas only stayed with us for a few months when he married and Harry not at all. It's been a year and a half. It is ridiculous to still be living with us. Never mind crowded."

"All right, Alice. Calm down. If it makes you feel any better, Mitchell came to me the other day and asked me to help him find a place. He didn't say so, but I think it is just as uncomfortable for them. He also reiterated his desire for more responsibilities at the bank."

Charles paused, looking out the window. "It's odd, Alice. Mitchell is your son I worried about the most. The one I least warmed to, if I'm totally honest. It's not just me. You know Watson worried also and harbored the same fears of Mitchell's masculinity as I do. Mr. Stone made it pretty clear to me that there was more involved in how Mitchell was let go at Lincoln. But he has impressed me with his good work at the bank and with his choice of May as his wife. I like her."

"Charles, you just like her because she flirts with you. If you haven't noticed, she flirts with every man. She's a hussy. I bet that *situation* she got herself into was of her own making. If Mitchell is so interested in more responsibility, maybe you can find another job for him. At another bank. In another city. Maybe in another state. You bankers are all so cozy with each other. Someone in another town must have an opening. Especially for a member of the famous banking Plummers." She picked up her skirts, spun around, and left the room.

Alice went to the solarium, her favorite room in the house, and rang for tea. "Very hot, Beulah, and with honey. And maybe just a touch of Charles's Jamaican rum." She felt herself calming as soon as she entered the warmth of the room.

She did not understand her feelings either. For someone so in control, this was an uncomfortable position in which to find herself. It was true that in the beginning, she had warmed to May, impressed by her quick adaptation. It was that three-week period after the birth of Frances that remained in her mind, erasing everything May had done so ably.

Alice had never been exposed to someone suffering from melancholia; for whatever else could it be called? It was unnatural. Do we all have this failing in ourselves? Is it possible it could come upon anyone at any time? Does being near someone in the throes of this misery increase the chances of it appearing in oneself? What about Mitchell who had exhibited weaknesses as well? What if their children are affected? That's all we need, she thought. Crazy children running around.

These thoughts baffled Alice and frightened her. They alarmed her enough that she did not want to be living near anyone who could be prone to such attacks. Never mind living in the same house. She absolutely could not handle it.

20—CHRISTMAS REDUX—1889

What Alice had to handle instead was the death of Charles. Shortly after her temper tantrum in the library, he became ill. His speech became slurred, the left side of his face drooped, and he stumbled when he walked. "Cancer," Dr. Clark announced. A large tumor in his brain and inoperable. Alice brought him to Boston and to New York City, to all the best doctors. But they all said the same. She brought him home to die, which he did on July 9, 1889.

Alice mourned quietly and envisioned her future life. She was forty-seven and had buried two husbands. Her children were grown, though one still lived in her home with his wife and baby for heaven's sake. And Marion, of course, she was only six. Alice was still considered an attractive woman and certainly eligible. Too eligible, she thought. Charles had eagerly made his intentions known soon after Watson died. Charles was no Watson Plummer, but he was attractive in his own blustery way, and most importantly he was independently wealthy. There was no risk to her social status or to the Plummer estate.

Alice did not want or need another man in her life. It would be a pleasure to not have to persuade another self-inflated male to accede to her wishes. Maybe she could travel around the world. Visit Montreal again where she and Watson had spent their wedding trip. Spend a summer in the south of France.

Thomas Plummer had assumed Charles's position as president of both branches of the bank. Mitchell prodded his brother about assuming more responsibility at the bank. He felt he should be earning his way up the banking ladder. May felt it was an insult that Thomas, as much as she liked him, had not promoted her husband, especially after Charles died. It was Mitchell's due as a Plummer, May reminded him.

He had savings, enough to make a down payment on a house. He and May had narrowed their search for a home, but he needed to make more money to support his family. His growing family—May had found herself pregnant again in early September. This time she was practically bedridden the first three months with terrible morning sickness. The search for a house was abandoned until the following year after the baby was born.

Mitchell and May spent this Christmas as they had the first two since they had married: Christmas Eve with the Plummers and Christmas Day supper with the Stetsons. May was enamored of her in-laws' evening traditions. Her own family did little on the eve; their traditional meal was a holiday supper on Christmas Day. It worked for everyone.

This Christmas was, so soon after Charles's death, more subdued than usual but still up to Alice's elegant standards. Harry had arrived the day before from Asheville and was staying with Thomas and Louise. Just as he had jokingly predicted three Christmases before, Thomas had built Louise a grand new house in West Bangor, still called the Little City in Itself because of its rapid commercial growth—where he and his stepfather had so presciently built the second branch of the Bangor Savings Bank.

The family gathered in the drawing room, chatting and reminiscing. This year Alice did away with the age limit. Marion was the only one under twelve, and Alice thought it would be cruel to isolate her. Frances, at seven months, was upstairs with Betty, the new nurse. Alice had insisted to May that she have one. It was what people did, her voice indicating she would brook no argument.

Mitchell was chatting with Harry. "How is it in the South? Is everything still ruined? Do they accept you?" he asked. "After all, you are a Yankee."

Harry smiled. "It is a little different, and sometimes I can hardly understand the people; their accents are so strong. Southerners, though, are very friendly. Much more so than we New Englanders. North Carolina's nickname is the Rip Van Winkle State because of its late arrival to industrialization, and Ashville is at the forefront of all that business.

"Asheville is trying to put the Confederacy behind itself. It must if the city expects to be competitive with the rest of the country. And if my bank is any indication, it seems to be doing a good job of it. After all, it is twenty-five years since the war."

"And you don't miss Bangor? I could be amenable to a move away from here, but May's not too keen on moving. She's so close to her sister and her work in the store."

"Not really. I miss the family of course. But it's a new world for me—exciting. And I can make my own path, not necessarily Father's or Charles's," said Harry. He lowered his voice. "I heard you and May were looking for a place of your own. About time, isn't it?"

Mitchell answered defensively. "Well, there has been a lot going on lately. It's not just me I have to worry about."

"I'm sorry, Mitchell," said Harry. "I didn't mean it that way. It's more like, how can you tolerate it?"

"It's not that bad, at least not for me. It is for May, but now that she's expecting again, it seems best to just stay until the baby is born. Between that bout of depression with Frances and then the issues with this one in the beginning, we all decided, including Mother, to just stay put. May's doing fine now, thank goodness."

May was talking with Thomas, now the patriarch of the family. She had always liked him, and he felt the same about her. The whole family had become fond of her, except for Alice. "You know, we were looking for a place of our own," said May. "But between Charles's passing and my recent health issues, we put it off until later. And I can help Alice," said May, hardly feeling guilty about the lie. Alice surely did not want any help, especially not from May. Nor, except once as a curtesy, had May offered it.

"That's kind of you," said Thomas, going along with the obvious white lie. He looked at her conspiratorially and moved a little closer. "And I'm sure difficult. She is my mother, and I love her, but she is not an easy person. Louise and I lived here for the first few months of our marriage, waiting until our house was ready. I thought Louise might move back home to her family," he said.

"Really? Louise? I didn't think anything bothered her," May said. She smiled, glad to know she wasn't the only one tortured by Alice.

"Well, my sainted wife has her limits just like anyone else."

"Louise has always been caring to me, like a big sister," May said. "Your mother is difficult, no doubt about it. She wasn't in the beginning. I know I was a project, but she helped me immensely and not unkindly. Sternly and coolly, yes, but I was all right with that. In fact, I appreciated her distance. But now matters seem to have gotten worse."

165

"Yes, I thought I sensed her coolness to you. More than her usual. She can be icy when she cuts someone out of her life," said Thomas. "I'm sorry. I didn't mean to imply she had severed your relationship."

May looked at Thomas with surprise. "I don't know her well enough to have seen that before. But, yes, it is exactly how I felt—severed."

Alice moved gracefully across the room and chatted with them both for a bit. Then taking Thomas' arm, she announced it was time to sit for dinner. The dining room was splendid, causing the youngest children to gasp in awe. Family members found their places, then Alice took her seat with the others following.

Mitchell was between Louise and Caleb, Louise's eldest son, both favorites of his. He didn't know how Alice did it, but the hours she spent planning the seating usually resulted in successful dinner companions. May was between Thomas and Harry. Good. She'd be happy with them both and they with her.

Mitchell chatted briefly with Caleb, now sixteen and attending Kent's School, where Mitchell had gone. Hearing Caleb's stories brought

Mitchell back to his days of teaching at Lincoln. He still missed it sometimes, but he'd become comfortable in banking. And banking paid more. Well, it would when he was promoted, which had to happen soon; it was almost embarrassing now.

Louise turned to him. "I'm so glad Alice put us together. How does she know?"

"I was just thinking the same thing about Mother's perception. It is a little unsettling to realize she knows so much about us all. But I am glad. Two of my favorite people," said Mitchell. "Still liking it out in the territories?"

"Oh, Mitchell, it is not that far out anymore. And I do like it. It's not so formal. The buildings are new, not steeped in history. You can make your own history, sort of. Must be what the people on the wagon trains feel. You and May need to come out more," said Louise. "And you don't need a covered wagon."

Later, in their quarters, Mitchell and May were having a heated discussion. "I'm telling you, Mitchell. I just do not understand your mother. If she were any colder to me, it would be because she was sitting on ice. Louise and Thomas both commented on it," said May, as she climbed into bed. "We cannot get out of this house fast enough."

"I know, May. I know," said Mitchell wearily. "Harry noticed it too. She's not even trying to hide it. She has been imperious in the past, even to Louise when she first came into the family. Maybe it's when the new wives move into her house," he said jokingly.

"It's not funny, Mitchell. Though maybe she was jealous. You know, protecting her territory. I just don't know, but I can't take much more of it," May said. She was near tears. "As soon as we have this baby, we'll move. If you can't find something in Bangor, then we'll move elsewhere. I will hate being away from Edith but not as much as I'm hating it here. And hating your mother."

Later that week, Alice met Thomas in his office at the older bank in town. They chatted briefly about Christmas Eve. Thomas noted how difficult it must have been for her without Charles there.

"It was, but life goes on as they say," said Alice, sighing. "It was nice to have all my children there. And Louise, too, of course. And my grandchildren."

168

"All right, Mother. What is really going on? You look like you're sitting on hot coals," said Thomas, resigned to hearing her out. Without Charles, Thomas had become Alice's financial advisor and, regrettably, her favorite venting recipient. "Should I take a guess and assume it has something to do with the unmentioned family member? May?"

"Wait, Mother, before you go on," said Thomas, cutting off his mother just as she had opened her mouth. "During the party I heard both Mitchell and May talking about moving. I know how badly you want them gone. It's mutual, Mother. They want to move too. I even heard May asking Harry about Asheville."

"You know that's only party chatter. I heard the same," sniped Alice. "I told you before, Thomas. I think she is determined to stay here in Bangor. Between her family and the store, I don't think she'll ever leave."

"That's a bad thing?" Thomas asked, astounded at his mother. "What is this antipathy you have for them? I just don't understand it."

"Never mind, Thomas. You will never understand. And it is not worth arguing about. It does sound, though, as if they are at least talking about moving away. Another state would be even better," said Alice. "I want her gone from Bangor. The further the better."

"You're right, Mother. I will never understand you. And this aversion to May."

Edith Stetson Plummer was born June 6, 1890. May had become increasingly anxious as the delivery date neared, worried about the aftereffects of her pregnancy. There was nothing she could do to ward off that insanity, Dr. Clark had said. He reassured her that just because she had had one episode of postpartum depression, it was not a guarantee that she would have another. Edith was an easy birth, and May, blessedly, suffered little to no emotional mood swings.

By now their family and the nurse, Betty, had taken over the whole of the upstairs, including Alice's large rooms. Alice had moved willingly downstairs, converting the library and the adjoining solarium into her own suite of rooms. She was more than content with her quarters; in fact, she wished she had remodeled long before. Though both women were still not happy with each other or the living conditions, an uneasy, undeclared truce prevailed.

Mitchell continued to push Thomas for more opportunities. May reluctantly agreed that Mitchell should begin looking elsewhere. In September, Mitchell was on a routine horseback ride when

171

Laddie, his favorite horse, spooked by two boys leaping out from behind bushes, reared up and threw his favorite rider. Mitchell broke his leg, requiring a lengthy recovery. He was able to return to the bank after four weeks, working at a desk as a senior cashier—a small step up in the banking hierarchy. Once again, their search for their own home was delayed.

One day in mid-January of the following year, Thomas went up to Mitchell's window. "How about I treat you for lunch? We can go to the hotel if that's all right with you. It's close, and I have a board meeting later."

"Great," said Mitchell. "I'll meet you over there in fifteen minutes."

"This is a nice surprise," said Mitchell, as he pulled out a chair. "So, is there anything special you want to talk about?"

"Yes, but we can catch up a bit first," said Thomas. "I never really got to talk with you at Christmas. Even someone as obtuse as me couldn't help but notice that Mother feels icily cold to May."

Mitchell took a bite of his Welsh rarebit. "Yes, you aren't imagining it. Neither of us know why, but it is really wearing on May. We know we will probably have to leave Bangor. It's obvious there is nothing here for us," he said, hoping he was hiding his resentment.

"Well, before you put down roots elsewhere, consider my other reason to see you," Charles said. "How would the job of head cashier in my bank suit you? You know that lone bank in the hinterlands I run? The position will open in March. I naturally thought of you. I have been impressed with your work, as was Charles believe it or not. But there were no positions at either bank until now."

"Oh, Thomas, that would be wonderful. I'd accept right now, but I should really talk it over with May." He was elated and could hardly wait to get back home to tell her the good news.

After the board meeting, Thomas went to his office. Alice was coming in to sign more papers regarding Charles's estate. He was thinking about his offer to Mitchell, feeling good about it and glad he was the one to finally help Mitchell. His father and stepfather had not made life easy for Mitchell. When his mother arrived, he told her his plan.

She reacted angrily. "Thomas, I wish you had consulted me before. I do not approve."

"You don't approve? Mother, what in the world are you saying? I am the president, as you well know. I've been making my own decisions for a while now." Thomas was furious. "I already offered him the job, Mother. Even Charles had become impressed with his work. He was planning on promoting him."

"I'm sorry, Thomas. It will not work. You need to find Mitchell another job, in another bank, in another city. Another state would be best."

Thomas was dumbfounded. She said this as if she was telling him the time of day. As if it was completely normal to demand him to arrange for the exile of his own brother. Her own son, for God's sake. How and why had his mother developed this dislike, no, hatred of May? It was ruining all their lives. He had thought it was just the close living quarters, but it was way more, to Alice anyway. She wanted them not just out of Bangor but out of the state.

"Damn it, Mother. And don't even think about telling me not to curse. I damn well will curse when I want to. I knew I sensed one of your ice storms toward May. I had thought maybe what I, and by the way, the rest of the family had seen the

174

previous Christmas was over. But no. It was obvious this last Christmas too. Everyone noticed it. I have known you to freeze us out sometimes, but it never lasts, at least not with family. Going after someone you consider a rival in the social world, now that's another story." Thomas slid his hand down his face. "I'd hardly think that May is a social rival. What in the world did she do, Mother, to deserve such a fate?"

"I don't know if I can ever explain it to you," said Alice coldly.

"Well, just try, Mother. I have to have some reason."

"It's just a feeling I have. She is going to be the ruin of us all. I feel it in my bones. If they are far away, and she wants to ruin their lives, let her," said Alice, this time with emotion in her voice.

"Look at her. Pregnant so soon after her first, like *Irish twins*. Maybe she's not Catholic, but her brothers-in-law are. And her sister converted. And that uncle of hers, Sean Mahoney. He's Catholic too. But most importantly, there's something unstable about her. She nearly killed herself after the first baby, remember? Then she

175

was sick as a dog for this one. What will she do if she has another one? Burn it at the stake?"

"Mother, God almighty, stop it! This is not like you at all. It is unseemly of you. People in our family do not talk this way," Thomas said, almost shouting.

"Thomas, watch your tongue when you're talking to me. I am your mother, lest you forget."

"And I am the president of this bank, Mother. I will see what I can do. I think you had best leave now, before I say something I will truly regret."

Thomas was at a complete loss. He knew he did not have the intestinal fortitude to take on his mother. He was going to have to rescind his offer to Mitchell immediately, before he goes home and tells May. Mitchell would bear the brunt, yet again, of another male in the family disappointing him. Damn her, he thought to himself, looking around the room guiltily. She had really put them all into a quandary.

Just before closing, Thomas came back to Mitchell's window. "Before you go home, come see me upstairs when you get off," he said.

Mitchell was crestfallen. And baffled. He was just beginning to feel his brother respected him and his work at the bank. So much for that thought. Mitchell was never going to rise in his family's eyes, ever. It was Lincoln Academy all over again. Thomas appeared embarrassed. As well he should be, thought Mitchell with disgust.

How could Thomas, the president of two banks, do something so unbusinesslike? As he told it, the manager of the West Bangor Savings Bank had already installed someone else to do the job. Without consulting Thomas? Isn't he the president for god's sake. He can overrule that offer, can't he? Did Thomas think Mitchell was stupid enough to believe that story? Mitchell could not help but believe their mother had had something to do with it. How else to explain it? Thomas never hinted at any such thing, of course.

Mitchell was not going to say anything to May about it when he got home. But she knew right away he was upset and wheedled the story out of him.

"It's Alice," she said, enraged. "She's behind this. I just know it. She is going to make it impossible for us to continue to live in Bangor. And

177

not just here but in the whole state of Maine." She was pacing the floor of their sitting room, her skirts rustling, Edie happily gurgling in her arms.

"I would have thought Thomas had enough character to take on his mother. I'm angry at him, too, and disappointed to find out he's such a weakling. But I can get over that; he's just human. She is not. I don't know if I can find the strength to move away. And I think we are going to have to move far away."

The next day, Mitchell sent applications to banks in Maine, New England, and upper New York State. He quickly received two offers for interviews nearby in Portland and Machias. By the time he arrived at the banks, the offers had apologetically been rescinded. Maybe May is right, he thought. His family wants them gone, and the state of Maine is not big enough for them all.

There were no other responses. When asked by Mitchell, the clerk in the bank's mailroom uncomfortably shook his head when Mitchell asked about his mail. When asked the same question by May, Maureen gave a similar response, as she guiltily averted her eyes.

"Good Lord. It is a Shakespearian tragedy. *Macbeth*," they said to each other. "Alice, standing over the boiling cauldron and whispering curses. It's just too awful."

Mitchell called Harry asking him about banking positions down his way—immediately available. Harry, on hearing of the rift going on in his family, was shocked and angry. He was surprised his mother felt so strongly about May, a woman he found smart and charming. And he could not help but wonder about Thomas' strength of character.

"I'll find you something, not to worry, Mitchell. I think it is high time we get you out of this mess with Mother. She has really gone beyond the pale on this. And I'm really sorry you've had to go through all this. I won't let you down."

Mitchell told May he had called Harry. What else could they do? May was distraught. "In the South? I will never fit in. What about the store? I love it there. Edith and Edward? Will I ever see them again? The girls will have to grow up without their family. Their *real* family, not this family. Not the creature in this house."

Three days later, Harry contacted him about a bank in need of a head teller. In Alabama. There were looking forward to a letter from him with his particulars. May nearly swooned, crying that she should have stayed in her crazed postpartum state. "At least that way I wouldn't know what was happening."

Mitchell received a response to his letter the following week from the British American Trust Company Bank of Mobile, Alabama. They were happy to offer him a position to be the cashier of their new branch opening in Scranton, Mississippi. Mitchell would report to Mobile for a few days at their main bank then go to Scranton. He could start as soon as he was able.

British American Trust Company Bank understood this would be a long and arduous move for Mitchell and his family. The bank would be happy to pay for his moving expenses and to provide housing in the Scranton Hotel for him and his family until Mitchell found a suitable home, the searching and initial financing of which they would also be happy to assist with.

"Mississippi? Is that better or worse than Alabama?" May cried. Mitchell waited her out.

They had to take the offer. There were no other options.

22—A HOME—1891

Mitchell and his family, including Betty, their nurse, left as soon as they could. Betty had tearfully begged to join them. "It's only my sister here, ma'am, and she's the housekeeper at the Goshens' house. She doesn't need me, and I love these girls."

The Plummers arrived in Scranton on April 1, hoping the date was not indicative of what their future might be. After assuring himself that May, Betty, and the girls were comfortable in the Scranton Hotel, Mitchell got back on a train to Mobile, Alabama, only forty miles away.

"Mr. Plummer have a seat, please," said the president, Mr. Harlan Johnson, warmly welcoming him. "I have been looking forward to your arrival. We've delayed the opening in Scranton until we found someone qualified to fill the position, so when I heard from Harry that he had a brother wanting to relocate, I couldn't believe our luck and the timing of it."

"Yes, sir. I guess timing is everything, isn't it," said Mitchell. If you only knew, he thought. "I'm happy to be here, too, and look forward to working with you. I have heard good things about the

British American Trust Company Bank. And not just from Harry."

Four days later, after a crammed immersion into the bank's ways of doing business, he was on the train back to Scranton. Looking out at the landscape rushing past his window, he reminisced. How naive he had been when he started at Lincoln Academy and then the fiasco of his departure, his start at Bangor Savings, his marriage to May and their two lovely daughters, and now a nearly two-thousand-mile move to the South, away from everything he'd ever known. In a span of five years, so much had happened.

Back in Scranton, May had quickly realized their new town was just an outpost. She was aghast at the differences but determined to make the best of it. After breakfast the first day, she and Betty put the girls in their prams and took a stroll around town.

They had moved from a bustling, thriving city of 19,000 inhabitants to a town of 1,150. Scranton was no Queen City. If it weren't for the Louisville and Nashville Railroad, Scranton and its sister towns, East and West Pascagoula, would still be trading villages on the Pascagoula River, which flowed lazily into the Mississippi Sound. The *Pascagoula Democrat-Star*, the once-weekly published newspaper, described Scranton as "The Seat of Justice of Jackson County, a growingly important town." May snorted.

Pascagoula, she learned, translated to "bread eater" and was the name of the peaceful tribe of Indians who had lived in the area long before. In fact, they were so peaceful, that a local legend told of how the tribe, as one, chose to walk, singing, into the river and drown rather than fight an enemy tribe. Ever since, the Pascagoula River was also known as "The Singing River." Well, she thought. If all else failed, she could always walk into the river and drown.

She pretended she was just a visitor and that she would leave eventually. It was the only way she could keep her composure. This is a temporary move, she whispered to herself over and over. It is a step up in Mitchell's progress. He will prove successful in this endeavor, and after a respectable tenure, they will be able to move back. Maybe not to Bangor but to some other city in Maine.

May and Betty walked with Frances and Edie twice a day, morning and afternoon. There were only a few sidewalks, just wooden walkways in front of the stores. The streets were oyster shell, packed down hard with a two-inch limey haze over the road surface that dusted the women's shoes and the babies' faces. Horse-drawn wagons and carriages passed by, raising clouds of dust behind them. More than once, all traffic was stopped by a slow-moving ox team as it hauled a load of charcoal across the street. She had already been warned by the hotel manager that the roads became impassable to ladies after rains.

They soon became familiar with the streets and shops in the town, the babies proving to be magnets. People introduced themselves, asked questions, chucked Frances under her grinning, drooling chin, and pinched Edie's chubby cheeks. May's alarm waned. Maybe it could be good here. For a while at least.

Each walk took them along Krebs Avenue and in front of the British American Trust Company Bank, the *Opening Soon* sign hanging on the front door. The Scranton Post Office shared the building, using a side door as its entrance until the bank opened. On one side of the bank building was the W. M. Canty Store and on the other side The

Noyes Hotel, smaller than the Scranton Hotel. Further down was Veillons's Blue Store, the Palace Drugstore and other stores, including Valverde Bakery, where they often stopped for a rest. Sarsaparillas for May and Betty, while Mrs. Valverde fussed over the babies and fed them little pieces of *churros*—fried dough sticks rolled in sugar. And there was a theater, grandly called The Ritz. At the far end of Krebs Avenue was The Hanging Tree. When May realized what it was, she studiously avoided that end of the street, wondering if they had moved to a town of barbarians. She could only hope it was not still being used.

By the time Mitchell returned from Mobile, his family was already known in the town. The Grand Opening of the bank on April 8, 1891, was well attended. Members of the bank's board, the mayor, various business leaders, and citizens of Scranton were all in attendance. Mitchell cut the large red, white, and blue ribbon, and the doors were opened. Many of the townspeople complimented Mitchell on his lovely wife and daughters and looked forward to bringing their business to his bank.

By chance, they had moved to a later version of the early Bangor boom years. The whole area was profiting from the lumber and timber industries just as Bangor had. Pascagoula was one of the largest ports on the Gulf of Mexico, shipping millions of board feet of lumber to the Caribbean, Central and South America, Europe, and Africa. The Port of Pascagoula had been modernized and declared a Port of Delivery in 1878, after Congress appropriated $100,000 for the enlarging and dredging of the current port, a new lighthouse, and a customs house.

As in Bangor, the railways lent their abilities in the transporting of lumber and in passengers. There were five to six trains daily to Pascagoula, bringing visitors to "enjoy its recuperative healthfulness and natural offerings," according to a Mobile newspaper, resulting in an increase in the construction of housing, especially on the waterfront.

Scranton, as the county seat, bustled with legal and business opportunities. The two Pascagoulas, East and West, Ocean Springs, and Moss Point all depended on Scranton for their mail facilities and now for most of their banking.

Mitchell's small branch was busy. He had three employees, only one of whom, Ted Mason—on loan from the Mobile branch—had previous banking experience. When Mitchell asked Ted why he hadn't taken the position when it was still open, Ted answered that he was to be married soon to a young woman who had no interest in moving; Ted did not have to say "to Scranton". Mitchell smiled, saying he understood completely.

May's daily excursions took them past houses, and she wondered which ones might be available. The spring weather was pleasant, and after the bank closed in the afternoons, Mitchell joined them for their afternoon strolls. They were becoming known. A member on the bank's board, a Mr. William K. Mead, offered to help them find a house.

He told Mitchell of quite a few he might be interested in. "May is the one to talk to," Mitchell said.

"Are you sure, Mr. Plummer?" asked Mr. Mead. "Isn't that a big decision for a woman to make?"

Mitchell smiled. "We try to make most of our decisions together. I trust May's instincts and I think you will find her well informed and with a good eye. When she has narrowed it down to two or three, I'll be happy to join you both. In the meantime, I'll be here at the bank."

Mr. Mead was quickly charmed by May. Her instincts were sharp, and she appreciated a building's lines and structure, the way the rooms flowed inside. "One thing, Mrs. Plummer, you might not be familiar with is our weather. Our summers are long, hot, and oppressive, our winters short, cold, and windy. Not like your Maine winters but nasty nonetheless."

"Thank you, Mr. Mead. That's important to know," said May. "The homes you've showed me seem to have been built with the weather in mind. Solid and sturdy with wide verandas and good ventilation," she said appreciatively. Mr. Mead beamed.

After a week of looking, May had narrowed it down to four. "Saturday, we'll look at the two I think are best," she said to Mitchell. "If you don't like either of these, we can look at the others. I'm not telling you anything else about them." She was excited, like a child giving a handmade gift at

Christmas. "I don't want you to have any preconceived notions."

They chose a house in town, an easy walk for Mitchell to the bank. May had noticed it the first day she went out walking, and it had become her first choice. It was on Canty Street, next door to the First Presbyterian Church, of which Mr. Mead was an elder and where she had already begun attending services.

Furnished, it had everything they needed and was available for rent. The owner, a Mr. Gautier of Pascagoula, worked for the railroads and had been transferred to Hattiesburg. He himself was hoping his move was temporary, so he was amenable to leasing the house. Both parties agreed the Plummers would have first option to buy if the owner wanted to sell. They could all pretend they were in temporary exile.

Mr. Mead suggested Mitchell get insurance for his household belongings and recommended the man he had used, a John Smith. He worked at the Robinson Mill but sold insurance on the side. Mitchell met him at his home that afternoon. "Sorry you have to meet me at home, but my company, Woodmen of the World, does not have an office here yet, and I don't think it's proper using Robinson's for my insurance business. I don't know what you know about us, but the Woodmen is a fraternal benefit society, one of many that formed after the War. When you join, only a small yearly membership fee, you get access to insurance, amongst other member benefits."

"I'm sorry, but I had never heard of your company before. I thought I might have to be a lumberman or something. I'm not very outdoorsy that way," Mitchell said, laughing.

"Oh, no. No axes needed. Our founder apparently had been moved by a sermon he heard from a pioneer woodsman, one of many clearing the forests to provide for their families. As our founder's last name was Root, I guess he thought naming it *Woodsman* a happy coincidence."

Later, with keys in hand, Mitchell and May went to explore their new house. They entered the house through the front door on the veranda, Mitchell carrying May dramatically across the threshold. The vestibule opened into the dining room. "A gracious room," said May. A door to the right of the vestibule led into the parlor, with a fireplace and windows onto the side yard and to the

191

front porch. The kitchen was behind the dining room, with a small bedroom for a cook, a door onto the back porch, and a privy outside, behind the house for the help.

There were three small bedrooms upstairs. "We'll need to fill them up," said Mitchell to May, laughing as he raised one eyebrow lecherously. Theirs, the largest, was above the parlor and had a fireplace and a window overlooking the front yard. A water closet finished the upper floor. Though the toilet was plumbed, the sink was not. Instead they would use the wash basin and pitcher standing on the small table. "Quaint" said May.

The kitchen was primitive compared to the Plummer mansion. A large cast-iron stove in the middle of the room took up most of the space. There was running water to the sink, but the sink was not plumbed; one had to empty the bucket underneath when it was full. Two tables and a cupboard were all there was for workspace and storage. Neither Plummer found the lack of basics upsetting, their ignorance of cooking and entertaining blissfully blinding them. However, they were not blinded by the huge copper tub in the corner, wondering how in the world they could learn to take baths in it—in the kitchen. "More than quaint," they said in unison.

The big kitchen stove and the two fireplaces, one in the parlor and the other directly upstairs in their bedroom, would keep the house warm. In addition to the wide veranda that ran along the front of the house, windows provided good light and cross ventilation. The furniture was tasteful and enough for them to move in right away. May's imagination was already thinking of ways to frill it up a bit.

Mr. Mead said Mr. Gautier's maid was available and arranged to have her come by the house the next day. "She's a Negress, Mrs. Plummer. Most of our help down here are negroes. They all live up yonder in Creole Town. It's not a place for a white lady."

He stopped and looked at May, who looked surprised. "Have you never had a colored maid?"

"No. All our help is mostly Irish or German. There are not many negroes in Bangor, Maine, I can tell you. Some that work on the lumber drives. But if that is who you use down here, I guess that is what I will use too. Are they different from us? Apart from their color, that is?" May asked.

It was Mr. Mead's turn to look startled. "Well, Mrs. Plummer. Yes, they are different from us," he said, deciding to not go further. He would let her find out herself. There was no way he could explain the complicated relationship between the white and Negro communities to a Yankee.

The next day, Mr. Mead drove Eva Ransom, Mr. Gautier's maid, up to the house. She was available and more than happy to return to her former place of employment. "Miz Plummer, it'll be fun havin' babies in the house. Mista Goatier (she pronounced it goTAY) was a widow man, you know, so it were easy, but too easy. I like bein' busy. I used to live here in the week but Mista always drove me home on Saturday afternoons, so's I could be with my husband, Roosevelt. So's we could go to church. We sing in the choir. Can I still to do that?"

"I think that could work for us. If we entertain, we will try to do parties on Friday nights. But if we had to do one on Saturday, could you stay over? Mr. Plummer would gladly arrange for you to get home on Sunday morning," said May, thinking it would be a long time before she had any kind of party.

194

"Yes'm. I like that," said Eva, happy to have a job again and one with such a fine young lady. And babies.

The Plummers celebrated Edie's first birthday in their new home. Just another day for her but significant for her parents. They finally were living in a house of their own. They might be in exile, but May was going to make it a homey exile.

For May, it was a chance to finally use her natural aptitudes of design and decorating on her own place. W. M. Canty, General Merchandise became her store for groceries and staples. Veillons's Blue Store, the whole building painted a bright blue, which appealed to May's sense of whimsy, became her favorite for dry goods, textiles, and other supplies. The owners, the Veillonses, also happened to live next door. Some things she ordered through catalogs, usually Montgomery Ward.

In June, Mitchell and May took a trip to Mobile, a work trip for Mitchell but also a small vacation, leaving the girls and the house with Betty and Eva. The bank was left in the hands of Ted Mason, who would be moving back to Mobile the next month. If Mitchell wanted to take some time off, it had to be before Ted left.

Mr. Mead, who had become a close friend of the family and felt a responsibility to educate them in the ways of the South, especially in the norms of negro servants, expressed his concern.

"I know Mr. Gautier swore by Eva. But he sent her home when he was gone on trips. We do not usually leave our houses to them when we go away. Never know which one of their *acquaintances* might come around. And your white nanny has no idea about overseeing a house with a negro maid."

May almost laughed then realized he was speaking from concern. She answered, seriously. "It will be fine. I trust them both, and they have our children's welfare first in their hearts."

On the train to Mobile, May could hardly contain herself. "Our first trip together since Newport after our wedding," said May, settling into her seat. "Well, excluding the major undertaking of moving here, which was something I hope never to have to repeat."

"You are right about that," said Mitchell. "Absolutely right. Although, in retrospect, I guess it wasn't that bad."

"For you, maybe," said May. "I just kept looking at Edith and Edward and Clarence lined up at the station waving us off. It was as if I had cut off my arm. That's how badly I felt looking at them and trying not to cry. You at least had a job waiting for you. And that first week alone in the hotel was awful. If it weren't for Betty and the girls, I'd have gone into that black hole again for sure."

"I know, May. I do know. I felt the same way looking at them. You know how dear your family has become to me. At least Thomas and Louise did show up to say goodbye."

"Humpff. He's the one who took back his own job offer. Don't forget that," said May.

"I haven't. And he won't either. He felt terrible about it, and Louise was furious at him."

"I don't really hold it against him," May said. "We both know who's to blame. Mark my words. Someday, someone in your family will set that woman straight. But you're right, they did defy her and came to see us off, and I was glad they came." May looked at Mitchell. "On another subject entirely...I've been thinking. What if I asked Mr. Veillons if he would let me convert a corner of the Blue Store into something like I had at Stetson's? I could ask Mr. Canty, too, but I just love that blue color of the building. It stands out and feels like it would fit my concept of a boutique. We would rent the space, he would buy the products, and we would split the profits fifty-fifty. What do you think, Mr. Banker?"

"I'd think that Mr. Banker man married a very clever woman. When we get home, write up a plan," he said. "And we will present it to him. Maybe split forty-sixty, with you getting the sixty. This banker man is looking out for your best interests."

"I never thought when we met, that not only would we marry, but that you would be so open to allowing me to continue to do work outside of the home. Alice educated me in the ways of society, but with your help, I've been able to expand on her ways. Thank you." May sat up straighter in order to look out the window. "So, what are we going to do in Mobile? I can't believe we'll be in a real city."

"Don't get too excited. Remember what I told you. Between the war and other disasters, it is a city whose fortunes have changed dramatically, and it's still coming out of its last depression. Things are picking up though," Mitchell said. "And

199

it should be pleasantly uncrowded, not crushing like it is during Mardi Gras. June will be hot in the daytime, I'm afraid, but hopefully cooler in the evenings."

They were staying in the Battle House Hotel, built in 1852 on the old military headquarters of Andrew Jackson during the War of 1812. The hotel had opened to great fanfare and continued as the place to stay when in Mobile. The lobby delighted and impressed May. "I had no idea, Mitchell. It is special." She leaned over and whispered, "Isn't it very expensive?"

"It is. But I am here to do business, so the expense can be written off," Mitchell said grandly, enjoying his sudden elevated status. "It was Winifred, Harlan's wife, who suggested the hotel. She's looking forward to meeting you tonight."

"So am I. I can't believe she's hosting a dinner for us, and I'm only just a little nervous. Who would have thought? No matter what I think of your mother now, I am thankful she taught me how to be a *society matron*."

Harlan and Winifred Johnson lived within a half mile of the hotel, and May and Mitchell chose to walk there for dinner. "We can get a carriage later to get back if we need to," he said. "I thought you would like to see some of the city. You'll be impressed with the buildings. There are so many influences here, from all those early years of colonial rule by the French and Spanish. Even African influences. This was the center of the slave trade after all."

Dinner was a gathering of ten, friends and relatives of the Johnsons, who peppered Mitchell and May with questions about the contrasts between the north and the south. May and Mitchell surprised themselves by defending their little town of Scranton.

The next day, Winifred took May shopping at Gayfer's Department Store. May felt like a child in a candy store. Bangor, as big as it was, did not have a department store. The closest was Varick's in Manchester, New Hampshire, or Filenes in Boston. Alice would make twice-yearly trips to those stores, but that was a luxury May had never been able to afford. She bought two dresses, some shoes, and scarves but spent most of her time in the home furniture departments, eying the latest in designs and fabrics.

On their return, their house, their children and the two women were safe and sound. Betty did say that Mr. Mead stopped by twice to make sure they were not wanting for anything. "Such a nice man. He even offered to take Eva home on Saturday, so she could go to church. She was tickled riding off with him in his carriage. And he brought her back on Sunday night."

May and Mitchell invited Evan Veillons and his wife, Elizabeth, the owners of The Blue Store, over for tea and to discuss May's proposal. Mr. Veillons was intrigued by her offer to open a small, ladies home section in their store. Intrigued and eager to cultivate the good will of the new banker in town and agreed instantly with the sixty-forty split. May's Boutique opened a month later.

"May, guess who's coming to town," Mitchell yelled, as he came into the house, taking off his coat, hat, and gloves. It was November, and just as Mr. Mead had warned, it was cold and damp. "I got a letter from John saying he would be here next month. For the week of Christmas. You get to do holiday entertaining to your heart's delight."

"Oh, Mitchell, that's wonderful news," said May, coming to meet him at the door. "Tell me all about it."

They went into the parlor where a brisk fire crackled. "Ev'nin Mista Mitchell. A bit chilly out there, ain't it?" asked Eva. "Roosevelt come by and brung in the logs to start this here fire. He said if'n you want, he can come agin tomorrow and chop a bunch more."

Mitchell poured himself and May some sherry. "Thank you, Eva. The fire feels wonderful. Tell Roosevelt for sure to chop more. I meant to ask him, but winter came earlier than I expected. Make sure he writes down his time, so he gets paid. I think I may have shorted him when he fixed that leak in the roof."

He and May were still adjusting to being master and mistress of their own house and the myriad things that had to be done in order to maintain it. And to appear knowledgeable in front of the help. The Plummer mansion in Bangor had purred along seemingly by itself. Now Mitchell had an inkling of how much work went into that quiet, invisible hum.

He sipped his sherry with his wife beside him, warm and comfortable in his own home. For the first time in his life, Mitchell was truly content. He had had to move far away from Maine to find happiness, but Bangor and the Plummers had never been a warm place for him. He was establishing himself here in Scranton, with none of his family's history or expectations to hinder him. He was proficient at his work and an enthusiastic and able member of the Scranton business community.

Mitchell had joined the Pascagoula Wing Shot Club the previous year, the memory of his schoolmate who had shot himself fading. It was not forgotten. In fact it flew through his thoughts at unexpected times, startling him and still making him wonder what that boy's thoughts could have been. But with time he had separated that incident from the sport he enjoyed.

Joining the club offered him good fellowship amongst men in the community, not to mention the opportunity to enjoy something he excelled at. Just as in Bangor, most men in Scranton and Pascagoula had gun collections. Mitchell still had the Smith & Wesson .38 revolver his father had given him and the rifle from Charles that he had used in his earlier competitions. He had since bought a Parker Brothers VH Grade shotgun, which surely helped to account for his routinely high scores.

The *Pascagoula Democrat-Star* published the news of the club monthly, with Mitchell mentioned in the paper frequently, always one of the high scorers. The last edition grandly told of his exploits, which Mitchell read to May with great gusto: "The numerous friends of H. M. Plummer are much elated over the magnificent score made by him at the recent tournament of the Pascagoula Wing Shot Club."

May, sitting beside him, comfortably doing her needlepoint, was thinking similar thoughts about her new life. Though she missed her sister terribly, she, too, was making her own way. Her boutique was new, but there had been some customers. This holiday season would be a good test. May still felt strongly about being a benefit to her community and putting the lessons she had learned from Alice to good use.

There was a small room in the Masonic Lodge, purporting to be a lending library, but with less than thirty books. May remembered the stories Alice had told her about the growth of the Bangor library which had started out with seven books in a footlocker at the Mechanics Hall. Its growth was a result of fund raising by Alice's Library Club. Perhaps little Scranton could support a decent library also. She floated the idea of a fundraiser to William Mead and to Evan Veillons, all three now on a first-name basis with May.

May, with William, her patron in all things business, presented the idea to the mayor.
What would he think about establishing "The First Annual Scranton Holiday House Tour" to support the newly formed Scranton Library Building Fund? Each house on the tour would charge a small fee toward the fund. Say, one dollar? After all, the houses were owned by people of some means, as

206

would be the people touring them. Surely, they could afford the donation. And all for a good cause. The mayor enthusiastically approved. Who knows, May thought? She and Evan might even see a small jump in their sales as homeowners primped up their houses.

Eva came to the door and announced dinner. Whatever Eva made, they welcomed. Neither of them cooked. May knew some cooking from her sister, but three years of living in the Plummer mansion had spoiled her. Eva's cooking style was country southern, and it had not taken long for Mitchell and May to adapt to the style of food. Both had put on some pounds from the deep-frying and large quantities.

Eva's style of serving, however, had left something to desire. The first night she served them dinner, she shuffled out in her old housedress, wearing...slippers? Whispering silent thanks to Alice, May quickly put a stop to that. She bought Eva two new dresses and a pair of new shoes. The Meads, who entertained lavishly and frequently, suggested a way for Eva to become more proficient as the cook and housemaid; May could lend them Eva to help their cook and staff during their larger events. The result, after a few months, was that the Plummers had a polished cook and manager of the house. Though, she still wore her slippers during the days while cleaning and cooking.

"Well, now all my decorating will have a more personal meaning with family coming," said May happily. "Did John say why he was coming? It is a very long way. And I am thrilled, of course, but he'll be missing Christmas in Augusta with Uncle Sean and Aunt Lucy."

"He only said he was able to wrangle the trip for business. I guess Edwards Manufacturing is thinking of expanding more into the South. Remember, they already opened a factory in Asheville. He's going to be staying at the hotel, not here, so we don't have to fix up a room for him."

"I wonder what we should have for dinner. And who shall we invite?" mused May. She was off in another world. Mitchell listened, as a good husband must. Mostly, he smiled inwardly, delighted in hearing her prattle on.

25—A VISITOR—1891

John arrived on a blustery, damp, and bone-bitingly cold day. After checking into the hotel and cleaning up, he walked over to the Plummers' for dinner.

"I thought the South was warm," John commented. He was standing with his back to the crackling fire, turning occasionally to warm his hands. "You didn't even get decent weather out of your banishment. The Plummers really know how to exile someone, don't they?"

Mitchell laughed. "That they do, John. Although, in a way I'm glad for it. The exile, I mean. Both of us are, aren't we, May? I'm enjoying my work, and next month I will be the Cashier of the new Scranton State Bank. Well, it is still the same bank but with a new name, no longer British American Trust Company. The one in Mobile will be the Mobile State Bank. Same with the one in Jackson. More local and more consistent, I guess. It's a promotion and more money."

Mitchell continued. "The only downside is Harlan will be retiring in six months. I am sorry about that. I get along well with him. A new president, name of Judge O. Randall, will be his replacement. I have my doubts about him. Just things I've heard. But he'll be in Mobile, away from our little place."

"Well, that is good news. Someone finally appreciates you. You deserve it. You sure as hell earned it," John said, toasting his friend.

"Still cursing I see," said May, but smiling fondly at her cousin. "Mitchell's right. I'm adjusting too. I miss Edward and Edith and you and your parents terribly still. The twins must be practically grown up by now. I have opened another shop, which has been showing a small profit. We're in this lovely home, and it's only us. 'Praise the Lawd,' as Eva says."

May continued. "And two sweet, little girls upstairs getting ready for bed. They'll be down in a bit to meet you and say good night. Life is good here in little Scranton. Especially tonight, with you here to share it. Thank you so much for coming all the way down here. I can't tell you how much it means to us." She was nearly in tears.

"Yes, it does, John," said Mitchell, putting his arm around May and giving her a squeeze. The three of them sat companionably near the fire, chatting and sipping their sherries.

There was a small commotion at the door as the two girls walked shyly into the room, Betty staying behind at the door. Frances was three and Edie was a year and a half. Both were in matching nightgowns, robes, and slippers, their hair neatly braided.

John's face broke into a delighted grin. "You two have been busy, now haven't you? Maybe *Irish Twins* were too much for Lady Macbeth. I have never forgotten your apt nickname for her. Well, it's just her damn loss, isn't it? They're beautiful," he said, bending way down to shake hands with the two little girls. They were laughing at this new person, their little hands lost in his large ones, which he was shaking vigorously up and down making them giggle even more.

"John. No cursing in front of the children," admonished May, though said in humor. She was thrilled to have John there, even with his curses. He was familiar to her. Mitchell felt the same. This was John, his best friend, who had come all the way to see them.

"So, tell me. What do you two do down here? How are you filling your days?" John asked during dinner after Mitchell and May had pumped him for information about home and his life.

"You mean in between work and a house and two children?" May asked. She filled him in on her boutique and some of her other plans. "Mitchell's the one who's really come out of the closet. He belongs to everything."

"My friend, Mitchell? So shy and retiring?" asked John. "I see you're still smoking cigarettes. No more pipe? It gave you that scholarly aura."

"No. I pretty much quit smoking a pipe. It was fun when I was teaching, but since I got into banking cigarettes just seemed easier."

Mitchell laughed. "It's true, John, what May said. It is like I get to start over. I joined the Wing Shot Club. I've still got the skills, I was pleased to find out. In the spring I'm thinking of joining the local baseball team. Don't laugh, but they're called the Mullet Catchers. I've been told they need a catcher. And of course, I have joined some civic associations. One must in my position." He laughed at John's expression. "Come on, John. I bet you've done the same. After all, we're the businessmen of this generation."

Later, in the parlor, the three sat enjoying coffee and a special port wine John had brought. They reminisced and talked of what they would do in the coming days. John had business obligations on two days but was available the other two. May told him she had planned a dinner party in his honor.

John looked at her uncomfortably. "I have a friend who is arriving the day after tomorrow. He's only here that one night, and we had planned to have dinner together. The night you've planned your party."

"That's fine, John. Bring him. It's only a few people. One more is welcome," said May.

Mitchell felt a small stab of jealousy. They had been looking forward to having John to themselves. "Is he here on business too?" Mitchell asked, trying not to show how he felt. He looked at May, who looked at him sympathetically. She shared Mitchell's feelings; she didn't want anyone else here either, despite what she'd said.

"I think so. His name is Edgar Hamlin. I met him a year ago at a convention of textile manufacturers in New Orleans. He was a reporter for one of the papers there. I met him at the hotel

213

bar, no surprise," John said, laughing. "We got along right away. He's older. Maybe in his late thirties now? I don't know. I think he visions himself an author, though, I don't think he's written anything of note."

"Well, he's welcome," said Mitchell, magnanimously, taking a page out of May's book of etiquette.

The day of the party May spent getting the house ready, and Eva was busy in the kitchen. The Meads, who would be attending, lent one of their housemaids to help May with the house, then later to help Eva in the kitchen and with serving. The dining room looked quite lavish when May was done decorating it.

May's knowledge of dinners and entertaining was still limited. She let Eva choose what she wanted to cook—her usual country cooking but fancier. May wanted it to be a good sampling of Mississippi foods for John. And if she was totally honest, a way to show off her continuing assimilation into her new community. This would be her first real dinner party.

The first course was to be fried green tomatoes with Comeback Sauce, Eva's take on the remoulade usually used. "Roosevelt always says 'comeback with that sauce' when I make it," she said, giggling. Followed by pompano with a spicy vinegar-laced butter sauce, a corn pudding, brandied glazed carrots, and collards. For dessert, Eva would make a Mile-High Meringue Pie, famous throughout the county, but a first for her.

William and Mary Mead along with Evan and Elizabeth Veillons were in the parlor enjoying drinks when John was shown in with his friend, Edgar Hamlin. Introductions were made, and questions were aimed at the newcomers.

After checking with Eva one last time, May announced that dinner was ready, and they moved into the dining room. Edgar was sitting on her left. "So, Mrs. Plummer, how have you adjusted to living down here in the swampy south?" he asked, in a subtle southern drawl. "Certainly, in regard to the menu, you've adapted well. Those fried tomatoes were some of the best I've had."

"Please, call me May. And thank you, but the cooking is all Eva. She is quite the wonder in the kitchen. Both Mitchell and I have become fond of the cooking down here, especially hers. Too fond, I think. It's more varied and flavorful than New

England dinners, and richer. We've both put on weight," she said, sitting up straighter and smiling ruefully at him.

"Oh, I don't know, May. You look lovely to me," said Edgar.

She squirmed a little in her seat. Goodness, she thought. He's as bad as John. No wonder they get along. "So, what are you working on now for your paper?" May asked, changing the subject.

"As I was saying in the parlor, I work for the *New Orleans Daily States*. I have my own column, and they allow me to write about most anything I choose. I like to go to different places and stay awhile, get the feel of the place."

"What do you write about? And what exactly do you mean by a column?" asked May.

"A column is just a way to write a story. It's more in-depth, and I can express my opinion, so it's not just the dry facts. It comes out once a week, sometimes every other week. It just depends on what I'm writing about. Sometimes the paper will suggest a subject, but usually they go along with whatever I have chosen. I spent more than a year doing columns on the presidential campaign, Cleveland versus Blain, which I told you all about in the parlor. And I covered a mafia story in New Orleans. It involves a lot of travel, going from town to town, covering different subjects. It's perfect for an itinerant like me."

"And what brings you to Scranton?" asked May.

"John. I had been in Jackson the last few weeks writing about its latest voting fiasco. When I heard John was going to be here, I came down to see him."

"Yes, he is quite the magnet, isn't he," said May.

Eva entered the dining room carrying the dessert. *Mile-high* was the perfect name for it. The meringue towered on top of the coconut cream pie. Perfectly browned, it soared, about to topple from its height and the movement as Eva slowly walked (in her good shoes) and placed it on the buffet. Always serious about her cooking, she couldn't keep herself from grinning. This was her first real dinner party too.

"Fran, my sweet. Tell me what you did today," said Mitchell. He and May were eating dinner with Frances, who was four and old enough to start eating dinner with them occasionally. Despite her liveliness and good humor, she took her place as the elder child and big sister seriously. She was quite delightful as a dinner companion and basked in the joy of having her parents to herself.

"Papa," she said, sitting primly in her seat. "Betty taught me how to braid Edie's hair, but she wiggled too much, and it didn't look nice. Betty said practice will make it perfect. And I made a little bed for Dorie."

"Dorie?" Mitchell asked, working his mouth to keep from smiling. "I don't know a Dorie. Mother? Do we have a Dorie living in our house? Who is that?"

"Well, there's my friend Dora, but she's back in Maine. No, dear, I don't know a Dorie either," May said, stifling a laugh.

"Papa, Mama, you know who she is. The doll Santa Claus brought me. You're just teasing me, aren't you?"

"Yes, Fran, we are. Tell us about the bed," said Mitchell. He delighted in these conversations with his girls. Playfulness had been so lacking in his childhood; he was surprised it came to him so naturally. And he loved that they were girls. There were no girls in his family, except for his half-sister, Marion, but he was sixteen when she was born.

"Well, Eva found a box in the pantry just the right size. And she gave me some small towels to use for blankets. I already tucked Dorie in, and she's waiting for me to kiss her good night. Tomorrow, I'm going to make her a little house."

"You're very creative, Fran. You were a good girl and ate your meal and very neatly too. You can be excused if you want," said May. "Go on upstairs and kiss Dorie good night. Give her two more for Papa and me."

Fran stood up and curtsied. "Thank you, Mama and Papa, for having me to dinner." Her parents smiled proudly at how she was learning her social graces. Fran then went into the kitchen. "Thank you, Eva, for a delicious dinner."

"Oh, you sweet chile," said Eva, stopping what she was doing to drop to her knees and give Fran a hug. "You is jes the most precious."

"I need to spend more time teaching her," said May. "I've been lax. All she knows is her ABCs. She's very smart and eager to learn more. And we should read to them more. I read in *Ladies Home Journal* that early reading is very important for little children."

"I'm sure you're right. We can take turns. On a totally different subject, I got a note today from Edgar Hamlin. You remember. The fellow John brought to our party last year," said Mitchell.

"Oh, yes, I remember him. What is he up to?"

"He's going to be here next month," said Mitchell. "He's invited us to dine with him at the hotel."

When spring arrived, May decided she was going to learn how to garden. She remembered wistfully how Edith's face lit up when she talked about her flowers, and May wanted that for herself. And she thought it would be good to know a little about the subject for her boutique. There were a lot of men, and some women, who came into the store asking Evan about agricultural supplies, mostly seeds and tools. May thought there might be a market for women gardeners, something along the lines of horticultural and landscaping supplies.

Well-armed with articles she had read in magazines, she set out determined to begin her Eden. Roosevelt helped with the digging and the heavy lifting and subtly taught her the right way to garden. As with most help, white or colored, he had perfected the manner servants had of giving information to their employers in ways that made them think they had thought it up themselves. May was not fooled but played along; it would be stupid not to, she thought. He did know what he was doing. It was a game. Just as Alice had told her seemingly years ago.

When Edgar Hamlin arrived, it was in the middle of an early heat wave. "It's frying out there. I feel like I'm back in New Orleans. These Gulf towns don't offer much air, despite how they advertise themselves," said Edgar, his southern accent seemingly more noticeable in the languid heat.

The three of them were sitting in the restaurant of the Scranton Hotel, the two men having removed their jackets while May fanned herself. She said, "I don't know the differences between the cities in the South. But I do know that it is far hotter and way more humid down here than in Bangor. And slower, too, it seems anyway. The heat leaves me feeling ennervated, it saps my energy so."

"Sorry we were a bit late. I know I said I had a meeting that ran late," Mitchell said. "But I have to confess. It wasn't a real meeting. I joined the Mullet Catchers, the local baseball team. I'm looking forward to playing again. What brings you to Scranton this time?"

"Research. I was in Jackson, thinking I might find something intriguing to write about. It is a hotbed of political machinations, but now I'm not sure. As long as I was there, I thought a quick visit down here to see you both would be nice."

"It is nice," said May. "We don't get many visitors. I guess in your work you have to do a lot of research, don't you?"

"Well, yes, in fact I'm always researching. Not just the document research in old newspapers, journals, and such but in interviews—formal and informal—talking with people. And listening. I hear everything. Staying in hotels is perfect for information gathering. They are close to everything, popular with the locals, and they usually have bars, which really bring out the stories.

"I heard a story today which I think I can plump up into a short article. An old geezer at that bar, right over there, told me how Scranton got its name. Around 1870, the surveyor for the railroad, a Mr. Scranton, got confused about the two Pascagoulas, East and West. He didn't want to add to the confusion by naming the depot another Pascagoula. So, he just named it after himself."

"Another little surprise about our town," said Mitchell.

"You're right," Edgar added. "After all, this area has been settled for hundreds of years, first by the Indians, then the French and the Spanish, and now us. The history alone is interesting, never mind whatever else could be percolating under the surface. I think there are probably quite a few surprises bubbling away here in Scranton."

After his trip to Mississippi, Edgar was between assignments. To him, this was the hardest part of journalism. He complained about deadlines, then when a column was submitted, he was at a loss about what to do next. Surprisingly, small Scranton and its environs continued to hold his interest.

There was something homey about the place. Maybe at thirty-seven, he was finally ready to give up the city lights and dramas. Leave New Orleans, put down roots somewhere and settle down in one place. Despite being small, Scranton could work well as a new base. He was able work anywhere if there was a railroad station with a Western Union telegraph nearby and rapidly rising telephone service would enable even more freedom.

This time, though, the ennui Edgar was feeling between assignments was stranger than usual. It was discomforting to find himself entertaining thoughts of moving, especially to a small town. Truth be told, it was the Plummers who held his attention.

***

Writing a novel had always been Edgar's dream, though, thus far he had not taken his writing to that next level. He fell into reporting, which he figured would be just a step along the way to becoming a famous author. But reporting was like a bad habit; once he started, it was impossible to stop.

In the 1880s, New Orleans was one of the top five cotton futures exchanges, the others being New York, Liverpool, Le Havre, and Alexandria. Edgar came from a formerly wealthy New Orleans family, once big in the business of cotton trading. Time, bad decisions, investments gone wrong, dreadful gambling debts, and disastrous marriages had sent their once-thriving enterprises into oblivion, just another speck on the city's timeline. The Hamlins, with the extended families of their spouses, still lived in the crumbling family mansion.

Edgar had no intention of falling to their level. At seventeen, after high school, he severed relations from his family. He was hired at the *New Orleans Daily States* as an apprentice, a *printer's devil*, then advanced to typesetter. One quiet news day, the editor allowed him to write an article, a small nothing about a broken water main. One story became another and in time, he became a regular reporter with a small following. Initially, he used E.H. as his byline; eventually he dropped the periods and kept the space, thinking the separated initials looked more vivid.

He became enamored of the process of reporting. It allowed him to be part of and yet remain aloof from events, most of which had great impact on the parties involved. The research and the required digging were fascinating. It was like detective work and filled him with a sense of importance. Writing articles came easily to him; writing novels proved elusive.

Mark Twain was his exemplar. They had both started in newspapers, first as devils who worked up to typesetters and then to journalists and satirists. Additionally, of course, Twain had become a noted novelist. Both men were self-taught, Twain having left school after the fifth grade and started his apprenticeship when he was twelve. He also had that excitingly, romantic adventuring on the Mississippi and his trips out west. Edgar did not reproduce that for himself, but he still felt a kinship to Twain. Certainly, there were worse people to emulate.

In 1884, when Edgar was twenty-nine, he begged the paper to send him to Chicago to cover the party conventions for the presidential candidates. Both were being held in that city, the Republican in June and the Democratic in July. Grover Cleveland won the Democratic, James Blaine the Republican. Edgar's columns were praised, and he was assigned to cover the national campaign which was surrounded with scandal and controversy.

A group of reformist Republicans, mugwumps, saw Blaine as corrupt and withdrew their support. Blaine had also alienated Catholic voters when one of his supporters gave a speech accusing the Democrats of being the party of *Rum, Romanism, and Rebellion.* Additionally, it was alleged that Blaine, while in Congress, had used his influence by pandering to businesses.

Cleveland, in contrast, was known as Grover the Good. But it was charged that Cleveland had fathered an illegitimate child. Cleveland admitted to an illicit connection with the woman, telling his supporters, "Above all, tell the truth." He admitted to paying child support to the mother, despite questions about the child's paternity. The child's first and middle names were those of the candidate's law partner—its last name was Cleveland.

Yellow journalism was coming into its own at this time, and those papers eagerly reported the lascivious details on each candidate. Edgar covered the campaign with restraint, writing objective, thorough pieces. His columns were well received and increasingly quoted in other national papers. The *New Orleans Daily States* circulation increased, pleasing his editors.

E H's name recognition climbed proportionally, pleasing him.

Edgar's next large and popular story was a feature about the Italian American mafia in New Orleans. Two families were vying for supremacy, the Matrangas and the Provenzanos, resulting in a war over the grocery and produce business. Edgar's resulting articles won him a loyal following. He wrote a follow-up the next year, when the police chief was shot by masked attackers while walking home. The chief's last words, choked out before he died, were: "The Dagoes shot me."

Edgar was neither introspective nor an intellect. He was not a great writer, but he had a style people liked, succinct and accurate. As Twain was known to say, "Use plain, simple language, short words and brief sentences...don't let fluff, flowers and verbosity creep in." Edgar took those words to heart. Most importantly, he had an innate intelligence and a doggedness that kept him searching for answers. Early on, he realized he needed to cultivate sources, protect them, and use his carefully gleaned information prudently. He was a good reporter and his dreams of writing the Great American Novel faded.

An apartment in the French Quarter overlooking St. Anthony's Garden was his home. The fact that the garden was behind St. Louis Cathedral only made the place more attractive to him, despite the riotous bells on Sundays.

His family was Catholic, though less than avid in their practice. As an altar boy, he had loved the rituals and pomp of the Catholic Church. As an adult, not so much. He had disobeyed almost every commandment and had no intention of ever confessing those sins to anyone. But the proximity of his apartment to the cathedral made him feel not completely ex-communicated.

Edgar had risen above his family's decline. The stigma on his family's reputation gave him an air of mysterious tragedy, which he did not discourage. He had never married; the memories of his family's disastrous unions having left a permanent stain on his brain. He had, however, a long and varied history of female companions from both extremes of New Orleans society. He was invited to events of the city's upper crust. He relished the acceptance into his family's former social class but was also resentful, knowing he was there only by invitation when, by rights, he had been born to it.

Edgar was intrigued by the patrons who frequented the many establishments in New Orleans, a city of artists where painters, writers, and musicians mingled comfortably. Mark Twain had frequented the Old Absinthe House thus making it Edgar's favorite, though, he wasn't particularly fond of the spirit—la fée verte, the green fairy. But he was amused by its bad reputation and the French pouring ritual: the clear liquor poured into the bottom of a special absinthe glass, a sugar cube on a uniquely slotted spoon was placed over the glass, and then ice water dripped over the cube until it dissolved, turning the absinthe opaque.

He knew his city intimately, the good and the bad, and had acquaintances in both worlds. When he tired of high society, there was the seedier side of New Orleans with its many bars and brothels eager to satisfy his baser instincts. There were rumors about Edgar and his past, his relationships, and how and where he got some of his information.

The gossip, alluding to parties and visits to New Orleans's prostitution district, only added to his mystery. There were many such houses in the city of "sex, sorcery, and song" that catered to any penchant of sexual activity. One was owned by Fanny Sweet, a colorful woman described in one paper as a "thief, lesbian, Confederate spy, poisoner, and procurer." Another was a homosexual brothel run by a large man named Miss Big Nelly. Edgar was a friend to both and more.

As a correspondent, a title he had assumed after the mafia story, reporting gave Edgar entry into worlds he ordinarily would not be part of. Because of his columns he had become a person of note, one who people wanted to know. He traveled often, another part of his profession he enjoyed. In each city, he established himself in a good hotel, introduced himself to the police, the mayor, committeemen, lawyers, bankers, shopkeepers and whoever else he needed to know in order to do his story. He was usually welcomed and invited to parties, dinners, and meetings. It always amazed him at how easily people naively spilled secrets and gossip. It was a life and profession he mostly enjoyed.

The past year, 1892, had been a tumultuous one for New Orleans. Streetcar conductors had gone on strike, winning a shorter workday and overtime pay, which in turn led to unrest with many other workers wanting the same. Across the country, labor unrest and the nascent unions became forces to be reckoned with. In the South, this discontent in the workforce was not as common as in the rest of the country. But Edgar and his editor believed these strikes were a harbinger of future conflict and that it was only a matter of time before severe labor unrest spread in the South, especially to the ports. Edgar thought there was a story to be written, and with the board's approval, he began researching it.

He intended to focus on Mississippi, stopping at the ports of Gulfport and Biloxi, up to Jackson and then back down in Pascagoula. With its confluence of businesses—lumber, the sawmills, shipbuilding, shipping, and the canneries—and its workforce made up of a mix of negroes, whites, and islanders from the Caribbean, Edgar felt Pascagoula was the port most at risk. This past year, Pascagoula had seen its biggest boom in the lumber business. He was sure the two Pascagoulas

233

and neighboring Scranton hid goldmines of information; most towns did.

Edgar left New Orleans in January of 1893. After he had visited Gulfport and Biloxi, he detoured north to Jackson, the capital and a viper's nest of legislative intrigue. Its preoccupation with all things political had slowed its recovery from the war, and it was still adjusting to the times with difficulty. Jackson, thankfully for Edgar, was not the setting for his story, but as the capital, its actions on any strikes could be pivotal to their outcomes; getting to know a few of the important personages couldn't hurt.

Edgar arrived in Scranton from Jackson in late February. He was looking forward to a lengthy stay and to seeing the Plummers. He moved into the Scranton Hotel, the best establishment he had yet stayed at on this assignment. Another reason to stay in Scranton, he thought. He had written to Mitchell earlier telling him of his arrival. The next day, they met for lunch in the hotel.

"It's great to see you again," said Edgar. "I just spent the last month and a half in Gulfport and Biloxi, with a last stop in Jackson. You people in Scranton are nicer, and your town is much more welcoming. Jackson might be the capital, but I felt as if I was in a place that time forgot."

Mitchell nodded. "I've not been there myself, but I hear that from many people. I think they still have not gotten beyond the "War of Yankee Aggression." Certainly, they are not alone in that thinking, but Scranton does seem more forward-thinking somehow. After all, they hired me," he laughed. "Can't get more Yankee than Maine. Maybe it's because Scranton is at the bottom of the state, away from the rest of the country. And because of the yards and the railway, we have a more mixed population. Perhaps that creates a more open feeling. I don't know."

"Well, that's why I'm here," said Edgar. "My paper thinks that labor strikes, like what we had in New Orleans, will spread to other places in the South. Your port of Pascagoula is much like New Orleans, and I would not be surprised if the same thing happened here. My paper wants to be on the forefront."

"Maybe," said Mitchell. "I haven't heard anything. But then I don't have your nose for news. The *Pascagoula Democrat-Star* has not written anything even hinting at that. If it does happen, I

235

just hope it stays in the port." He continued, lowering his voice and leaning forward. "What I have heard, though, through the banking grapevine is of the spread of a financial crisis brought on by that failure and receivership of the Philadelphia and Reading Railroad. They greatly overextended themselves."

"Yes, I heard that too," Edgar said. "This month, just before Grover Cleveland was sworn in. Nice thing to do to a new president. I still have a warm spot in my heart for old Grover. My first real column was about his earlier election. Who would have thought eight years later that he'd be in the White House again? Poor devil."

They finished lunch with Mitchell telling Edgar he and May would invite him over for dinner soon.

29—COMMUNITY—1893

Edgar's sense of imminent strife at the port caused solely by labor unrest did not come to pass. Mitchell's prediction of suffering caused by the nation's financial failings, however, did. The crisis affected the whole country, each state and every city, town, and village. Businesses failed, banks closed, farms went under. Railways closed, marine commerce fell, shipyards closed. Pascagoula was no different.

Edgar continued in Scranton, writing his column for the *New Orleans Daily States*. His editor warned of proposed cutbacks and told Edgar to return home. The paper might keep him on if he was local to New Orleans, but they could no longer afford a traveling reporter. Having anticipated such a situation but still wanting to stay in Scranton, Edgar had formed a loose arrangement with the *Pascagoula Democrat-Star* and had also signed on with the American Press Association, a press syndicate. Shortly thereafter, the *New Orleans Daily States* let him go.

He could not continue living in the hotel. He checked out rooming houses, but even the nice ones left him feeling depressed. He may have come

237

from a family whose fortunes had wasted to nothing but living in a rented room was far too long a fall.

He overheard a patron at the hotel bar complaining about tenants he had evicted from one of his houses. Edgar said he might be interested. It was a small house with only three rooms, an outbuilding on an estate gone to decay. Just like home, he thought, and considering that a good omen, signed a lease on the spot. May, of course, insisted on decorating it once Roosevelt had made it habitable.

Edgar made a melancholy last trip to New Orleans to pack up his apartment and say his farewells. He had few real friends, his editor being one. Over dinner they told tales of great stories, some published and some not. They promised to keep in touch, each knowing they probably would not.

Scranton suffered from the financial crisis but less than the big cities. It had never been a wealthy town, and its inhabitants had not overextended themselves. Mitchell's bank remained solvent due in large part to his foresight and conservative management. Mitchell worried constantly about the bank and how the recession was affecting his town and his family.

He had laid off three employees, leaving himself and one other doing the work of five. Neither complained, each considering himself lucky to be working at all and for pay. They had heard stories of others in banking who had lost everything. Mitchell knew he and his family could become destitute in an instant. He became distant to May about his work, not wanting to burden her with his problems.

May closed the boutique, a luxury no one could afford. The Blue Store remained open though Evan had to let his paid employees go. His wife, Elizabeth, and May took turns filling in. The Plummer household had not been affected that much. Their help remained, unpaid but fed and housed. Betty had nowhere to go, and Eva continued as before, still returning on Saturdays to her Roosevelt. May fretted about the same things as her husband and, like him, kept her fears to herself. A vacuum slowly grew between them.

Her social conscience pushed her to switch her talents from growing flowers to gardening vegetables to feed the needy. The Scranton

239

Community Garden was conceived by May along with Elizabeth Veillons and Mary Mead. After getting approval from the mayor, they took over some empty acreage on the outskirts of town. Roosevelt and his friends from Creole Town helped the ladies turn the land into a farm, resulting in much curiosity and gossip about the group of white women and black men clearing and preparing the ground.

People who had no gardens of their own were free to stake out a plot. Word spread, and within a month there were several gardens. Most were tended by workers from the port and the railroads, only a few of whom had actual gardening experience. Those new to farming were helped by their more knowledgeable garden neighbors. There were some negroes from the port, but most of the local coloreds had their own small gardens in their yards.

The garden club maintained a large plot, selling their produce to hotels, restaurants, and some wealthy homeowners. The proceeds were used to purchase more seeds and equipment. Roosevelt had staked up an awning behind the club's plot, offering some shade and seating on rickety old chairs. Often a gardener brought a pitcher of tea or lemonade; sometimes, someone brought cookies or breads. The amateur farmers made for a motley group with a genial air of pride and conviviality in this time of impoverishment.

The Plummers often invited Edgar to their house for dinner. The three had become close friends. Edgar enjoyed their domesticity and their presence, allaying their concerns with his numerous stories. Edgar became cover for their undercurrent of silent worry.

Opposite in their origins and their family histories, they nonetheless found themselves attracted to each other. Edgar told them about New Orleans, the high-society galas, and some of the less scandalous happenings in the infamous French Quarter. He told them about his family and their decline into poverty. He told them about his old dreams of writing a novel.

The Plummers reminisced to Edgar about how they had met and married. Mitchell told about his teaching then banking, glossing over the reasons for the abrupt changes in professions, and their move to Scranton. May spoke wistfully of her family and how she missed them, about how she had started into the boutique business, and her feelings of community responsibility. The three became closer, lingering long after dinner in the parlor over brandy or port.

Edgar was risqué, Mitchell earnest, May flirtatious—expatriated, kindred souls. To May, Edgar was a romantic, with an air of lost grandeur. To Mitchell, Edgar reminded him of John. Each was slightly besotted with Edgar and his sophistication.

Edgar, too, was beguiled by them. His fondness for Mitchell was disquieting, illuminating that side of himself he kept well hidden. His feelings for May were far more than fondness. She was a composite of everything he wanted in a woman. He knew it the first time he met her when he had come to dinner with John.

Having no desire to ruin the bond between the three of them, Edgar chose not to act upon his desires, surprising himself. He would have easily wooed May in the past. He came to their house for dinner, or sometimes took them out, and privately coveted May. Mitchell was oblivious. May felt a spark.

Mitchell had to travel to Mobile for an emergency regional meeting of area banks. He would be gone a week. May was at loose ends. She went on a cleaning binge of the house. She weeded her gardens, her own and the community garden. She was restless and agitated, something she had not been in years. Since Ivan, she thought, sending a disturbing shiver through herself and a sudden desire to have Edith's calming influence near.

She invited Edgar for dinner. It's only dinner, she said to herself. He's been over here a hundred times. She needed an actual conversation with another adult, not Eva or Betty. Eva's usually kind, open face closed when she saw Edgar.

Edgar was intrigued. He had always assumed his feelings for May were one-sided. She was always flirtatious, which certainly added to his affection for her, but she had never indicated she felt anything but friendship toward him. Don't get too far ahead of yourself, he thought. Do you really want something to happen?

During dinner, May was slightly giddy, especially after two wines. "I missed our dinners. It's always more fun to have people over. Especially you, Edgar. Mitchell and I always have such fun when you're here." She realized she was prattling.

Edgar toasted her with his wine glass. "May, it is always a pleasure to be here. And Eva's cooking is the best in Scranton," he said, smiling at Eva as she took his plate away. Making no eye contact, she barely nodded her head at him.

"I don't think she approves," whispered May, leaning in closer to him. "But I can have a friend over when I want. And you're a good friend."

Later, after Edgar had left, May had misgivings. She knew it was not acceptable to have a single man over while her husband was gone, even if that single man was a close friend of the family. But surely, she was not doing anything wrong. Yes, they had flirted. But only a little. She remembered that first dinner when he had visited with John, when he said she looked just fine to him. Her heart fluttered, and a twinge shot through the increasingly disordered circuitry of her brain.

Mitchell sent word he would be delayed in Mobile another week. By now, May was obsessed with Edgar, having worked herself up into a fever of infatuation. She had him over for dinner twice more, though, Eva's icy disapproval was blatantly apparent. Their flirting was more intense, their occasional touches more electric. After the last dinner, cleared away noisily by Eva shuffling loudly in her bedroom slippers, the two of them retired to the parlor with the door closed, lingering and talking quietly.

Edgar was overwhelmed. His own feelings for May were strong, but for them to be returned was not something he was prepared for. He had reconciled himself to desiring May from afar.

"May, I don't think you should invite me for dinner again. Not without Mitchell here. It is already ruining your relationship with Eva. Luckily, Betty is upstairs with the girls, but servants talk with servants in their house and with servants from other houses. You don't want to ruin your reputation," said Edgar.

"Oh, Edgar. Don't be such a worrywart. We're not doing anything wrong. And my reputation is fine. I know about reputations. I went through a time before I met Mitchell when we all thought I was doomed to spinsterhood because of something I had done," May said, thinking she should just stop now. She wanted to talk with

Edith. It was a brief stab of sanity that disappeared as quickly as it had surfaced.

"It's not only you I'm worried about. It's Mitchell too. I'd hate to have him hear rumors." Edgar stood up to leave.

"It's very gallant of you to be so concerned. It's one of the things I love about you," May said, walking him to the parlor door. Impulsively, she leaned in and kissed him lightly on the cheek, triggering another twinge in her brain. "Thank you for being so concerned."

Edgar stood still. And then he did the one thing he knew would change the course of all their lives. He kissed her, fully and completely on the lips.

Edgar was near tears when he stopped. "I am sorry, May, so sorry. I have been wanting to do that since I first saw you. I should never have let myself kiss you. It will never happen again. I'll let myself out."

May touched his arm. "Maybe it was meant to happen."

If Mitchell had been worried about the economy before he left for his meetings, he was in a full-blown panic when he returned. The forecast for banks across the country was dismal. He did see his brother Harry, who was there representing his bank in Asheville. Thomas, their brother, was in the same predicament in Bangor. Additionally, Thomas had had to close the second branch of Bangor Savings and his new house and move Louise and the children into the Plummer house with Alice and Marion. Mitchell could not help but grimly smile at that, though, it did nothing to ease his concerns. If anything, knowing about Thomas's troubles only made his worries worse.

Mitchell's state was such that he was unaware of anything else going on around him. He spent increasingly longer hours at the bank, coming home late, sometimes too late to see his two girls. They and Edgar, when he came for dinner, were the only things that brought any relief to his constant state of angst. And May, of course. She lit up his life.

She also lit up Edgar's. In fact, May burned like a bolt of lightning. Her energy delighted all

247

around her. Her girls laughed with her when she danced with them or told them funny stories, sometimes scary ones that left her daughters feeling uneasy. She directed the first harvest of the community garden and the second planting for fall. She helped at the store and she volunteered at the library. She was a wonder to all.

Except to Eva, who had no wonderment at all of what had happened to her mistress. Eva knew the minute she came out of her room, the day after she had displayed her disapproval, shuffling in the forbidden slippers. She knew by the way the sofa cushions were depressed, the pillows rearranged, the carpet wrinkled. She knew when May came down that morning, talking a stream, not looking her in the eyes. Nor had May looked Eva in the eyes since. Eva knew every time May snuck out in the daytime to meet Edgar, every time he snuck into the house at night. The knowledge sat inside of her like a stone.

Eva disapproved, and her heart broke every time she looked at May and each evening when Mitchell returned from his long days at work, totally unaware of what was going on right under his nose.

Financially, there seemed no end in sight to the, now, Depression. People resigned themselves to their impoverished lives, creative in their ways of adapting. The last plantings had gone in, in September for harvesting in December. Luckily, the growing season was most of the year, with frost only during December through February. May had to laugh. Did she say luckily? But compared to Bangor during the winter, Scranton was downright balmy. Three years had gone by, and she no longer yearned for home, only for her sister.

Sometimes, in the rare moments she allowed herself to slow down and contemplate her life, May wondered how she did it all. It should have exhausted her, but it invigorated her, this life of loving two men. And she did love them both—differently.

Mitchell, of course. He was her husband and the father of her girls. She worried about him and the weight he carried providing for them, his bank and the community. Her worries made her want to take care of him, protect him. Protecting him included having marital relations with him, frequently. It satisfied him and gave him a few minutes of relief from his daily travails. And oblivious of the irony, it assuaged her feelings of guilt.

Her feelings for Edgar were passionately electric. She needed that electricity and the power it gave her knowing she made him feel the same way. He was a man well versed in the ways of love and May luxuriated in his attentions. Edgar and she were in a state of acute, guilty ardor. Perhaps if the economics of the country were different, Mitchell might have become aware. But business occupied most of his brain. They were all still friends who found great enjoyment in their many dinners together.

By the end of October, May knew she was pregnant. The question of her baby's paternity increased her feelings for both of her men. This pregnancy was easy with no morning sickness, and she chose not to tell anyone right away. She felt voluptuously sexual and continued relations with both men, enchanting them and herself with her sensuousness.

One night after dinner, the three of them still sitting at the table, she told them about her condition. Each man was separately proud and awed; only one could show it.

"Mitchell, if she's a girl, we'll name her Alice after your mother. I know, I know. I certainly have had my issues with her, but why not? After all she turned me into a lady. And she gave me you. And this Alice will be different. She'll be sweet, I just know it. Like alyssum—sweet Alice. If it's a boy, we'll name him Harry," prattled May to her two stunned dinner companions.

Mitchell, buoyed by wine and masculine pride, said, "Edgar, you are part of the family now. We'll use Hamlin for the middle name. It can be used for a boy or a girl. How would that be?"

Edgar was not at all sure how that would be, but he certainly couldn't say anything. And he was a bit put off by May. Emotionally, he felt the jilted lover. Objectively, it should not surprise him she was still having relations with Mitchell. After all, he was her husband. But did she do it out of duty? Did she enjoy it with Mitchell? As much as with him? Was she just a calculating woman covering her sins? He couldn't decide if it made her more or less seductive.

During the Christmas holidays, May harnessed her energy to again direct the Holiday House Tour. But this time she included their house also. Eva and Roosevelt were exhausted by the added work to get the place ready. And Eva was exhausted by May with her insane energy and the continuing affair with Edgar. Their dinners were particularly galling to her. It was all she could do to not scream at them all—May and Edgar for carrying on and Mitchell for his ignorance. She considered leaving, but there was nowhere else to go.

By the sixth month of her pregnancy, May finally crashed. Not to reality but into a blackness she hadn't seen since after Frances's birth. She stayed in her room, refusing visitors. Her hair hung dankly along her face; her eyes had lost their sparkle. Usually she stared ahead at nothing or stood at a window gazing out in a daze. Sometimes she wandered the house, still in her nightdress.

When she was in her frenzied state, her head had zinged with ideas that she acted on immediately. Now, what thoughts she had pushed thickly through her brain with no resultant action. Her only thought was that she was surely going directly to hell.

Betty went to Mitchell. "Mr. Mitchell, you must do something. She's scaring the girls. You must call a doctor. He can give her something," she said in tears. "Remember when I first came to work for you? It was after Frances was born. She had something like this going on then, right?"

"You're right, Betty. Dear, Betty. And I think the doctor gave her a tonic or something, didn't he? What would we do without you?" asked Mitchell. "We must do something. I'll arrange for a doctor to come today."

Mitchell had been overwhelmed to the point of paralysis. Now, thanks to Betty, he had at least one thing he could do. For Mitchell, it was important for him to help. He also wrote a letter to May's sister, Edith. In the past she was the only person who could handle May's deep moods. Maybe he could convince her to come to Scranton.

Mitchell had contacted a Dr. Cox who came that afternoon. He was unable to find anything physically wrong other than her obvious apathy and her unhealthy appearance. "She is obviously suffering from a nervous disorder, common to women of certain makeup, especially during pregnancy," he said to Mitchell. "I suggest laudanum. It might ease her distress. We use it frequently with women as it is especially helpful for their female troubles. It is very bitter, so we mix it with a bit of rum and cinnamon, making a tincture. Just give her a teaspoon or two in the morning and at night. It will make her sleepy, but it should calm her so she is not wandering the house."

It did indeed make her sleepy, and amenable to care from Eva and Betty. They could get her bathed and dressed and downstairs to eat. Sometimes she read to the girls. Mostly she sat or laid on the sofa in the parlor, a book on her lap, staring at nothing—but not restless. No one thought this was normal, but it was better than before.

Edgar was bereft. And he was on the outside. This was a family crisis, and as close as he was with them, he was not family. He went to the house several times, pleading with Eva to let him in to see May. Eva refused, not unsympathetically, surprising herself.

"I cain't, Mista Hamlin. I cain't do that to Mista Mitchell. It's just unseemly. And the missus don't want to see no one, 'specially you." She softened when she saw his face. "I know you care for her. But she's pitiful. You don't want to see her."

Edgar took Mitchell out to lunch a few times, hoping to learn about May's condition. Edgar truly cared about Mitchell also. But his love for May made him selfishly blind. He pushed Mitchell to tell him everything that was going on with her. Had she asked for him?

"Edgar, you don't understand. She does not ask for anyone. Not me, not the girls, not Mary or Elizabeth. No one. Certainly not you." He looked at Edgar. "I'm sorry. I didn't mean that the way it came out."

"I know. I know," said Edgar, through his hurt. "I'm just so fond of her. Of you both. We all are so close."

Mitchell smiled wanly. "I think those days are over, Edgar."

32—AN INTERVENTION—1894

Alice Hamlin Plummer was born on July 20, 1894, after a normal delivery. In attendance were Dr. Kell and Edith, May's sister. She had arrived two months before, after Mitchell had sent a second letter with a train ticket included, literally begging her to come. "Edith, May's life depends on it. All our lives depend on you coming. You're the only one who can save her," he had written. Edith left the day after receiving the letter.

May was worse than Edith had ever seen her. When Edith came into the room, May just looked at her. Unable to speak, she cried silently, the tears streaming down her cheeks. Edith, near collapse, gathered herself enough to crawl into bed with May, to hold her and weep with her.

All May said when she was able was, "I'm so sorry. I should never have done it," slurring the words over and over.

Edith was shocked. May was unable to get up without help. She could not dress herself. She was incapable of doing anything by herself. Undernourished, pale with dark circles under her glazed eyes, she looked like a ghost with a large belly. At the girls' bedtime, Mitchell would bring the girls in for story time. It took a superhuman effort for May to sit up while he read to them, each girl nestled on either side of a nodding May. Edith talked with Eva and Betty. She questioned Mitchell, gently.

Dr. Cox had been back at the house only once after he had started her on the laudanum. She had suffered a bout of intense itching, resulting in scratching herself raw in places. After examining her, he had said to Mitchell "pruritus." In response to Mitchell's uncomprehending look, he looked down his nose over his glasses and said, "Itching. She also has pinpoint pupils, another side effect of laudanum. Perhaps morphine would be an easier drug for her to tolerate? She could take it the same way, as a tincture twice a day."

At Edith's insistence, Mitchell called for Dr. Cox. Edith, with Mitchell beside her, told the doctor his services were no longer needed. "My sister has suffered from deep mood swings since she was a child. Never was she drugged. She is at the point of unconsciousness with what you have given her. How in God's name do you expect her to be healthy enough to deliver her baby? She's not even eating. Mr. Plummer has decided to let you go. We will use Dr. Kell." She paused to catch her breath. "You can let yourself out."

She was furious. She did not know much about medicine, but she knew that what May was going through was not right. To Edith, his treatment was typical of a man. He could not handle (or more likely did not know how) May's moods, so he just drugged her instead. Edith tamped down a wayward thought that included Mitchell in this opinion. In fairness to him, she knew how difficult May's moods could be.

Dr. Kell, upon examining May, agreed with Edith, though he worded it in such a way as to not openly disparage Dr. Cox. "From what you both have told me, it's apparent that Mrs. Plummer is suffering from a deep depression. It could be from the pregnancy. All the hormones and changes to a woman's body can cause chaos in a woman's mind. Morphine *can* be used to help alleviate that. However, it is obvious she is now incapacitated from the drug. And you are right. She needs to be stronger for when she delivers.

"One cannot taper off these drugs; it has to be done all at once. The trouble with opium products, both morphine and its cousin laudanum, is that they can become habit-forming. They are all right for short term use, but not long term. We are just discovering that. They can also build up in the body, making the effects stronger and of longer duration," said Dr. Kell. "Certainly, the withdrawal will be devastating for the people around her. And someone needs to be with her day and night, so she does not harm herself. It is not a pleasant duty. As soon as the worst effects are over, we can start her up and moving and get some good food in her." He looked at Edith and Mitchell seriously. "There is also another concern—the baby. There's new information that has found that these drugs can seriously affect the unborn baby also."

The same lethargy that had overtaken the mistress had stricken the house. With Edith there, the relief felt throughout the household was immediately apparent. Eva cleaned and cooked with a gusto she had not had in months. The girls were happy having their aunt there paying them some attention. Betty helped Eva with the house. Mitchell worked with a renewed energy. Edith tended to May.

Edith suggested Betty move into the girls' room, Mitchell move to Betty's room and Edith would stay with May in their room until the worst was over. It was going to be difficult for anyone to get a full night's sleep if they were with May, and he needed to be at the bank. Mitchell agreed, maybe too eagerly. But Edith knew he needed to be at his best to continue supporting the household.

Despite Dr. Kell's instructions to Edith on how to care for someone coming off morphine, she was not prepared for the quickness of symptoms once the drug was stopped. Within hours, May's eyes were tearing up, her nose was running, and she was sweating. By the second day, she had chills, her pulse raced, she shook with tremors, and she paced. She suffered from stomach aches, muscle aches, nausea, vomiting, and diarrhea. She railed at Edith, at Mitchell, at her life. She continued chanting, "I'm sorry. I should never have done it." Edith finally yelled at her. "What did you do that you're so sorry about?"

Once the torpidity wore off, May's awareness returned, riddling her with guilt about the affair with Edgar. How could she have risked everything for him—her family, her husband, her girls? Why? Did she really love him that much to put everything she had in such danger? She could not possibly tell

Edith about it, especially considering her past with Ivan.

Irritability became her mood, and Edith was its usual target. Edith did not really mind. The doctor had warned her that ill temper was common in people withdrawing from morphine, so she took it as a sign of progress.

Edith was more worried about which May would surface once the drug was gone from her system. Mitchell described how *up* May had been during the months before her abrupt fall into depression. That coincided with Edith's experiences with May's moods, though, the severity of this one was new. They were cyclical, with long periods of normalcy interrupted by euphoria lasting for maybe months. Then the sudden slide into gloom, sometimes for months also. Would she still be in the depression when her due time came? Edith could not help but remember how May was after Frances's birth.

By the third week, Edith felt confident that the May returning to them was the normal May; neither mood extreme seemed to be present. She was full of self-recrimination and sadness for putting her family through such distress, but Edith thought that was what any woman would feel after what May had been through.

After a week, May had built up some strength. She dressed and made herself walk up and down the stairs and around the house. And she took her meals downstairs in the dining room with Edith and Mitchell.

Eva's face lit up each time she saw May. "Missus, I'm so glad you're up an' about. Lawdy, I missed you," she said, speaking volumes with those last four words. May looked at her gratefully.

Once May was over the worst of her withdrawal, Mitchell moved back into their bed and Edith took Betty's room. With Eva downstairs in her room, the Plummer house was close to bursting. Before her dramatic slide into depression, May had planned with Mary Mead to borrow her birthing bed. "I'll never use it again. That's for sure," said Mary. Foldable, it had been stashed in a corner of Betty's room, which would become the birthing room when the time came. Then Edith would move downstairs to the parlor.

By the time of the delivery, May's health was close to normal. The delivery, too, was normal. A look of concern flitted over Dr. Kell's face when he held tiny Alice. Her color was a bit dusky, but she pinked up when he spanked her, hard, making her take her first breath. She cried a weak, mewling cry, but a cry, nonetheless. On examining her, Dr. Kell found her small for a full-term baby, but she seemed otherwise healthy, if a bit listless. He handed the baby back to May where she clumsily latched on to May's breast, suckled some, and fell asleep.

"Looks like she'll be an easy one," said Edith, smiling at the baby, stroking her head and hiding her worry. She had seen the passing look on the doctor's face.

"She's our *Sweet* Alice," whispered May.

A busy, welcomed normalcy settled over the Plummer house. Edith stayed another two months, helping May with the baby and running the house. As May grew stronger, she and Edith began venturing outside for walks with Alice. It was high summer, but the mornings were fresh, and the air and exercise brought color to May's face. They were stopped often by friends and neighbors, all eager to see the new baby and welcome May back. Apparently, the timing of May's breakdown was such that her absence was attributed to her confinement.

Edgar had stopped by the house three weeks after the birth. Edith had wanted to meet this man, so close to the family that the parents had used his last name for Alice's middle name. She met him at the front door where they chatted briefly then brought him into the parlor where May was sitting, holding a sleeping Alice.

The look that passed between May and Edgar told Edith everything. It was electric. It pulsed. It filled the room. Could it be hidden? Edith feared not. She was afraid for her sister. She backed out the door, shutting it tightly as if to hold back all that was in there. A wave of nausea passed through her, sending her to the kitchen where she fell into a chair.

"Eva, perhaps I could have a cup of tea? Chamomile? My stomach is off," was all Edith could say.

"Yes'm," Eva mumbled. She knew exactly what was wrong with Miz Edith's stomach. She wanted to lean over and give this woman a hug, to share the secret she had hidden for a year, to cry with someone over it; she had not even told Roosevelt. But it would not be proper, her a negro servant confiding in a white woman. So, she only allowed herself to put her hand on Miz Edith's shoulder and give it a squeeze when she brought the tea. A person can tell a lot from a touch, cain't they? Maybe she won't feel so alone in her knowing, Eva thought.

Edgar's visit was short. He had brought May flowers—white alyssum. "Oh, Edgar, dearest. Sweet Alice for my garden. Thank you," she whispered, crying softly. He looked different to her. Thinner and more haggard. To him, she looked sad and fragile. They sat side by side, holding hands around the baby. For them, what was in the room was

265

anguish. After a time, Edgar touched Alice on her cheek. The baby gazed solemnly back at him. He leaned over and kissed her forehead, then slowly kissed May goodbye. Blinking his eyes, he stood up, opened the door and left the house.

Edith tried to talk with May about this descent into depression. She felt it was more important than ever for May to be vigilant about her mood swings. Maybe it might help her if she could somehow be prepared.

May brushed off Edith's concerns. Not that she was not worried. She was, but she could never discuss it with anyone, because only she knew about Edgar. It was all intertwined. "Edith, dear. I'm not being difficult," May said with a sigh. "I know you're trying to help. But I don't know if it's possible to prepare for these black periods. The ones I wish I could prepare for are the opposite ones. The exciting, busy, crazy ones. The black ones always come after, suddenly with no warning. But those wildly high moods that start slowly and sneak up on me. They're seductive," she said; in more ways than one, she thought. "By the time I'm aware I could be in its throes, it's too late."

Edith took the risk to speak of Edgar to May. She had to tell her that their feelings for each other were not invisible. At first May denied the affair but then told Edith the truth. "Just as I told you, it started during the high time. And Mitchell was gone for two weeks. I knew it was wrong. So did Edgar. The three of us had become so close, it was almost an extension of our friendship," said May, embarrassed. "I know. Crazy, isn't it? There was no reason for Mitchell to suspect anything. We had continued our marital relations. When I told Mitchell I was pregnant, it was at the same time I told Edgar. Here at the dinner table."

May was stopped for a minute by the look on Edith's face. "Edith don't get prudish on me now. You asked and I am telling you. And yes, it is shocking. That's what I mean about being in the throes of my moods."

With great effort, Edith tried to be nonjudgmental. "Good Lord, May. What a heavy load you carry. I wish there was a magic wand I could wave over you to make it all go away."

"I wish it too, Edith. And it is heavy burden. It was at that dinner when we talked about names that we decided to use Hamlin as the middle name.

It was Mitchell who suggested it, not me, and if I had said no, he would have been crushed. He would have asked me why not. It might have made him suspicious. We were a close unit, and except for John, Edgar is Mitchell's closest friend. So, I think I can find the strength to continue this friendship. Which is all it is now," May finished.

Edith said, "Well, you had better find a way to hide the emotion you both emit when you're together. It was like a living being when I was in the room with you both."

May nodded. "We'll figure out a way. Maybe it was because that was the first time we had seen each other, and Alice was right there. You know how it is after pregnancy. You're a jumble of emotions. But thank you for telling me how obvious it was when you saw us together. It is something we'll both have to hide."

Alice, "Sweet Alice," as she was constantly referred to, defined sweet. She was quiet and undemanding. She woke, nursed, and slept. She cried or fussed rarely. May and Edith had never seen such a baby. No croup, no colic, no gas, no diarrhea, no maladies. She seemed too good to be true.

Edith left in September. The whole family came to the station to see her off. May was reminded of their last farewell, in Bangor, when she and Mitchell and the girls had been the ones leaving and waving goodbye to Edith and her family. Could it really have been only three years before? This was a happier time, though bittersweet for the sisters.

"My dear, May, I wish we all lived closer, and I could be with you," said Edith, holding her in a tight hug. "Maybe I could see when your moods are coming on and warn you. Though, to be honest, I never saw them coming when you were younger." She was crying.

"Well, you came here when we needed you, and that's all that matters. You saved us all," said May, blinking back her own tears. "No, Edith, don't say anything. Do not belittle what you have done. If it weren't for you, Sweet Alice might not be here at all. We are all so deeply grateful to you."

Edith smiled through her tears. "All right. And I thank you. It was worth it."

Inside the train, Edith's breath caught in her throat as she looked out the window at her sister and her family. Would the furies that May suffered come again? she wondered. Would this family be able to withstand them another time? A crushing sense of foreboding overtook her.

A normal routine returned. May started back with her gardening. Roosevelt, bless his heart, had maintained the home garden. The community garden was flourishing, the gardeners becoming more accomplished with each new planting. There were now sixty plots growing. Impressive, May thought. She wasn't quite as indispensable as she had felt herself to be.

She had to do something about Edgar. He weighed heavily on her mind. She still had feelings for him, strong feelings that she found reassuring. At least this wasn't like Ivan, just a dirty fling. If she was going to risk everything for a love affair, it should be one that had meaning. And as it was more than possible that he was the father of Alice, that made him intimately more a part of her life. Her family's life.

Despite the state of the country, no longer in a panic but settling into a depression, peace prevailed in the Plummer household—from Eva and Betty to the girls and Mitchell and May. The relief in having back the normal May was obvious.

In September, Frances started first grade at Scranton Academy. Schooling had not been on May's list of necessities when she was house hunting. But luckily for them, it had been on William Mead's mind. He had brought it to her attention that the academy was just six blocks away.

She reminded herself to thank William when she saw him next. It became routine for May, pushing Alice in her pram with Edie holding one of the sides, to escort Frances to school each morning. Edie hopped along excitedly and jabbered away wondering why she had to wait two *whole* years to be able to go to school.

Despite the peace of routine in the household, there were concerns amongst the adults. Alice was not advancing the way she should. The first to verbalize her concerns was Betty. "Ma'am," she said nervously to May in January,

271

after all the Christmas hustle. "Alice is the sweetest baby I have ever seen. But...she's almost six months now. Oh, I don't know how to say this. Maybe it's just nothing."

"Go on, Betty," said May. "It's all right. I think I know what you're going to say."

"She's off. I don't know how else to describe it. It's almost as if she's too sweet. She just lies there, not moving a lot. She hardly ever cries. What baby doesn't cry? Or wriggle around? She should be turning over by now. And I know you hide it, but when she nurses, she gives up easily. She's still so small." Betty finished, unable to look May in the eyes.

"I know, Betty, dear," said May. "I've noticed the same, but I was too afraid to say anything out loud. Even Mitchell, who knows nothing about infants, hinted at it," said May. "I think he's afraid I'll go crazy again." She paused when she saw the look on Betty's face. "Don't worry, dear, I'm all right. I'll arrange for the doctor today."

Dr. Kell came the next afternoon. Alice lay quietly while he took his time examining her. Mitchell had come home—no reason May should go through this alone. They stood still, holding hands, watching. When the doctor was through, the concern on his face made them sit down.

"It is worrying. And I do not know if I can give you an adequate explanation," the doctor said. "You're right. She is not progressing the way she should. She is not in any acute distress, which is positive. But she is certainly small for her age. And she is a little lethargic. Her arms and legs have not developed good musculature, probably one reason she doesn't turn over. You say she nurses poorly. And as sweet as she is, she doesn't really engage with you, correct? You know. Laugh or gurgle back at you?"

May nodded. Neither she nor Mitchell was able to verbally acknowledge his questions.

"She has a rash around and in her mouth. It's called chillosis. That could make it difficult for her to nurse. And her skin is dry with some scaling. These things alone would not be that concerning. But with the other symptoms you have described, it adds up to something we in medicine call *failure to thrive.*"

May fell against Mitchell. They looked at each other through their tears. Mitchell was the first to speak. "What exactly does that mean?"

"Well, we don't know exactly what causes it. Some say it could be hereditary. You did say, Mrs. Plummer, that you had two brothers die young? One at birth and one at three? Others say it is not a disease but malnutrition. Maybe a form of malabsorption. Her body may not absorb nutrients the way it should," said Dr. Kell. He sat down heavily, thinking, this is too hard.

"Is she going to die?" May managed to get out.

"Maybe," said the doctor, who after seeing the look on her face, qualified his answer. "We just don't know. She might survive, though, probably always in a weakened state. I just can't predict."

He continued, trying for a positive approach. "Death doesn't always occur. We can do exercises to increase her muscle tone. We can encourage her to stay awake. We can stimulate her emotionally by laughing and playing with her. Let her sisters play with her. It is proven that infants react positively to children's faces and sounds. Take her on walks. Don't hide her."

May had to ask. "Remember what you told us when you first saw me? You said morphine can affect the baby. Could it be that?"

Dr. Kell chose his words carefully, not wanting to add guilt to May's already overburdened mind. "Usually that is seen at birth. As time goes by, the babies seem to outgrow the effects associated with the drug. So, no, I do not think it's that," he said, remembering well how he had been worried at her birth with her color and her lethargy. He had had to spank her harder than most babies to start her breathing.

He stood up to leave. Mitchell and May walked him to the door, somehow able to remember their manners, and thanked him for coming. "I'm sorry I could not give you better news. My prayers will be with you," he said to them. He turned and slowly went down the stairs of the porch, taking their hopes with him.

They took his advice. Betty and May took turns working on Alice's muscles. Betty introduced cereal in addition to May's breastfeeding. May and the girls took the baby for a walk. Once. Too many people stopped them, wanting to chat and excited to see the baby. It was all May could do to get them all home before she fell apart, in the kitchen, away from her girls. After that, it was Betty who took Alice out, alone and in the early mornings.

Mitchell fell back into work. There was plenty to worry about there too. The Depression did not appear to show any signs of recovery. He would come home every evening wearied by the country's economics. Frances and Edie were his path out of that exhaustion. Both girls now dined with them most evenings. Their chatter was music to Mitchell's and May's ears, allowing them to relax. Frances told stories about school; Edie competed with her own stories. She had a vivid imagination and told long, convoluted tales of her dolls' adventures.

Edgar came for dinner frequently. After dinner, the adults would retire to the parlor and before going to bed, the girls trooped down to visit Uncle Edgar, of whom they had become very fond. He told them wonderful stories. No surprise there, considering he wrote stories for a living. But making them up on the spot was a talent he never knew he had. He enjoyed it immensely.

The girls' favorite story was about a magical land called Limerick that only little children could visit. Two of those children just happened to be named Frances and Edie. Cries of "Tell us about Limerick, pleeese, Uncle Edgar," filled the house when they entered the parlor. Everyone smiled then, even Eva and Betty, who listened from the door.

Occasionally, on a weekday, Edgar stopped by, ostensibly to interview May about her community commitments. May would bring Alice downstairs, and they would sit in the parlor, the door closed, with Alice between them. Their feelings for each other were still strong but muted. It was easier for May. She had been in such a dizzying state at the time of their affair that now, in her state of normalcy, it all seemed like a hallucination. For Edgar, it had been as real as the baby between them. But he had loved her from afar before, and he could do it again. The important thing was to be a support for her and Mitchell, his best friends.

On August 18, 1895, Sweet Alice died in her sleep. Betty never heard a thing, despite Alice's crib being in her room. It was not until the morning when she picked up the tiny cold body that she knew. May was guilt-ridden that she had not been with her daughter. All she could think of was that her poor baby had died with no one holding her close. One moment Alice was alive, the next not.

There was hardly a transition between life and death for her Sweet Alice.

Mitchell was at a loss about burial for the baby. "Who plans for these things?" he asked Edgar in tears.

Edgar, just as lost, somehow remembered John Smith, the insurance man. "Woodmen of the World," Edgar said. "God, what a stupid name. But I bet he can help you, Mitch."

Mitchell stumbled to the man's house that evening. "Mitchell, I am so very, very sorry for you and your wife. What a terrible thing to go through." John Smith sat Mitchell down and poured them both a glass of bourbon. "Please, have a drink. Be at ease that we can take care of your problem. That is what is meant by a fraternal organization; this is when we shine."

He took a file from his desk. "I have five children, and I have been having the same thought about a burial plot. I happened to be looking at one, but it is a steep price for me. If the cost was shared with another, it would be manageable. I'd be honored if you would consider buying half with me."

Mitchell nearly slid off his chair, so grateful was he that he did not have to worry any more about where Alice would rest.

They had a small service, just family, Edgar, and close friends, including John Smith. May and Betty dressed Alice in her christening gown; she was a year old, and it still fit. She was laid to rest in an infant's white coffin in Machpeleh Cemetery, the gravestone reading only "Sweet Alice" and the dates of her short existence. The loneliness of that small white box in the dark earth would stay with Mitchell, May, and Edgar for the rest of their lives.

35—DEPRESSED NORMALCY—1895

The past two years had been an unending whirl of trials for Mitchell—familial and financial. The country was still in a depression brought on by the Panic of 1893, with the receivership of the Philadelphia and Reading Railroad, and followed by successive bankruptcies across the country.

A simultaneous financial panic in London, along with reductions in European and South American trade, caused foreign investors to sell off American stocks. Some five hundred banks closed, fifteen thousand businesses failed, farms were abandoned; the unemployment rate rose to has high as 43 percent in some states.

There were strikes and demonstrations across the country, most met with quick, strict action by the authorities done in the name of maintaining order. One of the country's first major demonstrations was a march led by Jacob Coxey, an Ohio business owner who was upset at having to lay off many of his workers. He wanted to lobby the government to create jobs involving building roads and other public works.

"Coxey's Army" began its march in Ohio in March of 1894. It was a band of one hundred protesters with new members joining daily as they traveled east. By the time they reached Washington, there were some 6,000 members, the feeding of which had become a common expression: *Enough food to feed Coxey's Army*. The day after arriving in Washington, Coxey was arrested for the transgression of "Walking on the grass of the US Capital." His arrest effectively ended that protest.

The nationwide Pullman Strike occurred in that summer, pitting the American Railway Union against the Pullman Company, major railroads, and the federal government. It was effective. However, the other rail unions made up of conductors and porters were affected negatively and strongly opposed the strike. They joined with management who coordinated the opposition. The resulting riots killed workers and caused millions of dollars' worth of damages. Ultimately, President Cleveland ordered the army to collapse the strike.

Also struggling were the banks. Some had connections with private financiers who saved them from collapse but earned them disdain from those banks unable to secure such largesse. Ironically, in 1895, the government itself felt no such compunction at accepting similar generosity in the form of a loan of sixty-five million in gold through a private bond from the Wall Street banker J. P. Morgan. With more money in circulation and a providential (for America) failure of foreign crops and products, there began a slight increase in the purchase of American goods. A feeling of optimism, small that it was, began to take over, at least in the financial and banking sectors.

That optimism allowed Mitchell to feel some hope. There was a sadness that still hung over his family, but his home life was returning to normal. He worked normal hours, ate dinners with his family, and played with his daughters. There was noise again in his home.

He thought of his baby, Alice, often. There had been so little of her; it was as if she had been born a ghost. She had never been truly alive. He felt a guilty relief she was gone. He ached for his little baby, but he had ached more for himself, his wife, and his two girls. For someone so tiny, she had taken up the largest part of their emotions.

For May, Alice's passing had left a hole in her life. It was a hole she had been aware of the moment Dr. Kell had told them Alice was suffering from *failure to thrive.* Those three words described her baby exactly. That hole would be with her forever, never filled. In fact, she did not want it filled. It had become a part of her. Maybe that's just what people are, she thought. A collection of holes held together by their bodies. Maybe eventually the holes became too many for the bodies to contain.

She worried, as did Mitchell, that she would go into a depression again. She was certainly sad, but not the awful, oppressive despair that had taken her over in the past. Maybe it was because death was the only possible future for Alice, and thankfully when it came, it took her peacefully.

Edgar, too, was affected. He was convinced Alice was his daughter, and he dearly missed those afternoons in the parlor with May and Alice between them. For him, those were the most perfect of times—almost sacred. He had to laugh. Him of all people. A man of questionable morals, lacking any religious principles, had found something divine in holding an infant. An infant who was probably the result of an illicit union. An infant who was going to die.

The three continued with their weekly dinners, May and Edgar's passion having burned to

283

embers. It glowed softly, always there but no longer aflame, and it cast a warmth they both treasured. Mitchell continued unaware of the emotional upheaval that had occurred in their little group. Eva cooked and served them. She did not understand, nor did she approve, but she loved the Plummers, and despite everything had become grudgingly fond of Edgar.

36—CROSSROADS—1895

After Alice's death, Edgar thought Mitchell would benefit from getting involved in more activities to take his mind off things. Edgar suggested yachting. He had heard about a new sailing club starting up.

"Yachting? Are you crazy, Edgar? I don't sail."

"I thought you told me you sailed when you were a boy?"

Mitchell laughed. "Well, I did take sailing one year in college. One of my stepfather's brothers raced sailboats, and occasionally he'd take us nephews along, for ballast, he told us. All we did was move from side to side every time the boat came about. That's all I know."

Apparently, it was enough. On August 10, 1895, he found himself elected secretary of the new Yachtsmen Club, discussing arrangements for the First Annual Yachtsmen Regatta to be held on August 28.

As if that was not enough distraction, he had become a bicycle salesman, resulting in him becoming an ardent cyclist. He had an advertisement in the *Pascagoula Democrat-Star* that read "H. M. Plummer, agent for Falcon

285

bicycles and selling Kodak cameras. You press the button; we do the rest. Everyone owning a bicycle should have a Kodak." He entered himself into the first ever bicycle race to be held on the new quarter-mile track recently built in Pascagoula.

May found herself adrift. The whiff of economic optimism that elevated Mitchell had not trickled down to the townsfolk. She could not open her boutique; people did not have extra money to spend on frivolous items. She would have enjoyed doing work on her house, but anything she did would cost money. She backed away from her fundraising. Who had money to spare? Her elder daughter was in school; her younger would be going next year. She was bored, something she had never been before.

She read. What had started as a chore back in Bangor when she had first moved in with her in-laws had become a welcome pastime. The Scranton Library, thanks to her fundraising, now offered hundreds of books and took up half of the Masonic Lodge building. Since Sweet Alice's birth and death, May had found casual socializing difficult. She could not bear another sad look or questions about how she was doing. So, reading was something she could do alone, allowing her to feel she was at least working her brain.

She finally read *Wuthering Heights*. Alice had been right. It *was* difficult with characters exhibiting terrible behaviors. Alice had not been alone in her feelings. An admirer of the book, had written, "It is a fiend of a book – an incredible monster." Despite the tragic characters, all self-centered and malicious, May was drawn in, identifying with Heathcliff and his black moods. Here was someone with far worse melancholia than herself.

She still gardened, the process allowing her to feel close to her sister. Edith and May often compared their gardening exploits in their letters back and forth. The community garden was thriving, up to over one hundred plots. A great camaraderie had sprung up amongst the farmers; whites farmed beside Jamaicans, beside Chinese, beside Bahamians, beside Germans, beside Cubans. In addition to the regular plantings, the garden had become a polyglot of international plants. Families from the homelands sent seeds. Those workers who sailed on the ships brought back more seeds and plants. The resulting foods were sampled by all, introducing new flavors and meals to be tried at home.

Eva often went to the gardens with Roosevelt, now considered the head gardener. She was intrigued by the different herbs and spices, using them in her cooking, concocting new dishes. She never followed a recipe— she couldn't read. But she knew them by heart, the ones passed down by her family and the new ones she created. She had become, just as Edgar had said about her, the best cook in Scranton.

So good, in fact, that May lent her to others when they asked. For Eva's services, the person who hired her paid May, not Eva directly. Ridiculous, thought May, as she gave Eva the money. Almost thirty years after slavery and they still lived as if things had never changed. Maybe, May wondered, she could transcribe Eva's recipes, write a cookbook, and give the profits to Eva. That would turn the tables on all that antiquated thinking.

May did have some dinner parties—small ones. It was common during these times of deprivation and was an easy and inexpensive way to entertain, especially if the guest count was low.

One or two extra people hardly stretched one's budget. Eva loved it, the girls happily helped May with the table settings, and Mitchell loved seeing his wife in such good spirits.

Sometimes her spirits were *too* good. May had taken to having a few nips of Jim beam during the days. Sometimes she became a little inebriated during dinner parties. It was hardly noticeable to anyone but Mitchell. He still worried about her, so if it made her merrier that was fine with him. She was a delightful hostess, and their friends enjoyed coming to their home. Also, delightful, she usually maintained that merriness later when they retired to the bedroom. May was still the seducer, he still the seduced.

One night, after a dinner with Edgar, the three of them were in the parlor enjoying a brandy Edgar had brought from Mobile. Since Sweet Alice's passing and the cooling between May and himself, Edgar had begun traveling again for his reporting. Although the change in his and May's relationship was mutual, it was still hard for him, and getting away offered a distraction. He often brought back gifts of wines and other spirits for

May and Mitchell, as a way of reciprocating their hospitality.

May was feeling the effects of the brandy and was fetchingly flirting with both men. Mitchell found it seductive, enjoying watching her charm them both. Edgar found it less seductive, though, he did not discourage it. He, too, felt under her spell.

"Edgar," May said woozily. "Remember that night you came for dinner and Eva came out in her slippers."

Mitchell laughed. "He wouldn't know that May. You put a quick stop to that, don't you remember?" He looked over to Edgar. "May almost fell over the first time Eva served us dinner. She did. Eva was wearing her bedroom slippers. Thank God, my mother was not here."

Edgar hoped his face did not give him away. "I never heard that story before. My mother would have fainted too," and weakly took a sip of his drink.

"You're right, Mitchell, darling," said May, sobering quickly. "That was before we met you, Edgar. The night you came here with John. That's the night we met you."

Edgar left shortly afterward. "I hate to be the one to break up the party, but I have to be in Pensacola tomorrow," he said. "I know, I know. I never said anything. Half the time I don't even remember if I'm going or coming."

That was rather sudden, thought Mitchell. Usually he stays longer. But the thought slipped away when May kissed him and began walking languidly to the stairs. It wasn't until later, after May had gone to sleep, that Mitchell wondered about her slipper story. Odd, she got mixed up on that. Maybe it was just the alcohol.

John Mahoney had been in New Orleans on business. The plant in Asheville was doing well, and his company was looking to again expand their business into the South. He took advantage of his trip to make a short detour to Scranton on the way home. John had been promoted to director of sales at Edwards Manufacturing, a position that would require little to no traveling, certainly not so far south. This might be the last time he could see his friends.

Edgar met John at the hotel, and they strolled over to the Plummers' on an unseasonably warm November night. Despite the sense of sadness that still hung over the house from Alice's death, it was a happy gathering of old friends.

"John, you haven't changed a bit," said Mitchell. They had been regaled with John's stories throughout dinner and were now in the parlor. "Though, in this new job, you won't be able to get away with some of your hijinks."

"Maybe. I must admit, though, I'm not nearly as amused by the hijinks anymore. Maybe it is time to settle down, like you two. It seems to work for you both," said John, a foolish grin on his face.

"John!" blurted out May. "Oops. I think I am a little tipsy. Don't tell me you've found someone. Have you? It's about time. You and Edgar both should settle down. Find yourselves nice girls."

"I think so, May." John was slightly surprised at May's state. But they all were a little drunk, and Lord knows, she had been through a lot. "Her name is Evelyn O'Brien. A good Irish lass," he said, laughing at himself. "Aye, she is."

"Congratulations, old man," said Edgar, recovering his voice. May's comment about finding himself a nice girl had left him speechless. He *had* found a nice girl, and he could do nothing about it. He was envious of John, who had always said he would never marry. John had his wild side for sure, of which Edgar was well aware, having taken him around New Orleans—on more than one occasion.

"Well, I'm sure there's more to her than just being Irish. Tell us about her," said Mitchell.

Hearing about John's engagement left Edgar feeling adrift, as if he was being left behind. He had chosen bachelorhood and was usually content with that decision. Yet incongruous as it seemed, being so close to Mitchell and May gave him a glimpse into what a marriage could be like. Sometimes he longed for that normalcy for himself.

His love for May simmered in the back of his mind, always. His affection for Mitchell simmered also, on another burner, with John on a third. It was a busy stove he tended. He had always felt apart from the normal community. Obviously, growing up as he had in a fractured family consumed with their loss of status had contributed to that. But it was his inner self that ruled his separateness. Staying single allowed him to enjoy varied relationships and unfettered entry into the underground world.

It was true that Edgar and John had met at a bar in New Orleans. Just not at the hotel bar, as was always told, but at Miss Big Nelly's. Edgar could not deny he was jealous that John had apparently found love with a woman and would soon embark on a traditional life.

Did Edgar really want such a life? With a wife? Even if that wife was May? He adored Frances and Edie, but did he want children and those responsibilities? Did he want to give up travel, sleeping, eating, and drinking when he wanted? Sexual liaisons? He thought not. He had made the conscious decision to be single, and it had suited him well thus far.

Discussion followed about when and where the wedding would be, with the Plummers and Edgar vowing to attend. May longed for a trip back to Maine to see Edith and Edward. Clarence was a young man now. And her aunt and uncle and the twins, they were twelve now. She spent the rest of the evening teary eyed and sniffling, from happiness and longing.

Normalcy was returning to the Plummer household. May became more involved in the daily goings-on. She was running the house, helping at the store, and working at the garden and at the library. She and Edie continued walking Frances to school. She read to the girls. And Mitchell and May continued with their dinner parties.

Sometimes Edgar brought a woman friend to dinner. Scranton was not New Orleans, but it did have its share of attractive, unmarried women. Soon to be forty, Edgar was still considered a good catch, though, those who wanted marriage quickly realized that it would not be with him. There were a few women closer to his age who enjoyed his company as he enjoyed theirs. Having a companion allowed him to not stand out quite so singularly, as it also did for the lady.

At first May found it uncomfortable to see Edgar with another woman; with different women. One seemed a bit loose, a bit too brazen, though Mitchell was not fazed by her. May smiled to herself, wondering what people would have said about her if they had known about her and Edgar. Or, God forbid, Ivan Festair. Lately, though, Edgar seemed to have settled down with Amelia Harper, the librarian. She knew May and the girls through their many visits.

After one party, Mitchell and May were readying themselves for bed. They had hosted a dinner with the Veillonses and Edgar, who had brought Amelia. Already a larger than normal gathering, Mitchell at the last minute had invited another couple, the Randalls—Judge and Judith—visiting from Mobile. Five years earlier, Judge had replaced the retiring Harlan Johnson as president of the Mobile State Bank, the parent bank of Mitchell's.

"May, dearest," said Mitchell. "You were just a bit too tipsy tonight, don't you think? Even Evan and Elizabeth seemed surprised, and Edgar and Amelia were for sure. I know you get nervous when we have new people for dinner, but..."

"Mitchell," interrupted May. "I do get nervous, and an extra drink or two helps me. Especially with those people. Whatever possessed you to invite them? And poor Eva. She had to stretch the meal, which she did very creatively, in case you didn't notice."

"Lord, May. You're not the only one who suffered but I *had* to invite them. He is my boss, and he was in town. How was I to know they were teetotalers? And that she belonged to the UDC? When I had to ask her what that was, you would have thought I'd asked her if she believed in God. And then we all had to suffer as she clarified exactly what the United Daughters of the Confederacy stood for and all their good works. It was just as bad for me too."

"Well, Mitchell. If you got your nose out of that bank every now and then, you might know," snapped May in a huff. May had not known what the UDC was either, but she hated it when Mitchell commented on her drinking.

"I do understand why you had to invite them," a mollified May said, pacing around the room. "It's just that they both were so tedious, especially her. You must admit it, Mitchell. I was not the only one who had more to drink than usual. I think we all did. It was hard for all of us. I know a lot of people here still have holdover ideas from the Confederacy, but they don't go bragging about how glorious it was in the old days. At least not to our faces. 'How the South should never forget. That it will rise again. That it was the War of Yankee Aggression.'" May plopped down on the bed with a thump.

She went on. "Even when Elizabeth gently reminded her where we were from. And she said it humorously too. 'Judith, you do know Mitchell and May are from Maine? They certainly are not aggressive.' Everyone chuckled, even her husband, the one and only Mr. Judge O. Randall—goodness, what a silly name. But she didn't, the fool."

Mitchell took a deep breath, thinking he should just let it drop, but he too had been drinking. "Well, Edgar certainly drank a bit more than usual. The two of you were almost rude in your behavior toward the Randalls. They were our guests. And Edgar was with Amelia, and you both acted as if you were in your own little world. You have to be more careful in your behavior, May."

"Mitchell, I was just flirting, like I always do. Amelia doesn't care. They have an *understanding*, whatever that means. And don't give me that look. I've seen how you flirt with Elizabeth sometimes. Sometimes I think you flirt with Edgar too. Haven't we both always had a bit of an infatuation with him?" May added. She was tired of this petty argument. But it seemed like Mitchell was picking arguments with her frequently these days. Whatever. That Judith was awful. With luck she would never have to see her again. Or her fat ridiculous husband.

Mitchell stayed silent. Ever since the night May had mentioned Eva coming out in her slippers, he had wondered. Those doubts had become suspicious seeds festering in his brain. Could that have really been only a slip of the tongue? Could Edgar have been over here one night for dinner when he had been away in Mobile for those meetings—those incredibly stupid meetings that did nothing to stem the tide of what was to come to the country? He was gone for two weeks.

Something could have happened. It certainly was not unheard of. And May did have that indiscretion before he had met her. Edgar was no saint, for sure. Could they have had relations?

His love for May endured, despite his misgivings. Those doubts, strangely, only added to her desirability. He found it sinfully seductive that other men could be attracted to her. For some reason, he felt his fantasies were more of a sin than their actual affair, if indeed an affair had happened. And the fact that this liaison could have occurred with Edgar made it almost unbearably erotic. May was right. Mitchell did have an attraction to Edgar, as he did to John. Both friends brought out feelings in Mitchell that he kept hidden.

He remembered his stepfather's accusations about his *proclivities*. But he was married now and had children. That should say something about his manliness, shouldn't it? Plus, he had May. She was married to him, and he could satisfy his yearnings with her.

"Destructive Fire on Canty Street. Presbyterian Church and H. M. Plummer Residence Reduced to Ashes."

The headline in the *Pascagoula Democrat-Star* of January 17, 1896, screamed out to Mitchell. He was reading the article out loud to May.

"Last Friday night, about 11:00 p.m., fire was discovered in the church. The volunteer fire companies immediately responded...The flames had gained such headway that the church was apparently doomed...Efforts were directed towards saving the frame residence of H.M. Plummer nearby...there was a scarcity of water...Contents of the house were removed, many [*sic*] injured or demolished...After the flames were communicated to the Plummer residence, it was rapidly reduced to ashes...Both buildings were a total loss...The fire must have been of incendiary origin, as there had been no fire in the church since the previous Sabbath...The church, almost new, was insured by Liverpool, London, and Globe for $1,500...plan to rebuild on same site...Mr. Plummer's furniture was insured for $1,200. The residence owned by Walter

301

Gautier of W. Pascagoula was insured for $1,000 and will be rebuilt at once...A reward of $250 is offered for the apprehension and conviction of the incendiary...H. M. Plummer has, with his family, moved temporarily into the Blanchard dwelling, adjoining Noy's Hotel on Krebs Avenue."

"God, I still don't believe it," Mitchell said, placing the paper down on the table and shaking his head. He looked at May sitting across from him. "How did we all get out of there?"

"I don't know. But we did, somehow. We're all safe," said May. She wiped away tears. "I'm just still so emotional; I can't stop crying. I have to get hold of myself."

"It's all right, dear," said Mitchell, giving a small cough over the lump in his own throat. "I feel the same way. Who wouldn't, for God's sake?" He reached across and took her hand. "At least "the Blanchard dwelling" is big enough for us all. More than big enough. A little shabby but surprisingly tidy, considering old man Blanchard died six years ago, and the hotel uses it for spillover," said Mitchell.

True to the paper's reporting, the rubble of both buildings was removed quickly. Mr. Gautier, the owner of their house, had already consulted with a builder. The church would also commence rebuilding. Their street would be a noisy, dusty place.

"I hear the girls. I'd best get up there and help them get dressed for school. I am never going to get used to Betty not being here. She spoiled us all," said May as she left the kitchen. "Thank goodness she wasn't here during the fire."

The month before, Betty had come to May in tears. Her sister, back in Bangor, had fallen and broken her hip and needed help recovering. May could only wish her well. She would have done the same if it was Edith living alone. The girls were older now and didn't really need a nurse anymore. It was a sad little group that went to see Betty off at the train.

Despite the fire and Betty's leaving, the new year of 1896 had begun with a sense of optimism for the Plummers, at least financially. Economic signs continued looking up. Southern Bell Telephone Company was in the process of initiating service to the town, a big excitement to the business population. Mitchell was able to pay himself regularly, enabling him to pay Eva and

Roosevelt again. It wasn't much, but it was something. He felt he was again the man of the house, able to provide for his family.

May enjoyed watching Mitchell's successes. She remembered how insecure he was when they first married, when he was working with his stepfather. And how uncomfortable they were living with his mother. He deserves this, she thought. He has truly worked hard as the provider.

As for her, May seemed to have reached a plateau. She was resigned to the void that Sweet Alice had left in herself and her family. She enjoyed her girls. Frances, now in second grade, was thriving. Each day she came home with stories that she related to her family at dinner, her parents a proud audience, Edie envious. Once a week, May took the two girls to the library. May was looking forward to getting back to gardening once it was warm enough.

After the debacle of their last dinner party and the fire, they had cut back on entertaining, though, Edgar of course still came frequently when he was in town, usually alone but often with Amelia. Knowing how Edgar loved Eva's cooking,

May asked Eva to experiment with new meals on those days.

May had broached the topic of writing a cookbook with Eva. At first Eva just laughed. "Oh, Miz May. You is funny. It's all in my haid. Just like it was in my mama's and her mama's. What white lady wants a cookbook by a colored cook? And no colored would buy one. They cooks like me anyways," said Eva.

But the seed had been planted, and in time Eva agreed. Initially, it was difficult, especially the measurements. Eva just did it—a chicken or some meat, maybe a fish, some flour, some sugar, a dash of this, a dollop of that, a shake, a splash...

If May interrupted with questions, Eva got upset and needed to start over. Eventually, they worked out a system. May sat on one side of the table, directly opposite Eva with a notebook on one side, measuring cups and spoons at the ready on the other and she let Eva work with no interruptions. Eva happily chatted and worked at the same time, making it easy for May to take notes; Eva's comments would be integral to the book. Just before Eva went to add anything, May slipped a cup or a spoon under her hands to

305

measure it. After some awkward starts they got the hang of it. Sometimes the two women were in the kitchen for whole mornings or afternoons. It was a close, treasured time for them both.

In February, May knew she was pregnant. She didn't tell a soul until she felt the quickening, and then only Mitchell. He'd had an inkling; all sexual relations had ceased abruptly. And May had become pensively quiet, often sitting with her hand on her stomach, just staring. Waiting for something? He had wanted to ask but didn't dare. Was this a new manifestation of one of her moods? Could it be a pregnancy? And if it was, would this be a healthy baby?

When May told Mitchell they were expecting, they were both thrilled—and terrified. May had secretly blamed herself for Alice's death. She had been wicked with Edgar. She had been crazy, and she had taken morphine. There were a multitude of reasons she should be punished for what she did.

Mitchell, too, worried. Mostly about how another pregnancy could affect May. Which May, the crazy one or the loving one, would carry this pregnancy and care for the new baby? Dr. Kell reassured them the pregnancy seemed totally normal and that May appeared strong and healthy and could continue with her normal routines. "Just relax," he said.

Despite the doctor's advice, May did cut back on her activities. In March, she sat on the porch and watched (trying not to direct) Roosevelt as he put in her garden. She left the community garden to others, knowing how well it had survived before without her.

Recalling how weak she had been with Alice, she wanted to be strong for this baby. The magazines she read all encouraged keeping healthy and staying active, within reason. So, her walks with her girls continued, and in the evenings they all, including Mitchell, walked after dinner. And she and Eva worked on the book.

On November 20, 1896, Anna Holland (May's sister Edith's middle name) Plummer was born. She had been an easy pregnancy and an easy birth. She was not an easy baby. She was colicky and kept May working overtime. May hardly complained, and when she did it was good humored. The memories of Alice and her *sweetness* were still fresh on everyone's minds. A little tetchiness was a small price to pay.

May had not planned to have a nurse, but after a few weeks, she asked Eva if she knew of anyone who could help her with the children. "I know just the woman," said Eva. "Miz Aunt Mary Beck. She ain't my *for real* aunt. She ain't nobody's aunt that I know. But she takes care of babies like no one else. Don't be put off cuz she be old. Miz Mary gets around just fine."

Eva was convinced Anna's crankiness was a sign of strength. Eva had never been involved in the childcare, though, she loved having *her babies* in the house. But because of May's work on the cookbook, Anna as an infant spent long hours in a cradle in the kitchen, resulting in Eva being more involved. Listening to the two women talking seemed a tonic to Anna. She would lie quietly between sleep and arousal, almost in a trance. When she was awake, a measuring spoon kept her contentedly cooing.

"Mark my words, Miz May. You see. This girl got spirit. Someday she's gonna do big things. And I'll tell the people: I knowed Anna before you knowed Anna."

May had little desire to continue with her social obligations. She was content with her family and home. Her committees and her friends tried coercing her. They needed her. May was the one who did all the organizing. She was the creative one, not they. She fought off their pleas. "You'll do fine without me." She was content with her books, her garden, and her girls. They continued their walks to school, to the library, and in the evenings with Mitchell.

She reread *Jane Eyre*. Though it had remained her favorite, this time she found it too romantic. She remembered the darkness of *Wuthering Heights* and reread it, returning to its harsh drama of love, obsession, death and grief. May found it hauntingly familiar. She wondered about Emily Bronte and what state her mind had been in. She was thirty when she died, one year after the book came out; only four years younger than May herself. How she must have been suffering, to have written about such a harsh reality.

The family had a new, small addition: Blackie, a black fluffy kitten who followed her around everywhere. He had shown up at the kitchen door one morning and refused to leave. Eva swooshed him away with her broom, but he returned. Those actions might have worked in time, but once Edie saw him, the kitten's battle was won.

Not chairing the library committee was the only one of her charities May felt guilty about. But she went there so frequently with the girls and for herself she felt she was supporting the library in a different way. Amelia, who May had become quite friendly with, saved them books she thought they would like.

Before she had moved to Scranton, Amelia had lived in Chicago and worked at Poole Brothers, a publishing company. It catered to transportation companies, in particular to the railroads, printing railway maps, railroad tickets, brochures, and other associated documents. According to Amelia, almost every railroad in the country used their printed materials.

Amelia was thrilled when May told her about the cookbook. "I'd love to help, if you'd want me to. I can edit and proofread. It's certainly not railroads, but the process is the same when the time comes to put it together. I might even be able to use some of my old contacts and find you a publisher."

The cookbook was nearly finished. May had notes of Eva's recipes—about seventy of them—painstakingly written along with Eva's comments. May was now in the process of rewriting each recipe following May's notes, and it was slow going. May had to convert those notes into something understandable and, most importantly, reproducible. It made for creative dining.

"Miz May, don't you white folks have it all in your haids? You don't really take time to measure every little thing, do you? Lawd, have mercy. It take forever. No wonder you need a cook," Eva said, frustrated at having to follow the recipe. "It not natural. It slows me down."

"You can do it, Eva," coaxed May. "And, yes, we white folk have it in our heads too. My sister does. So did my mother and my aunt. I just never liked cooking that much, and once I married, we lived with Mitchell's mother. She sure didn't cook a thing, but her cook, Beulah, was fantastic. Like you, with it all in her head."

"I guess cooks all over do the same, no matter what color they is," said Eva.

"Think about it, Eva. If these recipes work, and I can write it so others can follow them and get the same results..." She had to laugh at the look on Eva's face. "Well, they'll never be *exactly* the same as yours. Don't worry, Eva. But if they come out close to yours, someone like Beulah or some cook in New York can cook your southern country cooking. You'll be famous. And rich."

Eva chortled. "Miz May, I don't wanna be famous. What am I gonna do being famous for? Put on airs? No. They'll just laugh me out of Creole Town." She got a devilish grin on her face. "Now rich, I knows I might could like that."

Not only did May discontinue her social obligations, she was not inclined to resume her marital obligations with Mitchell. Anna was four months old, and it was past time. She was the one who had usually initiated their lovemaking, but she had no desire for it. Occasionally, usually after a dinner with Edgar and several glasses of wine, she and Mitchell might be intimate.

Mitchell, now, was the one feeling restless. He found the change in their sexual routine upsetting. Sex was never something he *had* to have, not like John and Edgar. Not that they ever went into any details, thankfully. But he could tell by the way they talked together, that it was always on their minds. Sometimes he was uncomfortable around their closeness, that hinted at more than just a friendship; an intimacy that, if he was honest, he was jealous of. He suspected that something might have happened between them in their past. He longed for that closeness with each of them.

In his marriage, he had successfully put those uncomfortable desires out of his mind. His hungers were satisfied with May. As passive as he was in the initiating of their unions, he entered them eagerly and reveled in the feelings she incited in him.

But now that she no longer wanted to arouse his attentions, he found himself yearning for them. He began having graphic fantasies, initially with a fleshly May. But then the dream May and her voluptuousness faded into ghostly androgynous beings—beings increasingly familiar to his two best friends.

Mitchell tried to become the seducer to May, but it was difficult when she did not respond, and he was clumsy in his attempts. Sometimes he forced himself on her, leaving him feeling as if he

313

had defiled them both. Their marital bed had become a place of hurt.

"Mitchell, are you going to keep this up all night?" May shouted, in a whisper. "Why are you asking me this? Just because I didn't respond to your affections tonight?" She almost added "oafish" but had clamped an invisible hand over her mouth before going further. "What is it you want to know? You act as if I'm hiding something. I told you. I have a headache."

"Because you had too much to drink, again." Mitchell knew he was going too far. His thoughts of Edgar were eating him up, both his suspicions of him and his desires for him. Mitchell, too, had been drinking, resulting in this self-righteously emboldened state.

Trying to find relief in May's body was proving to be impossible. "May, I don't know what is going on with you. But I am your husband, and if I want to be with you...well, you must..." he said, his voice tapering off, knowing he'd gone too far.

"Lord, Mitchell. Do not act the *master* to me. Please. That is not you. You've never done that sort of thing," said May, almost crying. She did not want to hurt Mitchell. She just had no desire for lovemaking, with him or anyone else for that matter. It was rather astounding, considering how she had enjoyed it so much in the past. She could understand why he was hurt.

Mitchell couldn't help himself. "Tell me about you and Edgar. I know you both were together when I was in Mobile. You and my best friend. How could you?" It was out. He felt as if he had just vomited up a rock that lay between them. He lay there waiting for whatever was to come.

"Mitchell, what in the world are you talking about?"

"Don't lie to me, May. Not anymore. I know it happened, and I want you to tell me." There was still a chance he was wrong. There was no proof, just his inconceivable suspicions. They could still come back from the edge of the precipice he had brought them to. He would only look the fool.
***

When she finally finished telling him, Mitchell was curled up in a ball under the covers. "Mitchell, it's a lot, I know. But there's one more thing."

"Good God, May. What on earth else? Should we sew a scarlet *A* on your blouse? And you

315

can sew a red *C* on my shirt, for cuckold. Maybe something for Edgar too? A *B* for backstabber? Bastard? Then everyone can know what has been happening in my house. My house, May! Who else knows? Eva? The girls? I'll never be able to look anyone in the eyes again. You both have ruined my life."

He needed a drink. He got out of bed, quietly left the room, tiptoed down the stairs to the parlor, and poured himself two shots of brandy. His world had been torn asunder.

The next morning, the coldness between Mitchell and May emanated over the household, akin to a light mist visible only to someone highly attuned to their moods. Like Eva. She knew immediately when she served them breakfast. Lawdy, it's like Creole Town when the fog won't burn off, she thought. A curse. Something bad always happened on those low foggy days.

They were civilly polite with each other at breakfast. Mitchell read his paper, suddenly feeling like Charles. When the girls came down, he made a point of putting the paper down and chatting with them.

May sat at her end of the table, barely participating in the conversations. Her mind was spinning. Why did she tell him? Now he'll hate both Edgar and her. She needed to tell Edgar before Mitchell got to him. Though knowing how Mitchell felt about conflict, he might never say a word. She felt a serious headache coming on.

After walking the girls to school, May continued through town to Edgar's house. If he wasn't home, she'd leave a note. She was the one who had made this mess; she should at least be the one to tell him.

"May, what a nice surprise," said Edgar. He was still in his robe and slippers. "I'm not dressed to receive visitors. One of the advantages of my profession is I get to do most of my work at home, and sometimes I don't get dressed until the evening. My little secret," he said, only slightly embarrassed. She'd seen him in less.

May couldn't help but smile; he'd certainly seen her in less. "Speaking of secrets, ours is out."

"Oh no. Oh, dear. Is it Mitchell? Or does someone else know? I always knew it would get out some way. I just made myself a pot of coffee. Come in and have a seat. I'll make you a cup as soon as I get dressed," said Edgar.

Edgar brought out two cups of *café au lait*. He made as they did in New Orleans with chicory coffee, strong, and with hot milk. May loved it that way. She told him everything. At the end she said, "I was just about to tell him that you could be Alice's father when he cut me off. Just as well, really. He'll figure it out himself when his brain starts working again. So, what do we do?"

"At least it's only him. I don't think anyone else knows, other than Eva of course, and she won't tell anyone. She'll go to her grave with that secret, bless her heart. Better he found out through you and not some town wag," said Edgar.

Neither wanted to prolong Mitchell's misery. Edgar felt he should speak to Mitchell as soon as possible. Not so much to explain as to take Mitchell off the hook. He knew Mitchell would stew forever about whether and how to confront him.

"It's like a bad novel. Probably the one I would have written if I still wanted to write fiction," said Edgar. He was pacing back and forth in the room. "He's going to come to his own decision anyway. But if I talk with him now, he won't endlessly worry about what he thinks he has to do about me. Us."

Edgar told May he would wait until closing time at the bank to talk with Mitchell. "It might be quick. He could throw me out, but I doubt it. Hopefully, we'll come to some understanding. Maybe, somehow, our friendship might survive."

"You know, Edgar," said May, turning to go. "Each of us has had an infatuation with you since we first met you. I don't know if it's because John was the one who introduced us to you, and he's so special to us both, or just something about you. A little of both, I guess—you swept both of us off our feet."

Mitchell about fainted when he saw Edgar enter the bank. Did May get to him already? Could it be a coincidence? Edgar often stopped by at closing time to chat and take him out for a drink.

"Mitchell, don't throw me out." Edgar held up the bag he was holding. "I brought a peace offering. A bit of Jim Beam, in your office?"

Mitchell nodded tersely. After locking the doors, they went back to his office, and Edgar poured the bourbon into the two glasses Mitchell dug out of his desk. They sipped in silence for a short while, each looking uncomfortably around the room. Finally, Edgar spoke.

"I know how absolutely horrible you must feel, Mitchell. I have no excuse for what I did to you," Edgar said. "I don't want to lose your friendship, nor May's. I know that sounds absurd to you right now. But maybe in time we can repair our relationship."

Mitchell sat still, looking at the floor, and without looking up finally answered. "No, Edgar.

You have no idea how horrible I feel. Nor would any excuse suffice for the hurt you both have done me. I, too, am sorry, but I don't think it's possible for our friendship to be repaired. What we three had together was all I have ever wanted, and you ruined it."

Time numbs all wounds; Mitchell and May returned to being seemingly close; *for the girls,* they said to themselves. They had some dinner parties, small and without Edgar. Amelia came to help with the book, often staying over for the dinner they had made from the recipe they had tested that day, never commenting on Edgar's absence. May wondered what Amelia knew.

It was a turbulent time, especially for Mitchell. In addition to trying to navigate his new life with May, there were disturbing changes happening at work. Scranton State Bank had its own charter, separate from the Mobile State Bank, but the Mobile bank had always been considered the parent bank. Since Randall had become president of both banks five years before, each successive year found him taking his authority to new heights.

He often countermanded Mitchell's plans for Scranton's small bank in a smaller town. Its style of hometown banking was one that Mitchell had worked hard to cultivate. Randall had different ideas. He had big plans of expanding. Merging with a large, aggressive bank chain was something he had been working on since his arrival in Mobile.

In February of 1897, the two banks were bought by the Bank of Louisiana based in New Orleans. At the signings in Mobile, Randall was puffed with pride and importance, his wife Judith preening beside him. Mitchell just tried to get through the procedures, thankful May was not there, knowing full well her opinion of the Randalls.

Two weeks later, Mitchell was on a train to New Orleans for a week of orientation. Other than his business obligations, Mitchell was looking forward to going to New Orleans. He had never been there and getting away from his personal problems for a while would be a welcome relief.

Unknown to Mitchell, Edgar with full knowledge of Mitchell's presence, was on the same train. May had told Edgar that Mitchell would be in New Orleans for three days, and she had not disagreed when Edgar devised his plan.

"May, it's perfect. I have been meaning to go there for business anyway. He'll be a captive audience while he's on the train. You know Mitchell. He would never make a public scene. Hopefully, we can repair our friendship. With luck, he'll let me take him around town."

Mitchell was reading his paper when Edgar sat down beside him. "Good Lord, Edgar. What are you doing here?" He almost smiled—his first instinct being to welcome his friend—former friend, he remembered. This could not be a coincidence.

"May. It was May who told you, didn't she? Damn her meddling," Mitchell said. "And I suppose you both think I'll just naturally roll over and let you worm your way into my life again."

"No, Mitchell. I know it will take more than a chat on the train for you to forgive me," said Edgar. "But when she told me, I had to take the opportunity." Edgar moved uncomfortably in his seat. "Please don't let your over-proud, sensitive nature get the best of you. I must at least try to make amends. I miss you. I miss what the three of us had together. Perhaps we can get beyond what happened and move on."

"Maybe you should have thought about all that before you made a cuckold of me by seducing my wife." The angst he carried inside himself against Edgar (and May) was like a scab he couldn't stop picking at. He would like nothing better than to pretend it all had not happened. Can one do that? he wondered. Just a snap of the fingers and it will all better? Well, maybe this is a chance to find out. As far as he knew, no one else knew about their affair. It was not as if he had to save face in front of the community. It was between the three of them only.

Edgar interrupted Mitchell's musings. "How about we have dinner tonight, and we can talk more then? It just so happens I'm staying at your hotel," he said.

Mitchell went to the dreaded meetings during the days. Randall had told him to look up a Mr. Burnsby, the chief accountant of the Louisiana

324

State Bank. "He's looking forward to meeting you, Mitchell. He is the *man to know* if you intend to embrace this exciting new opportunity. He is also head of security, a new department that all large banks have now. They must if they want to remain in business; it is very competitive out there. He has a team of investigators to make sure our clients are who they say they are, and that they are, of course, solvent," Randall had told him over the phone.

In the evenings, Edgar took him around town. Mitchell couldn't help but wish May was with them. She would have loved New Orleans—its architecture, its design, its personality—refined yet risqué, not unlike May herself, he thought fondly.

Their time together did bring a thaw from Mitchell. Neither he nor Edgar went into the details of how, what, or where. It happened, it was over, and it was time to move on; they each did so with relief.

The Bank of Louisiana had made it clear that they wanted the same hierarchy of officers in each bank, and that they wanted each of their banks to be run the same way. Randall was president of the Mobile and Scranton banks, and he would assign a vice president to each bank as soon as possible.

Despite their differences, Mitchell had been led to believe that position would be his. He was the only logical choice.

While Mitchell was in New Orleans, Randall installed J. Ira Ford as vice president of the Scranton State Bank. On his return, an infuriated Mitchell called Randall. "How could you have done this? You told me it would be me. It should be me. To do this behind my back while I was away is underhanded."

"Mitchell, I never promised you the position. Perhaps you assumed too much. We both know we're not always in agreement. And as you learned, or I certainly hope you did while in New Orleans, the Bank of Louisiana is very high on all their banks following in lock step. It's how they've become so successful.

"It's vital," Randall continued. "Absolutely vital that I have someone who has the same vision as I do. And Mr. Ford is someone who comes from the South and grew up with the same background as me. It is obvious your northern upbringing and banking acumen conflicts with mine. I am sure in time you will come around. It's the new way of banking, and if you stay focused on the bottom line, everything else will fall into place."

How could he continue working for this man? Mitchell asked himself repeatedly. Randall was his boss, his superior. What could he do? Harlan Johnson had never once pulled rank on Mitchell. Ever. They had been equals. Mitchell had always prided himself on running Scranton State Bank with a personal touch. He had offered loans and services to everyone in town, including the poorer citizens of Scranton. There was many a family farm and small business whose success was a result of help from Mitchell and his bank. He was on a first-name basis with his clients, and he knew their families and what they needed. He could only hope this J. Ira Ford was not cut of the same cloth as Randall.

Increasingly unhappy at work, Mitchell lived for his times away from the bank. All his activities helped—shooting, softball, cycling, and sailing. But it was his family that was his best diversion. The estrangement between himself and May had been horrible for him. He was desperate to return to some normalcy in his marriage. Edgar, despite having committed the original sin, had now made it possible for Mitchell to reclaim his position of husband.

In the evenings, entering the house after work, he would shout out to the girls, waiting for Frances and Edie to clatter their way to him for hugs. The ritual filled his heart with warmth, which considering the cold house he grew up in was something he was thankful for every day.

Now, after the welcome from the girls, he and May could once again go to the parlor for drinks and talk to each other about their days. She was sympathetic to his complaints about work and her dislike of both Randall and his wife, Judith, was equal to Mitchell's.

"I'm sorry, Mitchell. I can't imagine having to deal with that Randall every day," said May one night. "Is it absolutely unbearable?"

"No, May. Not absolutely. Believe it or not, it is better for me now that Ira is vice president. I think he's going to be all right, and he takes the pressure off me. He can have the joys of dealing with Randall. But Randall will figure some way of making me miserable. I don't know how I angered him so, but I feel sure it's personal. He is out to get me; of that I am sure," said Mitchell pouring them each another drink. He no longer harped on May's drinking.

"Is it time to look for another job?" asked May. "Maybe things have settled down back home. I did always think of this move as temporary. A year or two and then back home. Though I must admit, I have become fond of Scranton. And Sweet Alice is here. How could we leave her all alone?"

"That's just it. I like it here too. I wish things had just stayed the same at the bank," said Mitchell.

They resumed their dinners with Edgar. The first few times he brought Amelia. She was a welcome foil against the initial awkwardness the three of them felt returning to their friendship. She and May had become close friends during their work on the cookbook.

May was unsure just what the relationship was between Amelia and Edgar. Did Amelia know about the rift between Edgar and Mitchell? Did Amelia know about Edgar's relationship with herself? May could have asked her outright, but she wasn't sure if they were that close.

"This mess with Randall sounds dreadful, Mitch," said Edgar. It was early spring, and they were out on the Plummers' front porch taking advantage of the warm weather. "Should I start asking around if there are any bank openings when I travel?" he asked, only half-jokingly.

Mitchell laughed. "No, Edgar. At least not yet. And with Ira there, he can deal with Randall. I don't know how much I trust Ira yet, but I like him. He joined the Wing Shot Club too. He's a good shot."

After pouring them all refills, Mitchell continued. "Randall has thought of a new torture though. He's sending us an assistant cashier to replace the one who left. When Ira said he had someone in mind, Randall said 'no' and insisted it be one of *his* cashiers. He was adamant about it. A man named P. Easton Jane. He told Ira he was just the man for us. That he's looking to move up." Mitchell snorted. "I just bet he's looking to move up. Right up to my position. I know that makes me sound crazy. But he's being sent to spy on me, I'm certain. Make sure I toe the bottom line." He had almost shouted the last sentence, embarrassing himself at the emotion in his voice.

"May is everything all right with you?" asked Amelia one morning. They were taking a break from the cookbook so that May could nurse Anna. "I've been worried about you. You've not your usual self, it seems. I can tell you're losing weight, and you look tired."

"I'm fine, Amelia. But nursing an infant and having two older girls can tire out any woman. And with everything going on with Mitchell at the bank, it is just draining us both. What really gets to me is these cursed headaches. They used to only happen once a month, usually with my cycle, which, if I keep nursing this little bundle, I don't get. So, I can't blame them on my monthlies. Stress, I guess. And I get hot flashes sometimes. No one can sleep through those," May said. "Maybe my body is out of order somehow. I tried taking Mrs. Winslow's Soothing Syrup. I used it when the girls were teething, and it worked great on them. After all it has morphine and alcohol in it so I thought it could work on me too. And it does a little, but I need something stronger. I even tried mixing it in sherry."

"Well, I know nothing about teething, but Mrs. Winslow's didn't work for me. I get terrible cramps," said Amelia. "Try taking a double dose and if that doesn't work, try Dover's Powder. You can get that at McVea Young's Drugstore. It has opium in it, which is purer and stronger than what's in Winslow's. And whatever I use, I take it with a good shot of bourbon—maybe two," she said, smiling conspiringly. "I know McVea's has a somewhat low reputation, but they're less stringent than the Palace. And they respect your privacy. Mrs. Watson has a tendency toward gossip.

"Really? That can't be good for business," said May. "You certainly are a fountain of medical knowledge. I should have talked with you a long time ago. I hope Mrs. Watson hasn't told others about what I buy there, or for what reason. I'd hate it if people thought I was going through the change already."

Amelia lowered her voice. "McVea's has the real stuff too, you know. Every drugstore does, but if I were going to buy it, I'd get it there. I even heard you can get it through a Sears Roebuck catalogue."

May was surprised at Amelia's knowledge. Though, on second thought, why should she be? Amelia was circumspect in talking about herself. She and Edgar must have an intimate relationship, May assumed, and he probably wasn't the first. Who knows? Amelia's well into her thirties now. In all those years as a single woman she may have had need of *things* far stronger than teething medication.

"Thanks, Amelia. I'll try the Dover's," said May, buttoning herself up. She put Anna over her shoulder, who promptly let out a loud burp. "Don't you wish we could do that? It sounds so satisfying." She stood up. "By the way, I did tell you about the party we're having, right? On July 1, to celebrate both our birthdays. Mitchell will be thirty-one in June, and I'll be thirty-four in July."

"I didn't know you were older than Mitchell," said Amelia. "You don't look it. You look younger than him."

"That's because he's always so serious. And don't say anything about my age to anyone. Well, you can to Edgar. He already knows. But no one else does."

"I won't. We all have our little secrets," Amelia said. "What woman doesn't?"

Mitchell's worry about the new teller seemed all for naught. Easton appeared a nice enough young man, and the clients liked him, though, Mitchell was careful to do everything by the book. If Easton was a spy, Mitchell was not going to give him anything to take back to Randall.

Scranton and Pascagoula continued to grow. Two years previously, the hotel had undergone a major renovation and remodel, renaming itself The *New* Scranton Hotel. The Pascagoula Commercial Club of Scranton, a civic and social association, now with forty members, including Mitchell, had organized a year ago. When Randall called telling him to join, Mitchell was delighted to inform him that not only had he already done so, he in fact was one of the founding members.

"I celebrate my small victories when I can," said Mitchell, after relating that story to Edgar. He raised his glass and toasted himself with the bourbon he allowed himself at lunch. Only one. It wouldn't do to be seen having more.

Edgar, too, celebrated his victories when he could. He had quit the *Pascagoula Democrat-Star*, at least as a regular reporter. However, he continued writing "Edgar Eats," a popular restaurant review column. When word got out that Edgar was leaving the paper, the proprietors of the local eating establishments insisted he continue his columns—a good review from Edgar guaranteed an increase in business. The owner of the paper agreed, grudgingly. As a result, Edgar and Mitchell could continue their (mostly) free lunches and sometimes even dinners for the two couples.

"It's my only perquisite," Edgar said. "I'd be a fool not to take advantage of it when offered, wouldn't I now?" He laughed. "Best of all, I love to think about how much it must gall that buffoon, Mayers, to have to keep me on while I get to eat free."

Edgar had resigned from the paper out of principal. The owner, P. K. Mayers had become a bitter enemy of Edgar's. "I can't be employed by him anymore. He's an avid, unapologetic, conservative Democrat. He censors my columns, and sometimes he omits them entirely. He still carries an allegiance to the Confederacy, and the paper is just his mouthpiece to espouse those opinions. He has claimed, proudly, that there have been a few attempts on his life because of those views. If someone does pop him off, the first person they would probably look at would be me. Even more reason for me to not be associated with the paper."

Mitchell chuckled. "For two people who seem easy to get along with, we certainly have our problems with our superiors. By the way, Randall is sending me to New Orleans again, for two days next week for a meeting. Apparently, there's some affair he can't miss, and he wanted Ira to stay at the bank, so suddenly I'm acceptable to go in his stead," Mitchell said, shaking his head. "It's odd. Considering how he treats me, I figured he'd never ask me to do anything again, especially anything to do with the *public image* of his precious bank. But he insisted I go and even gave me a list of topics to bring up at the meetings."

"Really?" asked Edgar. "Perhaps I could go at the same time. Why not? We could stay a day or two more over the weekend. We'll tear up the town."

"Well, you know I'm not known for my raucous behavior, but that might be fun. I could do with a break. Too bad May can't come. She was envious of my last trip. Will you be bringing Amelia?" asked Mitchell.

"No. We'll make it a bachelor party," said Edgar. "Speaking of parties. Are you two still going to have your party next month?"

"I think so. May's in charge of all that. Hard to believe I'm going to be thirty-one. Sometimes I feel like I'm still twenty, though, lately I feel a lot older. Like sixty."

"Oh, no, Mitchell. You have such a debonair and winning way, and you still look like a dapper young man to me," Edgar said. "All the more reason to get away and kick up your heels."

"I think Edgar's right, Mitchell," agreed May that night at dinner. His business meetings would be on Monday and Tuesday. "Go early and have the weekend there. If anyone needs a break, it's you. We can go together another time."

The two men left on Friday afternoon. "Best to get an early start," Edgar had said. "If we make the six o'clock train, we can be there by nine. Time for a drink at the hotel, maybe scout around. New Orleans never sleeps."

Mitchell, feeling quite giddy, turned to Edgar, laughing. "Don't forget, my friend. I'm no

John Mahoney. It's not in my nature to go out socializing after hours. I'm afraid you chose a tame partner to go with you."

"You just need the right environment, my man," said Edgar, punching Mitchell lightly on the arm. "And New Orleans is the perfect environment."

43—AWAKENINGS—1897

"Edgar, what were you thinking?" Mitchell said as soon as he saw the lobby of the Hotel Monteleone. "There is no way I can stay here. Randall would never approve of such luxury. I *am* on the bank's tab, you know. When you said you were picking out the hotel, I just assumed you'd choose something like the one Randall picked for me. I can guarantee that this is not one of them."

"Mitchell, it's all right. With us sharing the room, your half is the same price as that run-down place he put you in. If it's more, I'll pick up the difference," said Edgar. "Don't argue. You will love it here. This is the oldest and best hotel in New Orleans."

Mitchell looked askance at Edgar. "You didn't say we were in the same room either."

"That's a small omission, I know. But I knew you'd react exactly the way you are. Don't worry, Mitch. It's a suite with two bedrooms, a sitting room, and plenty of privacy. If anyone needs a dose of luxury, it's you. Now let's get to our room, drop off our bags, and go out for a drink. You're on holiday for two days."

339

One o'clock in the morning found them at a bar in the *Vieux Carré*. "It means the old square. Back in the day, that's what this area was called, and still is by the old timers. Now, it's more commonly called the French Quarter. But I still prefer the old French name, even if it makes me sound out of date," said Edgar.

"I don't think I've ever been out this late. Ever," said Mitchell. "So, this is what you and John do on your wild nights."

"Wild? You are such a dolt, Mitch," Edgar said. "I really had no idea how sheltered your life has been. Considering your wealthy upbringing, your life has been severely lacking in the enjoyments life has to offer. But luckily, you're with me, and I'm here to introduce you to them. This is definitely not a wild night," said Edgar. "It's just a warm-up."

"It's so different being in a place where everything is open at such hours," Mitchell said. "Bangor is a big city, and I know they have places that stay open late. But I certainly never went to them. I didn't even know where they were. Here, it's the whole city, not just certain establishments.

And you don't even have to look for them; you just trip over them."

"That you do, my man. That you do," laughed Edgar. "But I suggest we go back to the hotel and get some sleep. We'll get an early start in the morning with breakfast at Café du Monde in the French Market. Wait till you have their *café au lait* and *beignets*. We can plan our day."

It was a day of sightseeing. Trolley lines traced throughout the city. Most had been converted to overhead electric propulsion, though, some, especially on the outskirts of town, were still drawn by mules. It was easy touring; all one needed was a ticket, and a person could get on and off at will or switch to a different train on a different route. The trolleys took Edgar and Mitchell along grand avenues shaded by great live oaks and stately mansions, some of which were open to the public. It being May, the gardens were bursting with flowers at the height of their blooming. They hopped off at Edgar's favorite places, where he was able to give Mitchell interesting historical and personal viewpoints.

One trolley went through Gentilly, past Edgar's family home, the neglected building

341

standing out starkly in comparison to its well-kept neighbors. "Gentilly," Edgar said wistfully, (pronouncing it, jen-til-LEE). "Such a pretty name; it means in a gentle, noble way." He looked away. "You're the only person who has ever seen what I'm from," said Edgar, his discomfort obvious. Mitchell patted Edgar's knee, moved by his friend's emotion.

After a rest and a wash up at the hotel, early evening found them sitting at Le Petit Sazerac, a tiny bar on the corner of Chartres and St. Peter Streets, overlooking Jackson Square with the Mississippi River flowing by the square's edge. Edgar had been welcomed as if he was royalty, the bonhomie encompassing Mitchell as well. They were seated outside, the world of New Orleans passing by around them.

"So, here you are at one of my favorite spots," Edgar said, opening his arms expansively. "Really, the whole city is, but this little corner in particular." He paused as the waiter brought them their drinks. They toasted each other.

"To us," said Edgar. "And to your first Sazerac cocktail. It's made with Sazerac cognac, bitters, sugar, and a little absinthe. Later we'll go to the Old Absinthe House, and you'll have the real

342

absinthe, also known as the Green Fairy. She's very seductive."

"Lord, Edgar. I probably won't be walking by then," Mitchell said. "What a wonderful city this is. Tell me again where your apartment was."

"Right around the corner on Orleans Alley Sud—south in French. There even was a tiny bar next door to me, Pirates' Absinthe Bar; I liked to think of it as my own. I'll show it to you when we leave. The alley runs alongside the St. Louis Cathedral, right over there, and St. Anthony's Garden behind it. I loved living beside the church. Go ahead and laugh, but it suited me."

Everywhere they went, Edgar and Mitchell were welcomed like family. At Antoine's, Edgar translated the French menu to Mitchell with a flourish. As he ordered, the waiter, Austin Murray, a favorite of Edgar's, patiently nodded, committing each item to memory.

"A cocktail first, Austin. My friend will try the French 75. You'll like it Mitchell, it's originally from Maxim's in Paris. And you must have the Oysters Rockefeller for an hors d'oeuvre. I see your face. Don't worry, we'll share them. But one simply cannot come to Antoine's and not have them. We can share the chateaubriand, something else you must get here. And we'll have the *Pommes de Terre au Gratinée*, and the *Asperges au Beurre*. Oh, and Austin, please, a bottle of the Chateau Lafitte Rothschild Bordeaux, 1894."

Edgar smiled at Mitchell's astonished face. "There's more, my friend," he said, smiling up at Austin. "You know what we're going to order for dessert," he said to him. "The Omelette Alaska, Antoine, flambéed as only you can do it."

Aside from the oysters, which didn't appeal to him, the meal, along with the theatrical presentation, was easily the best Mitchell had ever had in his life, the flaming dessert a fitting finale. He could not help but think his life up to then had been completely banal.

They went to a few other spots, ending up at the Old Absinthe House as Edgar had promised. Mitchell felt delightfully decadent, watching the pouring ritual that clouded the green liquid then sipping the opalescent licorice-tasting alcohol. They stumbled back to the hotel, holding each other up, singing raucously.

Sunday morning found them at Café du Monde again, with beignets and copious cups of

344

café au lait. "Edgar, how did you survive with those damn clarions right beside you?" asked Mitchell, referring to the early morning ringing of the cathedral's bells. He dusted powdered sugar off his face and fingers as he reached for his third coffee.

Edgar smiled at Mitchell sympathetically. "I know. It is loud, isn't it? And our hotel is eight blocks away, not next door, as my apartment was. Excessive, I'll admit, but I figured it was a small cost to pay for whatever sins I had committed during the week. Call it a penance. We Catholics, even the good ones, always feel penitent about something."

"Edgar, why in the world did you leave this wonderful city for Scranton?"

"Timing, I guess. Remember, it was at the beginning of the Depression, when I came to Scranton to do that column on labor problems? My editors were pleased with it, but they couldn't keep me on, at least not in that capacity. I thought maybe a small town would be good for a change. Believe it or not, it was mostly because of you and May. I had met you both and liked being with you; you were foremost on my mind," Edgar said.

"I don't have any real friends here, other than my editor, whom you met briefly last night. Lots of acquaintances and drinking pals, as you've seen. You and May were my first good friends. You do have a sympathetic social character, Mitchell and it was what drew me to you, as it does to most people who know you. I'll bet you are totally unaware of that trait of yours, aren't you?"

Mitchell, who definitely was ignorant of his own traits, was overcome by the compliment and the affection it expressed. He replied fondly, "I guess it was the same with us. Except for John, I didn't have any close friends either. And neither did May, other than Dora and her sister Edith. We both felt more than just friendship for you. It was not only May. I felt a strong kinship between us also. Still do, even after what happened," he said, his throat tightening.

They spent the morning strolling through the *Vieux Carré*, visiting the cathedral and the St. Louis Garden behind it. Maison Blanche, the large department store, was closed, as were most of the shops on Canal Street. "It's Sunday. Even in New Orleans, it's considered a day of rest. Well, the morning is anyway. We do have Blue Laws in the city, even here in the Quarter. But once it turns noon, they're ignored and the restaurants will open."

"I had hoped to get something for my girls," said Mitchell. *Girls* included May, but he found himself reluctant to mention shopping for her with Edgar. He'd shop tomorrow, alone, after his meeting.

Lunch at Commander's Palace was leisurely. "This place opened in 1893, just before I left. It was fast becoming my favorite," said Edgar. "I always make a point of coming back when I'm in town. On a day like this, on the patio, well...what else can be said?"

"Not much," said Mitchell. "I feel as if I'm under a spell, cast by you and this city. And this drink," he added, referring to his absinthe frappé, a silly grin on his face.

"It is a spell. When we're finished here, we'll go back to the hotel and rest up," said Edgar. "Last night was calm in comparison to what I have in store for you tonight. We're going to see the other side of New Orleans. Storyville. No man can say he's truly been to New Orleans without at least going there once."

After a long nap, a restored Mitchell washed up and dressed for the evening. He found Edgar in their sitting room with a glass of champagne in his hand, sitting at the open window overlooking Royal Street. Mitchell poured himself a glass, pulled up another chair and joined him at the window.

"I don't know about you, but I feel wonderful," said Mitchell. "I needed that break. I probably don't need the drink, especially considering what you have in mind for tonight, but it seems somehow appropriate in this place."

They sat companionably, sipping champagne, smoking cigarettes and looking out at the sights. Royal Street, along with every other street in the French Quarter, was coming to life. Foot traffic had increased along with more horse-drawn carriages clip-clopping along the road. Trolleys rumbled in the distance, and voices called out to each other in different accents; it was a cacophony of sound.

Cigarette smoke from passersby wafted up to the window along with perfume from beautiful women in evening dresses and jewels. Spicy odors from the Creole restaurant across the street mingled with the pork roasting on the street vendor's brazier, and a small bakery down the street emitted the sweet smells of chocolate, sugar, and coffee—a mélange of aromas.

"Well, we've finished the bottle, so let's head out to our night of sin and debauchery," said Edgar with a wicked grin. "I'll tell you about Storyville on the way."

There had always been a large red-light district in New Orleans, but it was not until this year, 1897, that Storyville came into being. It consisted of thirty-eight blocks that allowed prostitution. Still not legalized, it was restricted to that one area, where it could be regulated. The city government had studied the legalized red-light districts of European ports and directed that the same be done in New Orleans. Originally called *The District*, it quickly assumed the name Storyville because of the alderman who had proposed the ordinance, Sidney Story.

The district started with *establishments* (houses of prostitution) ranging from cheap cribs, considered fifty-cent joints, to expensively lavish mansions charging ten dollars and up. Restaurants, saloons, and dance clubs followed quickly. All the various venues offered live music—usually just a piano player, sometimes a trio, rarely a band. Most Storyville audiences were not there for the music and not critical of what was played, allowing the performers the freedom to experiment with music styles.

Jazz was in its early days. It did not originate in Storyville, but it thrived there. Many a jazz musician got his start in the bordellos and saloons: Tony Jackson, Buddy Bolden, Joe "King" Oliver, and Alcide Nunez. Mitchell's eyes glazed over at Edgar's enthusiastic descriptions of each artist and his style. Mitchell's knowledge of music was limited. His knowledge of everything tonight was limited.

"Blue Books," were Storyville's guides to prostitution for visitors. They could be purchased for twenty-five cents and were sold everywhere in the district. The pages inside listed the establishment, descriptions, prices, services, and the *stock* that each house offered. They contained, in alphabetical order, the names of the prostitutes, the address of their houses, and their races—white, black, or octoroon. Landladies were named with descriptions and photos of their houses, especially interior shots. The fees for general or specific services at the listed establishments were not included.

Lulu White's Saloon was a welcome relief when they finally pushed their way in. "I never thought I'd ever be at a *madam's* bar, never mind finding it to be a relief," said Mitchell, taking a large gulp of his icy beer, the foam sticking to his upper lip. "I've never seen such a crowd. And so rowdy."

"Just men pandering to their more basic instincts," said Edgar. "They're just out for a good time. Here, I got you a memento. It's your very own Blue Book."

"I don't know if I should say thanks. It's certainly a memento I can't show anyone," said Mitchell, as he flipped through the pages. "Good Lord. It's just as you described—and so many houses and women. Hard to believe that there is a whole element of society in the business of providing these services. There's even pages of advertisements—lawyers, restaurants, drugstores, taxis...everything a man could need." Mitchell was laughing by this time, wondering if any of the men in his family had ever been to a place like this. He highly doubted it.

"What does this mean, Edgar? Is this a motto? "Order of the Garter?" But I can't pronounce the rest."

"'*Honi Soit Qui Mal Y Pense.*' It means 'Shame on Him Who Thinks Evil of It.' It's probably not a bad way to look at everything," Edgar said with a shrug. "Just mind your own business. Come on, let's eat dinner. Storyville is not noted for its cuisine, but Lulu White's offers the best meal in Storyville. And we're lucky tonight. Tony Jackson is playing here, so you get to hear one of the greats."

During dinner, Edgar continued his stories. "Mahogany Hall is Miss Lulu's brothel, one of the biggest and most lavish and built entirely of marble. The woman herself is very wealthy and an important businesswoman in these parts. As you can see for yourself, right here in your little blue book, she boasts that Mahogany Hall has the best women around, that they have 'beautiful figures and a gift from nature.' I'll leave it to you to wonder exactly what she means by that." He couldn't help but laugh at the expression on Mitchell's face. "Don't look so disapproving, Mitch. A woman has to make a living, right?

"It's a huge building, four floors, five parlors, and fifteen, so they say, bedrooms, each with an attached bathroom, and every suite with running hot and cold water and steam heat in the winters. The interiors of each chamber are furnished with chandeliers, elegant furniture, and potted plants...I feel like I'm reciting bad lines from the Marquise de Sade's *Justine, The Misfortunes of Virtue*."

"Well, it all is a bit sad," said Mitchell. "And sordid."

They listened to a few sets from Tony Jackson. "I can see why you like him," said Mitchell. They walked to Mahogany Hall, the most extravagantly lit-up place on the street. On entering the parlor, they were met by a conservatively dressed, statuesque matron who welcomed Edgar with a large hug and a handshake for Mitchell. "Welcome to my house. Any friend of Edgar's is a friend of mine," she said, escorting them to comfortable armchairs.

Lulu White was of mixed racial descent, not beautiful, not even very attractive. In fact, she was pug-like in her facial features. But she had an air about her that made every man in the room, of which there were about twenty, feel welcome and in for a special treat that only she and her girls could provide. Young women, seductive in their dress, yet (just) strategically covered, circulated the room, offering drinks and conversation.

"Thank you," Edgar said, smiling warmly to Lulu. "You know how I appreciate your offerings, but we just came for a short visit tonight. My friend here is from out of town and quite conservative. Very, in fact. When I told him no visit to our city was complete without a visit to Storyville and the famous Mahogany Hall, he agreed to come and see the place for himself. Maybe another time, my dear."

"If I didn't know better, I'd say I was with John," Mitchell joked later on the walk back to the hotel. "Do men like you go to a special school to learn to talk like that?"

"No, my dear friend. It's a natural talent some of us have. John is even better because he can put on the Irish blarney." He paused, serious for a moment. "Maybe it's not a talent we should necessarily be proud of."

When Monday morning arrived, before going to his meeting at the bank, Mitchell walked to the Baronne Hotel that Randall had chosen for him to cancel the reservation. It was not a hovel, as Edgar had implied, but it paled in comparison to the Monteleone. The desk clerk was reluctant about canceling the reservation, stating it was too late. Mitchell surprised himself by threatening the clerk with the loss of future bookings from Mr. Judge Randall, president of the Mobile branch of the Bank of Louisiana. He also asked for a written quote of what the price of the room would have been. He walked out with a doubtful smile on his face. Part of him was plumped up at his audacity; part of him worried that seedy Storyville might have changed him for the worse.

Later that day he made it to the department store, Maison Blanche, the luxurious interior making him feel like the rube Edgar had called him. He remembered how May had excitedly described her trip to Gayfers in Mobile with Winifred Johnson, Harlan's wife. God, how he missed that man. He conquered his insecurity and found a kindly saleslady in the jewelry department who led him to just what he was looking for—three small sapphire pendants for his daughters and a larger one with matching earrings for May.

Even though he and Edgar would still have the evenings together the next two days, Mitchell felt a bitter letdown. How could he spend the next two days at those boring meetings? How could he go back to his now mundane life?

On Mitchell's return to the bank, his expected meeting with Randall was delayed for unspecified reasons. Mitchell had paid Edgar for his share of their stay in the Monteleone, and other than their dinner at Antoine's, which Edgar had paid for, Mitchell paid for his own meals. His accounting of the trip was in order and with receipts, including the quote from the Baronne.

"You're not the first businessman on the boss's dime, Mitch," Edgar had said with a knowing smile. "Hotels and restaurants are used to it and are happy to accommodate. We've all done it. Changed a reservation, padded a tab or two. It's nothing new. To you, maybe, but not to the rest of the world."

Still, Mitchell felt nervous and guilty, and the wait only increased his anxiety. He was uncomfortable in his own bank, his distrust regarding Easton Jane having returned. It was almost with relief when Randall called and asked him to come to Mobile.

"Mitchell," said Randall, friendly enough. "Come in, come in. Tell me about the trip."

Once the give-and-take of talking about the meetings began, Mitchell relaxed. He knew he was prepared, and Randall seemed comfortable with his answers. He hadn't even glanced at Mitchell's expense sheet.

Just as Mitchell was thinking he was going to get out of there without a lecture, Randall's voice changed. "By the way, Mitchell. It is important that we remember our place. Just because we are in banking, we mustn't flaunt our closeness with the money we handle every day."

Oh, Lord, Mitchell thought. Here it comes. He's up to something.

"Mr. Burnsby, the accountant at the New Orleans State Bank of Louisiana, is a good friend of mine. You met him when you were there for your orientation in March, remember? He remembers you. He dropped me a note saying he saw you coming out of the Hotel Monteleone and leaving Antoine's on Saturday before the meetings had even started. It surprised him because he recognized your companion as the one who had been with you previously during your orientation.

"Later, that same night, very late, someone else saw the two of you coming out of one of the most disreputable bars in the city, the Old Absinthe House. You had your arms around each other, stumbling and singing your way back to the hotel."

He pursed his lips. "Mr. Burnsby also found out from the desk clerk at the Monteleone that you both were sharing a suite. Not, as your silly *quote* would have me believe, staying at the Baronne. You didn't really think you could get away with that trick, did you? The manager notified me immediately when his desk clerk told him.

"I am really surprised, Mitchell. I thought you were a smart Yankee. I even gave you a heads up about Mr. Burnsby being head of security. Didn't you think he might be interested in a man who works for me? I would have thought you would have been more circumspect in your dissolute behavior.

"Except for the Old Absinthe House, these establishments are very high-end places and ones I would assume you couldn't afford. At least not on the salary we pay you. I know you come from a wealthy northern family and maybe you're used to all that luxury, but we here in the South try to be more conservative in our tastes."

He put his hand up. "No, Mitchell," he said, as Mitchell began to explain. "I'm not done yet. As you know it gets worse. Storyville is a place no civilized well-bred man should ever enter, yet you were spotted there, and on a Sunday night no less. I thought you were a Christian man. Does your friend William Mead, an elder in your Presbyterian Church, know of your deplorable inclinations?

"Don't answer, Mitchell. New Orleans can test anyone's scruples. What you do on your own time really is none of my business. But you don't want to throw money around in outrageously expensive restaurants and hotels and flaunt your position for all the world to see. And, apparently, not coincidently, with the same male acquaintance you have been seen with often in Scranton. Your affection for him has not gone unnoticed even in your fair town." Still sitting behind his desk, he looked up at Mitchell, his lips barely forming a thin smile. "I just wanted you to know. You understand how we bankers must stick together."

Mitchell left feeling as if he had been publicly flogged. He rode home in the bar car, and by the time he got to his house, he was completely inebriated, a sight so rare that May took him

360

straight upstairs and put him to bed, whispering strong warnings to not come downstairs. She need not have worried. He was asleep soon after she closed the door.

The next morning was Saturday. At least Mitchell had the weekend to suffer his hangover in privacy and to think about his boss's very disturbing insinuations. He told May the whole sordid story—sordid at least in Randall's eyes. He had withheld telling her about Storyville when he had come home. Now he had to humble himself while he related that visit to her. What has happened to him? Before this last week, it would be surprise him if he had told a total of five lies in his life.

"God, May, I hate that man. I just detest him. How can I continue to work there? He does have spies. What is it about me he so dislikes?" Mitchell asked, looking imploringly to May.

"I don't know, Mitchell. I'm not upset about Storyville. I trust you, though, I wish you'd told me when you got home. I have no idea why he hates you so much, and I feel terrible for you. Maybe it is because you're from the north? Did he really call you a Yankee? Again? Maybe it's that miserable wife of his and her United Daughters of the Confederacy. I just don't know." Her mind was whirling. Mitchell might lose his job because of this overstuffed, stupid man. What then?

"But everything is still okay between you and Ira, right?" asked May. "Maybe you should talk to him. Give him some of the details, not all of them, obviously. I wonder if he even knows how Mr. Holier Than Thou Judge O. Randall, regards you. This is not normal. Has Ira ever indicated he's seen that side of the man?"

"He's hinted at how inflexible Randall can be but very circumspectly. After all, he's Ira's boss too," said Mitchell. "Ira is the vice president and he has his position to protect. But I think I will say something just in case Randall says anything to him."

May agreed. "I think we need to prepare for the worst. It looks like he might be preparing to dismiss you. You need to write Harry and see if he knows of any jobs in Asheville; swallow your pride and write Thomas too. If we do move back to Maine, and there is no banking job, I'm sure there'll be a job for you at Stetson's. At least until you find something permanent. I don't see how this is going to get better, and we should start preparing ourselves for whatever comes next." She gave a sardonic laugh. "Good Lord. It's like your mother Alice all over again."

Mitchell was uncomfortable with what was happening to him. He had never been a man of moods. He was a man of moderation, rarely subject to extreme happiness or the depths of depression. The opposite of May he thought, who knew well those opposing moods. His happiest moments were the day he married and the times he had with his girls. And when he was with John or Edgar. Mostly he felt duty bound to provide for his family, which had never been a burden. He did it gladly, for it was his purpose; what he should do. And this horrid man was threatening the meaning of his life.

He unburdened himself at lunch on Monday with Edgar. "He had spies on me. And the way he talked to me, like I was dirt. It is obvious he thinks you and I are having an illicit relationship," Mitchell said. "Maybe May is right, and we'll have to move."

He took a long gulp of his drink. "Working with Thomas would be just as bad, and I'd have to deal with my mother. Harry would be better. He's nicer and closer to here. And we could still see you sometimes."

Edgar, who had none of Mitchell's sense of obligation, was surprised at his friend's overwrought reaction. "I'm sorry, Mitch," he said, trying to be sympathetic. He was, but he was also uncomfortable with Mitchell's emotionalism. "But, if you have to move...well, just do it."

Mitchell looked at him. "I know I can just do it. Don't take me for an idiot, Edgar."

"I'm sorry. I don't mean to simplify it. But if that's what you must do, you will. You have always done what was needed. I mean, you packed up your family and moved here. I fervently hope you don't move, but you must do what's good for you and your family," said Edgar, trying not to think how badly he would miss his closest friends.

He continued, looking at Mitchell with sympathy. "It's too bad you're not more like me. I'd just ignore the bastard and outlast him. So what if he thinks you did sinful things in New Orleans with me? It's all in his dirty, little insular mind. You could stay, you know."

"I know. I know. Both decisions, stay or move, are unbearable to me. How can we stay while

I continue working for someone like that? But how can I pull my family away from all we have here? The girls are in school now. We have friends here. We have you."

As for May, she was almost as paralyzed as Mitchell. She certainly did not want to move, and the thought of being near her mother-in-law filled her with dread. God forbid they might have to live with Alice, even for a while. But foremost on May's mind was leaving her own little Alice. How could she abandon her sweet baby girl? The cemetery was on the other side of town, but often she would take a Hansom cab and go there to sit on the grass and tell Sweet Alice the news of her sisters.

May's headaches had increased in frequency and severity, often incapacitating her. On those days, Mitchell walked the girls to school. May found that if she took the Dover's Powder with a few shots of bourbon, as Amelia had suggested, she could be up and about by the time everyone came home. Hidden amongst the increasing collection of patent medications in her bureau was the last of the morphine tincture Dr. Cox had given her. Thus far, she had not taken any, but just knowing it was there soothed her.

Because of the headaches, May's work on the cookbook had slowed. The first draft was done, but it needed proofing and a professional eye, which Amelia had happily offered.

"You know I've been dying to get my hands on it," Amelia said to May on one of May's good days. "I promise I won't do anything drastic to it. It really doesn't need much. Just some editing, maybe some grammar corrections. You've done a great job."

Amelia paused, unsure if she should continue. "May, have you been to a doctor about those headaches? I hate to see you suffer so," Amelia asked. "Maybe you need stronger medication. Maybe there's something wrong."

"I did see Dr. Kell last month, but he didn't find anything wrong with me. He said I was healthy as a horse. 'Probably just stress,' he said. He made it clear to me how he felt about opium products the first time he saw me, so I don't think I'll get anything from him. I guess I could try Dr. Cox again. He seemed comfortable giving stronger drugs." May looked at her. "What can I say? It's just the way I am." She shrugged her shoulders. "On a lighter note, you're still coming early on Saturday,

366

right? I know I'll need help with last-minute party preparations."

The day of the party started off with showers then settled into a warm, sunny, muggy day. Maybe it will cool by the evening, May hoped. The guest list had been pared down to the usual friends and Mitchell's co-workers and a few from his clubs. Heaven forbid if the Randalls got wind of how the Plummers had held a gala for themselves, flaunting their wealth. Humpff, she thought, as if we have wealth.

The girls were thrilled by the goings-on and helped to set the tables and arrange flowers. Frances, now nine, made out place cards, and Edie, five, set them out at each setting as May directed. For this special night, they would dress up to greet the guests and serve *hors d'oeuvres*. Edgar, with his New Orleans background, had introduced May to this custom of small snacks with drinks before dinner.

"*Ma chérie*, May. *Tu es tres avant guarde*," said Edgar, giving her kisses on each cheek, playing up the French influence. He and Amelia had arrived early and had gone into the kitchen to say hello to Eva, still in her housedress and slippers, happily bustling around in the enormous kitchen along with two extra maids borrowed from the Meads and the Veillonses.

The Plummers' temporary lodgings, though much larger than their little house that had burned down, were dated and slightly frayed like a beach house one rents by the sea, which it was. The expansive front porch was set up with several tables and chairs for the cocktail hour. The dinner would be in the dining room, more than large enough for the guests. May had once again performed her magic with table settings, flowers and lighting.

At one point, well after the party had begun, Edgar and Mitchell found themselves together at the bar, which Mitchell had set up on a corner of the porch. They stood together, leaning against the porch railing, companionably looking into the candlelit dining room.

Edgar put his arm over Mitchell's shoulders. "This, Mitchell, is what I love about you. The friendly warmth you and May share with the rest of us. You are whole-souled and genial, totally free from affectation, and it's why people like you."

Mitchell smiled. "That's a formal way of describing me, Edgar. Is that your newspaper voice? You do that sometimes. But thank you. It

369

means a lot. I do love to entertain our friends, though, it doesn't come as naturally to me as it does to May. I'm just along for the ride." He turned and patted Edgar on the arm. "Let's get back and join the party."

Later, on the porch after the guests had left, Mitchell and Edgar sat at one table, May and Amelia nearby at another, enjoying a brandy and the time-honored tradition of post party critique—who was with whom, who had too much to drink, who divulged secrets.

"So, Edgar, did you hear anything useful for one of your columns?" asked Mitchell.

"Oh, nothing of import," said Edgar, lighting a cigar. "The usual gossip. I heard a lot of war mongering going on about Cuba and the Spanish, which probably will not amount to anything. Mostly from your shooting pals. For someone who seems to be a pacifist, that seems like such an odd sport for you to have excelled in."

Mitchell laughed. "It is, I know. But it was a good choice. It was manly enough to appease my stepfather, and I was good at it. Very good, in fact. It was the only thing I did better than my brothers. And remember, it is only wing shot; I'm only shooting down a piece of clay, for pity's sake. It's the skill that attracts me. As a boy I hunted some with my brothers, but when I shot my first deer, I felt awful. Still do. Clay pigeons are my style—no blood or death."

"Well, you certainly get your name in the paper often enough with your high shooting scores. The other day the paper said you had the highest individual score and that if war becomes a reality, you 'would carry many a scalp in your belt,'" Edgar said, laughing. "*Scalps?* Really? And it always describes you as the genial or clever cashier with your numerous friends. Talk about hyperbole."

Mitchell was laughing too. "Why, Edgar? Are you jealous of me? Though I did think that article was a bit over the top. Just goes to show you how the writing in that paper has gone to hell since you left."

"It has, if I must say so myself. It's that hack, P. K. Mayers. You know those columns in the paper, 'Scribus' and 'Hello, This Is Wade?' He writes them. Anonymously, as a way for him to pontificate without actually using his name. He shouldn't opinionate in his own paper, but he just can't help himself. He thinks we're all ignorant fools."

The following Friday in the next edition of the paper, there was the usual small social paragraph in the paper that described "the fabulous dinner party put on by Mr. and Mrs. H. M. Plummer at their temporary home abutting the grounds of Noy's Hotel." May and Mitchell were on the veranda having cocktails before dinner, Mitchell reading the paper while May did her needlepoint.

Mitchell suddenly sat up straighter. "Good Lord. That small paragraph I just read you about our party. It was fine, right? Just the normal little piece they always put in about events and parties. Wait until you hear this. You know that column, 'Hello, This Is Wade?' One half of it is taken up about our party. Describing our house as opulent, the food as lavish, the guests as *diverse*, as one couple even came from the Mormon state of Utah. Then it ends with an insinuating comment about me and a certain male guest seen with their heads together, talking intimately."

Mitchell jumped up and slammed the paper down on the table. "Good God! What on earth is he talking about? Remember Edgar told us the night of the party that Wade is really Mayers, the proprietor. That he uses Wade as an alias. And 'Scribus,' the other little social column? The one that's usually more about the negroes. That's by him too."

May was aghast. "Why in the world would he write something like that? He doesn't even know us. And who is it really about? You or Edgar?" She couldn't help but think that at another time, it could have been Edgar and her they were writing about.

"And that's not all. That comment about the diversity? Our guests were the same as always. Except the Browns, who brought along their houseguest, that man named Samuel something, from Utah. Nothing unusual in that, is there? Just on out of town visitor."

"Mitchell, where are you going with this?" May asked. All this talk was making her feel headachy.

"I'm sorry, dear. Didn't Samuel what's-his-name say his manservant was staying in Creole Town with relatives? I only remember because most people don't mention where their help is staying, especially their colored help."

Mitchell took a large swallow of his drink and wrestled with the paper. "This is what Scribus wrote in the column on the next page: 'The Mormon preacher, Irwin, is making his rounds, swooping down on the ignorant and illiterate element of the country with his false doctrine. As ever the wolf goes about in sheep's clothing...There is no more worthy work for Christian people than to prevent the spread of this dangerous doctrine...The sin of omission is as great as that of commission.' May, he wants everyone to make the connection that our *diverse* guests included Mormons. Who apparently are wolves? Good Lord. How can anyone even think that way? As if that even matters." Mitchell threw the paper to the floor. "What utter nonsense. That's it. I am never reading this rag again. It's garbage."

"Mayers certainly wasn't here. Where did he get his information about our party?"

They looked at each other and blurted out simultaneously, "Easton."

"The little bastard." Mitchell finished his bourbon in one gulp and poured them himself another. "Excuse my language, dear. But what else can I call him? We weren't even going to invite him, remember? But Ira said we should. We'd invited the other tellers, and if it got back to Mobile that we hadn't invited Easton, Randall would be furious."

May looked alarmed. "You don't think Ira had anything to do with this, do you?"

"Lord, I hope not. Mayers and that skunk, Randall, must know each other. How else could this have happened? We certainly don't know Mayers, and I don't think anyone else we know does either. How could he know us?"

On Monday, when Easton came in, Mitchell nodded at him. Easton looked him straight in the eye and nodded back, a small smile on his lips. Later at lunch, Mitchell and Edgar discussed the column.

Mitchell could not help himself. "Look at us. Just like what was said in the paper; we have our heads together talking, intimately. I hope this doesn't mean we can never be seen together in public. I know I saw people looking askance at me as I was walking here. A few people at the bank seemed aloof, but I might have imagined it."

Edgar smiled. "I'm sure you did. But even if you didn't, you need to develop a thicker skin, like me. Just ignore it. Plus, aren't you the clever, genial cashier with the legions of friends? I'll find out, Mitch. I am a reporter, after all. I bet there is a connection between the two of them. How good would that be for them? Randall gets rid of you, and Mayers gets rid of me.

"I wonder...one of my AP columns was published in the *Weekly Corinthian* a few weeks ago," said Edgar. "It was a satiric piece about small-town journalism, and it alluded to our town's pretense at a newspaper. I didn't mention it by name, but I didn't go to extremes to disguise it either. I may have crossed a line with Mayers and brought his wrath down on us both. Maybe I shouldn't have written it."

May continued with her suffering, her headaches increasing in their frequency and severity. And not just headaches. No longer nursing Anna, her cycles had returned, adding their own torment with painful cramping and excessive flow each month. Those times she would stay in bed for two or three days in her darkened room, cool rags on her forehead, and a hot water bottle on her belly. Eva brought her hot broths and teas, sometimes toast or crackers; it was all she could tolerate.

May's accumulation of potions and medicines had grown, and she took them with glassfuls of the Jim Beam she kept under her bed. The household had become used to her monthly schedule and crept about quietly. Once her ailments had run their course, she emerged weakened and thinner with dark circles under her eyes but glad to be part of the family again. Her last bout was one day shorter than usual. May was convinced it was because of the dose of morphine she finally allowed herself.

Their new house on Canty Street was nearly completed, as was the church. "Mitchell, the house is going to be so wonderful. Luckily, Mr. Gautier is happy to keep the same arrangements we had for only a small increase in rent, so we get to live in newly built luxury. The plumbing alone is a marvel. No more lugging pots of water to the tub in the kitchen. And no more privies. Your family should have stayed in the plumbing business. We'd all be millionaires by now. I'm sure the nosy Wade will have something to say about this luxury of ours."

The move back to their new house was a relief. The house was a near replica of the first but with some changes to the interior. Major amongst those changes was the bathtub with running hot water in the bathroom. "Mama!" cried the girls in unison. "No more baths in the kitchen."

There was a flush toilet in Eva's little water closet off the kitchen. "Thank the Lawd," said Eva. "No more privy."

May, excited as a child offering a gift, showed her the kitchen. "Look, Eva. The stove is against the wall now instead of in the middle of the room, taking up all the space. You have shelves all along one wall and a counter with cabinets along another. The sink drains into the sewer system now, so you don't have to empty that bucket anymore. And without the bathtub taking up room, that door on the other side of the stove hides a real pantry. All the space is yours," said May.

"Oh my Lawd, Missus. I'm gonna enjoy this," said Eva with a grin.

May, though, found herself unable to enjoy her new home as she would have liked. If it weren't for Amelia, and surprisingly Eva, who now thoroughly enjoyed talking about her cooking, she wouldn't have returned to working on the cookbook.

"May, I'm still worried about you. You're just not yourself, and you look so peaked. Isn't there something I can do? Are you eating?" Amelia asked her one day. She had finished proofing the first draft and wanted to show it to May. "Is it still the headaches?"

May nodded. "Yes, they're still bad, but I'm taking care of them. Don't worry about me, I'm all right. Let's get on with the task at hand."

May, in fact, *was* taking care of her headaches. During her last spell, she went to see Dr. Cox who was obsequious in his welcome of May. "I know these things are hard on you, but you are not alone by any means. Many women get these symptoms during their menses. Sadly, there is no cure, although they do go away during pregnancy or the change. But morphine can be used as an aid in the meantime. It is a pity a woman must go through such travails. I can give you another bottle of the tincture or, if you would prefer, a needle and vial. It is stronger and works immediately.

"I'll stick with the tincture, Dr. Cox. It works fine. I don't like the idea of sticking myself." She had heard about people who did that. Usually people of low class who were desperate and got addicted to the needle. That's the last thing she needed. The tincture was not habit forming and she could take less of it. She just needed a little to get her through those bad days.

Dr Cox nodded understandingly. "You know, my dear, what might also help, especially if you're feeling overly tired or a bit down, is Cocaine Toothache Drops or Metcalf's Coca Wine. Cocaine will aid in controlling the pain, but it is also a natural stimulant. It might combat the lethargy you feel from the morphine, which is only normal. Feel free to come see me anytime."

During May's good days, she overcompensated to make up for her absences. If she was up to it, sometimes she'd help Eva make dinners. Just as Eva had learned to take pleasure in describing her cooking, now she enjoyed teaching May how to cook.

Her girls needed her instruction on developing ladylike pursuits. Frances had become quite practiced with her sewing, and May was now teaching her embroidery. Edie had her own hoop to begin needlepoint, though, she lacked the patience, preferring to play with her dolls and tell them stories.

"Mama, why can't you be with us always? Why do you get sick?" asked Frances one afternoon. They were sitting together on the sofa, doing their stitching.

"Yes, Mama," chimed in Edie, never missing a chance to talk. She picked up the needlepoint hoop she had discarded just minutes before and sat down primly on May's other side, demurely crossing her ankles, ready for a ladies' chat.

May swallowed the lump that arose in her throat. Why, indeed? she asked herself. Right here, right now, the three of them together was all she needed in life. She was absent from their lives when she was indisposed, and when she was present it pained her doubly. It was her fault; she was guilty of not controlling her weak character.

She knew that one day she would have to talk with her girls about female issues, but not now; they were still just little girls, especially Edie. "I know, dears. I miss our times too. You're too young to understand completely, but when you get older...well, I can explain it to you then," said May. "I don't want you to worry about me. I am not sick. I just have an ailment. All women have these times each month, but mine are worse for some reason and there is nothing I can do about it but just go to bed. One day, a few years from now, they'll just stop. Or so I'm told."

Mitchell's life at the bank was bearable only because Ira Ford, who was aware of the tension between Mitchell and Easton, minimized interaction between the two. He was sympathetic to Mitchell and thought Easton was a prig, though, he could not say so to Mitchell. As much as he would like to, there was no way Ford could fire Easton. He was more than able at his job, and Randall had handpicked him. If Easton was there to spy on Mitchell, he was probably there to spy on him also.

Mitchell and Edgar's next lunch was at a small out-of-the-way place in West Pascagoula, not in Scranton. Mitchell had suggested it. At the table, Mitchell, obviously disturbed, waited until the waiter had served them their drinks.

"Remember, you asked me if I had checked for any openings at other banks? Fred Lindinger, the vice president at Peoples Bank in Pascagoula he called me. I know him and I trust what he had to say. Randall, that interfering prig, called Fred's boss regarding me. Fred couldn't help but overhear most of the conversation—his boss yells. Apparently, Randall had called all the presidents of the other area banks specifically instructing them not to hire me if I came looking," Mitchell said. "Not just anyone, but me. No one can say I am imagining things anymore.

"Fred thought I should know. He was pretty disgusted. Said they were ruining business for us ethical bankers. Then he added that he is sure all the increased negative comments in the paper are originating from Randall also."

"Interesting" said Edgar. "That goes with what I found out about Mayers. He and Randall *are* friends. But they're very secretive about it. They've got this town sewed up and they'll swoop down and destroy anyone who disagrees with them."

Mitchell shook his head. "And just to add to my misery, that damned Easton joined the Wing Shot Club *and* the Mullet Catchers—the two clubs I enjoy that are not involved with business. Bad enough he joined the Commercial Club of Scranton, but that's civic duty. This is an invasion of my private life. Randall has declared war on me, and it's ruining me."

"I knew about Easton. It was in the Wade column a month or so ago," said Edgar. He cleared his throat uncomfortably. "There was also something in last week's column about you— us actually. Mentioning a rumor that we were seen together in New Orleans. In essence, it states we visited Mahogany Hall in Storyville. And as only Wade can do, he described it as 'the most reprehensibly sordid house of prostitution known in that city of sin.'"

The two sat back in their chairs, staring at each other. "I'm doomed," moaned Mitchell.

***

During the hot months of summer, Scranton, The Pascagoulas, Ocean Springs, Moss Point, and their environs were popular with tourists, usually from the neighboring cities and states. They arrived on the trains wanting to take advantage of the advertised ocean breezes, the beaches, and the relaxation offered by hoteliers and restauranteurs.

Each year there was a new hotel or new restaurant. Guesthouses abounded. Beachfront mansions owned by out-of-town wealthy families overflowed with multiple generations, highlighted by the working patriarch's return for the weekends. Smaller houses and cottages were rented out for a week or more. With luck, the owners, who had probably squeezed themselves and their families into a relative's house for the season, could contribute a sizable increase to their finances for the year—often undeclared income.

In August, a fever had broken out in Ocean Springs, only seventeen miles west of Scranton. Yellow fever epidemics had occurred with frequently in the low-lying areas of the Gulf coast, the last epidemic having occurred nineteen years past in 1878. Assuming the worst, the local governments called in the Louisiana Board of Health. The towns' concerns were allayed by the physicians who declared the contagion was only a mild form of dengue fever.

The *Pascagoula Democrat-Star* on September 17, 1897, quoted a Colonel R. A. Van Cleave. "I have been through the yellow fever epidemics of 1875 and 1878, and according to my experience and observation, no yellow fever exists or had exited [*sic*] in Ocean Springs."

In late September, yellow fever, also called yellow jack or the black vomit, was officially named as the fever occurring in Ocean Springs, and the town was put under quarantine. During the time that had elapsed since the first incidence of fever, a month and a half before in August, excursionists, many already infected, had returned to their homes by ship or by railroad, spreading the disease to all the southern states and some further north.

In Jackson County two quarantine encampments were established. In all, nearly four thousand cases were reported, with five hundred deaths occurring in the country. New Orleans alone accounted for three hundred deaths. Ocean Springs, ironically, had only three.

By October, with the temperatures beginning to drop and the breezes increasing, the threat and cause of the contagion blew away—mosquitoes. In 1881, a Cuban physician, Carlos Finlay, had proposed that the cause was the mosquito, but that idea was not yet accepted by the scientific community.

***

People who had spent the last month irritably locked in their hot, humid houses escaped to the outdoors. In another time, May and Mitchell would have done the same, enjoying watching the girls play in the front yard and chatting with neighbors. But since the last nasty columns, they let Aunt Mary supervise them and had their drinks inside in the parlor, cooler now with the windows open. May did her needlework, and Mitchell read his papers or a magazine. They cherished this time together, with pleasant conversation, opting not to talk about their worries.

True to his word, Mitchell had canceled his subscription to the *Pascagoula Democrat-Star*. What knowledge they had of the rumors swirling around them came from Edgar or Amelia.

On Fridays on his way home, Mitchell would pick up one of the other area papers that were sold in the newsstand at the Palace Drugstore, though, *area* was debatable. The *Sea Coast Echo* was published in Bay Saint Louis, Mississippi, sixty miles away, and the *Weekly Corinthian*, out of Corinth, Mississippi, was four hundred miles away.

"I don't care where they're written. I will never read that thing again. The other papers do a better job of covering what's going on in the rest of the world anyway. And," Mitchell stated, "they don't upset me."

47—DOWNWARD SPIRAL—1897–1898

The anxieties the Plummers carried only increased through the winter, each suffering in relative silence. Mitchell didn't want to burden May with his problems, and May hid hers. Evenings still found them in the parlor, though, less frequently due to her episodes. Conversation was cursory and usually one-sided, with Mitchell reading aloud from his newspapers or giving superficial accounts of his days. May sat quietly beside him listlessly doing needlepoint. At suppertime, Eva sent in the girls to announce dinner. Frances usually took May's arm gently, Edie grabbed her father's, and with great formality they escorted their parents into the dining room.

Randall continued his harassment of Mitchell. He pushed Ira to fire him, but Ira held firm. "He's far too good to dismiss, Mr. Randall. And he is incredibly popular and heavily involved in the business and recreational aspects of this community. All of which directly impact the bank. And, as you well know, we are not the only bank in town anymore. You know how rumors can spread, and I worry about what would be said around town and what it would say about this bank if Mitchell was dismissed. Especially if it got out that the vice president disagreed with that dismissal," said Ira, over the phone, both knowing full well the chances of being overheard on the party line.

Ira knew his defense of Mitchell was weak, at best. Mitchell had always been popular in the community. However, the weekly attacks in the paper by "Wade" and the whispers fueled by Easton were taking their toll on Mitchell's good reputation. Randall intended to ruin Mitchell, of that Ira was sure. It was only a matter of time. Easton had increased his passive-aggressive behavior, spreading his innuendo and his unsubtle spying on Mitchell. There were fewer and fewer glowing articles in the paper about Mitchell's amazing efforts in shooting or baseball.

Easton's prime function in life seemed to be to make Mitchell's life a misery, and the odious man was successful at it. No matter how hard Mitchell tried to heed Edgar's advice to ignore Easton, he could not. Each day was a struggle just to maintain civility and accomplish his duties.

His feelings of insecurity increased. He became reclusive at work, preferring solitary secretarial duties rather than interacting with clients. His routes to and from work varied, as did the times, usually very early or very late, and he avoided making eye contact with others. His presence at his various clubs became sporadic. He was becoming a recluse.

As awful as his life was, his biggest worry was May. He anguished over her. "Edgar, I just don't know what's wrong with her. She is not herself. It's as if she's in a sort of cloud, a fog, that's separating her from the rest of us. These spells she gets set her back terribly. I took her to Dr. Kell last week. He said she appeared healthy enough, though, he agreed she looked weakened."

Christmas came and went with little fanfare. There was none of the frantic decorating, no participation in the annual house tour, and little socializing. Some social events, the business-related ones, were important for Mitchell to attend. He went alone or with Edgar, only adding fuel to the rumor mill. May did go with Mitchell to the bank's Christmas party, though, the proximity of Easton brought on such a state of anxiety for her that Mitchell took her home after an hour.

They attended some parties thrown by their close friends but again they often left early. More and more rumors surrounded the Plummers. Slight and in concerned whispers by their friends, more luridly commented upon in the paper. It was not just Mitchell who had been described as genial, clever, and charming. May's name had also been bandied about in the paper with the same adoring adjectives. Lately, though, the comments in the paper were less flattering: "Folks wonder about the health of the increasingly absent Mrs. Plummer...the low-profile Plummers...friends wonder where the socialite Plummers have gone."

"It's Mayers's campaign, Mitchell," Edgar said. "His and of course Randall's." Edgar still came for dinners, occasionally. The invitations came sporadically, when May was having a good week, though, her participation in the table conversation was minimal. Despite Mitchell not reading the local paper, Edgar kept them both up to date when he was with them, sharing the less judgmental comments. May seemed oblivious; Mitchell was angry enough for them both.

Mitchell and May did have their own annual Christmas party. May could still put on a show when she needed to. The house was simply decorated, just the tree, plus holly and pine boughs draped over the mantle and a multitude of candles scattered around the dining room. Only their closest friends were there: the Meads, the Veillonses, the Cantys, Edgar, and Amelia.

"A toast to our May," said Mitchell, looking at her with pride. "I'm sure you all noticed the small packages at the women's places. I'll let her tell you about them. I could not be prouder of her."

"Oh, Mitchell, dear. Thank you," May said looking thin and frail. With a small smile, she raised her glass to him and the others at the table. "Thank you all, dear friends."

She rose and went to the kitchen and brought out Eva, looking uncomfortable but hiding a smile that slipped around her lips. "You all know Eva and what a wonderful cook she is. The recipes we used tonight are now in a book. If you open your package, you, too, will be able to replicate her meals."

There was the noise of paper tearing then exited oohs and aahs from the women at the table. "They're cookbooks: *What Eva Knows about Cooking*. Eva and I have been working on this for two years along with Amelia, who did all the manuscript work and arranged for this small printing. Both Amelia and I have easily reproduced her recipes using this book, including some of tonight's dishes. If you enjoy this meal, and be honest ladies when I ask you later, then all the work will be worth it."

There was a smattering of applause. Eva, her smile now filling her face, curtseyed and fled back to her domain. The women flipped through the pages; the men returned to talking. May and Amelia smiled and toasted each other.

***

January of 1898 and the new year brought loud rumblings of a war with Spain. Cuba was involved in a war of independence from Spain, and the United States was concerned at having Spanish war ships so close to its borders. President William McKinley was against a war, as were most business interests, which lobbied heavily against it, especially so soon after the Depression.

But America's public sympathies lay with Cuba, and those opinions were becoming increasingly agitated over reports of Spanish atrocities. The USS *Maine* was sent to Cuba to protect US interests, but on February 15, 1898, the USS *Maine* suffered a mysterious internal explosion, resulting in its sinking in Havana Harbor and the loss of two-thirds of its crew. The press became inflamed in its accusations and argued for more direct action by the United States. The *Pascagoula Democrat-Star* was one of those papers avidly pursuing the path of war. "Remember the *Maine*! To hell with Spain," was quoted frequently in its pages, or so Mitchell heard.

Even the other papers Mitchell now read were also filled with news of Cuba, though, not in quite such incendiary form. In the parlor before dinner one night, Mitchell was upset after reading an article out loud to May from the *Weekly Corinthian*. "As if we don't have enough to worry about," he said. "This country is going to hell."

He looked over to May sitting quietly on the sofa, her needle point on her lap and staring vacantly ahead. "May, God damn it! What is wrong with you?"

He was shocked at himself. He was sure this was the first time he had ever yelled at his wife. Certainly, he had never used profanity aimed at her. "May, dear, I am sorry I cursed at you. But you worry me so. You're leaving me. Us. The girls. I can feel it. Tell me what I can do to help. Let me help you, please!"

May pulled herself together; everything was a never-ending effort these days. "I'm sorry, dear. I know I drift away sometimes. Daydreaming, that's all." She smiled at him. "What were you saying?"

May *was* dreaming; dreaming of her new way to get morphine. She had been getting her morphine tincture from Dr. Cox and McVie's; alternating every other week between them. But, lately, no matter how carefully she spaced the doses, she ran out sooner. Dr. Cox made her uncomfortable with his unctuous manner as did the druggist at McVie's. Either one might think she was intemperate in her use of the drug. She had even gone so far as to get two doses from the Palace Drugstore, but that gossipy Mrs. Watson worried her.

Then, she remembered what Amelia had said about the Sears and Roebuck catalogue. She laughed when she read the magazine. Not only did they carry morphine tincture, but they sold morphine, and cocaine *injection kits*. The kit consisted of a small carrying case with a syringe and two needles and two vials of drug for $1.50.

Amazing! Injecting the stuff still seemed a bit desperate to her. She really did not need it that badly. But she had ordered two bottles of tincture yesterday that should arrive next week. It was all so simple, and no one would know. Plus, it cost far less, and she would not have to ask anyone for it, which always embarrassed her. This way she could always have another bottle on hand.

48—UNHOLY MESS, REDUX—1898

Mr. Judge O. Randall, having no office of his own in the Scranton State Bank, had usurped Ira's office. It was a Wednesday, and he was sitting intrusively behind Ira's desk, the three officers of Scranton State Bank standing opposite, lined up like sentries at attention. Only P. Easton Jane looked at ease. He had been instructed to put the Closed sign up early, before lunch.

"Mr. Plummer," Randall said. Mitchell made himself look at him, desperately trying to hide his hatred. Was Randall almost smiling?

"Mr. Plummer, I, or rather we, at Louisiana State Bank have finally had enough of your disreputable behavior. These rumors are affecting the bottom line of this bank. We cannot have that, now can we, Mr. Plummer?"

Mr. Plummer stood like a steel post, willing himself not to betray his emotions.

"If it weren't for Mr. Ford here," Randall said, with a disparaging look at Ira, "I'd dismiss you right now. I should have done so when I first learned of your debauchery in New Orleans on that business trip, which my bank financed. Totally unethical. Even after I had counseled you about the temptations that such a *friend* could exert on a man of your weak moral fiber, you are still seen around town with him. Everywhere. You have continued to show a deplorable lack of character and, most importantly, a disrespect for your position."

He took a deep breath and leaned back in the chair. "You're often seen drinking alcohol during the daytime, at lunch. And more than one glass. How can you do the bank's business inebriated? And how can you continue to have intimate conversations with that same man? You even took him as an escort to parties over the past holiday season. Not your wife, who seems to have mysteriously disappeared. This is not how we live here in the South, Mr. Plummer. No sirree. It's amoral, unchristian, and an unholy mess."

Mitchell was driven to speak up. "Leave my wife out of this. She is of no concern to you." He worried he might faint from the effort of controlling himself.

Randall smiled piteously at Mitchell. "Maybe, Mr. Plummer. Maybe. Though the absence of a gentleman's spouse is always disconcerting."

He continued, obviously enjoying working up to his *denouement.* "Now, Mr. P. E. Jane here has been invaluable to us and as a result he shall, as of this moment, be the cashier of Scranton State Bank— the head cashier. Only because of Mr. Ford will you be retained—as the assistant cashier."

Randall stood up, attempting to close his jacket over his well-fed stomach. "Obviously, the salaries will be commensurate with each position. It pains me, Mr. Plummer, that you do not have what it takes to be an able banker. I have tried to be patient with you and lead you in the right direction. But to no avail. All your previous duties will be assumed by Mr. Jane. If you have a problem with this, talk with Mr. Ford, your immediate boss. You're lucky to have him. He seems to be your only supporter—in the bank and in town.

"I'll be leaving now. I'm late for a luncheon meeting with Mr. Mayers at the paper." With that, he left, seemingly taking the oxygen in the room with him. Mitchell sat down. Easton, unable to hide his smugness, at least had the decency to leave the room without saying anything.

"Mitchell, I'm so very sorry," said Ira. He had become more than a boss to Mitchell—a good friend, he would have liked to think, were it not for the position their boss had put them both into. What Randall had just done was repugnant to him. "I know I can't say anything to make you feel better. Later, when you've gotten over the shock, we can talk about options. There must be something we can do about this problem. You can stay in here if you need to, and feel free to take the rest of the day off. In fact, you can take the rest of the week off. I would." He left the room, closing the door quietly.

Mitchell sobbed. Other than when Sweet Alice had died, he hadn't cried since he was twelve, the last time Thomas had beat him up. He had wept tears of happiness when he married and when each of his girls were born. But these were tears of shame, frustration, defeat, and utter hopelessness.

He dreaded going home. May was having another one of her episodes. He couldn't tell her of this now; he had no idea what her mental state was. She might not even comprehend what this would mean for them. He had made a decent wage, enough to support his family and his help, with some put away in savings. He knew what Easton had earned, and it was noticeably less than what

Mitchell was making now. After all he was the one who did the books—had done the books. Things were going to be very difficult.

How was he going to hold his head up in town? What would that horrible paper print about this? He could just imagine it: "Mr. H. M. Plummer, the formerly clever cashier of the Scranton State Bank, has been replaced by the former assistant cashier, P. E. Jane, whose position the previously genial H. M. Plummer will now assume."

God, it's just too awful. His mind was awhirl, his jumbled thoughts like dreck, swirling down a drain. What would he do? How was he to care for his family? He had worked so hard and for naught.

He needed May. The old May he had married and loved. Who had made him laugh, who had made love to him, who had born his children, who had made this town her own. He would not be able to continue in this life if she were not by his side.

As it had been for the last few months, May was in their bedroom when he returned home, the ever-present *Wuthering Heights* lying open, beside her lethargic form. She woke, barely, when he crawled into bed with her. He wrapped himself behind her, spooning her tightly, cupping his hand over her breast, consoling himself with her heart's steady rhythm.

"May, dearest. You must come back to me. Randall has ruined me. I could continue on, but only if you're with me. Please, May. Please help me." The vision of them in bed together, him begging his unresponsive wife to help him, set him onto another round of tears.

This was abnormal enough that May roused herself enough to slur, "It's OK, dear. It's OK. Talk later." She returned to somnolence before he could answer her. Shortly thereafter he, too, fell into an exhausted sleep.

Eva was aware of Mitchell's return home. In the middle of the day, with no hello to her. He had just run in the front door and up the stairs. This is worse than with Mista Hamlin, she thought. Something awful is going on in this house. Miz May ain't been herself for most of a year, and now the Mista too.

She brought out a pitcher of lemonade and set her worried self on the front porch to catch the girls before they went inside. They were due home from school at any time.

Aunt Mary had taken Anna in her pram for their usual walk to meet the girls at school. Anna started jouncing around in the carriage, giggling and calling out in a language known only to her as soon as she saw her sisters. Frances felt too grown up to be walked home from school with her two little sisters, one still a baby, and her ancient negro nurse. She immediately felt conscience-stricken for thinking of Aunt Mary, whom she adored, as ancient. Edie of course went right up to Anna, laughing and giving her kisses.

They were surprised to see Eva on the porch, offering them all lemonade. Aunt Mary sneaked a sideways look at Eva, knowing something was up. Eva said, "I knows you girls are always good, but this day's been real bad on your parents. So, we all need to be extra quiet."

Frances frowned, and Edie looked about to cry. "I know it's hard on you, babies. You know your mama loves you. But she's got something off with her lady parts that gives her pain, and the only thing for it is to sleep."

"Go on now. Go upstairs, get changed, and quick come back down here. Do not go into their room, now, you hear? I made your favorite for dinner tonight—fried chicken—and when you come down, we'll make an apple pie."

They left, quiet as mice, making Eva tear up. She told Aunt Mary about Mista Mitchell coming home in the middle of the day and going straight upstairs. Aunt Mary shook her old, gray head that had seen just about everything, pursed her lips, and tsk-tsked.

Mitchell eventually woke but May remained lethargic. He splashed cold water on his face and ran a comb through his hair. Then he went down to the parlor as if it were perfectly normal to have arrived there from upstairs and not the front door. He poured himself two stiff shots. He thought about staying in the parlor, but that was his and May's routine. He did not want to be there without her.

He took the third glass into the kitchen where he heard the girls, Edith doing most of the talking. Other than perhaps getting a glass of water or extra coffee in the morning, he hardly knew what the kitchen looked like. Right now, it looked warm and inviting with his girls, dear Eva, and Aunt Mary. He sat in the rocking chair beside the warm stove, trying to swallow the seemingly permanent lump in his throat.

"Eva, would it be all right for us to have dinner in here, in the kitchen? All of us, including you and Aunt Mary? It's so cozy in here..." his voice trailing off.

"Papa. That would be fun," said Edie, ever the one to try new things. Frances looked at her father. At nine, she was aware that adults kept secrets from children. In particular, she knew that her parents had been keeping something serious from Edie and her for a while now. But she was still too young to know for sure, and she did not want to ask.

"Mista Mitchell, that would be mighty fine," Eva said graciously, her mind saying, Lawdy, Lawdy.

The next day, Mitchell dressed himself in his clothes from the day before. It didn't matter; he wasn't going to work. He walked to Edgar's house, trying to make himself enjoy the spring day. He knew Edgar was in town, as they had made plans for lunch.

"Dear God, Mitch. You look terrible," said Edgar. Mitchell never had anything out of place. Yet here he was standing on the doorstep unshaven, in a wrinkled shirt, tie loosened, and his jacket held in one hand, almost dragging on the ground. "One too many last night? Lucky for you, I just made coffee. That should fix you up."

Mitchell stumbled into Edgar's little house. "Don't be too kind to me. It makes me cry," he said. He somehow waited until Edgar had cleared off the table and set places with *café au lait* and rolls before he told him the whole wretched story.

"Jesus. What a horribly abysmal thing to do to anyone. Does that man have no morals? Any ethics?" Edgar was furious for his friend. "And that priggish ass Mayers was in on it surely. I'll bet you anything there'll be some nasty line in the "Wade" column tomorrow."

The two sat in silence for a while before Mitchell continued. "The worst of it all is May. She is in a constant stupor. It's that morphine; I just know it. I could maybe get through all this if she was beside me. You know she's always been the stronger of us. But it's as if she's dead already. And for me to live without her, I just don't know if I have the strength. How can I take care of the girls without her? How can I provide for them with the meager salary I'll now be making?"

"Mitchell, what are you saying?" Edgar asked, shocked at the way Mitchell was talking. "Come on, man. Pull yourself together. You're scaring me with this talk. You do have the strength, Mitchell. And together, we can help May too. Amelia will help too. She's been worried about May for a while now."

Edgar was pacing in front of Mitchell. "You have the girls to think about, for God's sake. What about them?"

Mitchell just looked at him. "Maybe they'd be better off without us."

Edgar cut him off. "God damn it, Mitchell. Listen to yourself. This is not you. You and May are wonderful parents. You love those girls. You have to stop talking this way."

After breakfast, Edgar suggested Mitchell nap in his bedroom; it was obvious he was exhausted. Edgar tried to work on his column, but to no avail. He was terribly frightened for his friends.

Mitchell sounded as if he wanted to end it all. How could he talk that way? This was terrible, true. And everything else that has happened to him for the last year or so. But he can't abandon all hope. Edgar, he of amoral behaviors, still had an inbred aversion to the sins of his lapsed Catholicism. He was greatly upset by the things Mitchell had said.

Edgar was grasping for solutions. All problems had answers, didn't they? Or at least they could be managed. Mitchell could back away. He did not have to stay at that job, subjected to Randall's abuse. Edgar was suddenly taken aback. May would never take it—have taken it. But May had been missing for most of the last year. The last time she had exhibited any life was at their Christmas party. Amelia had told him how concerned she was about May. More than once. Christ, what kind of a friend was he?

Edgar decided to invite himself for dinner at Mitchell's that night. Eva always made more than enough, and he hadn't seen the girls in a long time. They might need some distraction.

Frances and Edie had indeed missed their Uncle Edgar and climbed all over him, looking for the candies he hid in his pockets. He regaled them at the table with his stories, the laughter and noise a needed tonic to them all. His Limerick story took an especially long time to end, the two little girls in it surviving multiple adventures. Eva and Aunt Mary listened from the kitchen.

Edgar convinced Mitchell not to go into work the next day. "Let them stew in their own juices, Mitch. You can go in on Monday. I'll come by around eleven, and you and I will take a walk down to the beach. Dress casually. The fresh air and lunch at the Olde Fish Grill will fix what's ailing you."

Mitchell was more relaxed when he returned home late in the afternoon. It was good he was no longer agitated, as May was awake, still in bed and groggy. Mitchell opened the heavy drapes and the windows, letting in fresh air. He sat down beside her and held her hand.

"May, you're back to me. How do you feel?" he asked.

"Better," she said quietly, surprised he was there. He looked almost boyish, his hair

410

windblown, his face sunburned. She ran her hand through his tousled hair, smiling at him. "You look like when I married you."

"That's me," he said with a crooked smile. Now that she was awake, he didn't want to disturb her with his troubles. He would tell her later.

"Did you come to me the other night, dear? I thought I remembered you holding me. But it's been such a long time since we held each other. Maybe I was dreaming."

"Yes, May. It was me. I've missed you too."

Over the weekend Mitchell told May about what had happened at the bank. He made it sound routine, a changing of the guard, so to speak. Even in her drugged state, May saw through him.

"Oh, Mitchell, dearest. If I was only my old self, I'd march right into Randall's office and give him a piece of my mind—the pompous ass. And I sure wouldn't be polite about it. How dare he call himself a Christian man. But I can't. I'm stuck in this body that only gives me pain. I can't take care of my girls anymore. Or you. I can't help you. You're a good man, Mitchell. You deserve better from this world."

She laid back onto her pillows. She wanted only to go back to that blue haze the morphine enveloped her in; it was like velvet. Nothing else mattered. She reached over to the table and took a spoonful of the tincture.

"Maybe you should have some, Mitchell. Maybe it will take away your pain. I can't help you, Mitchell, but maybe this can."

Why not? He could do with a loss of consciousness. He took a spoonful then laid down beside her. In time he felt peace fall over him and drifted off to sleep. When he awoke, it was evening. With only one dose, he felt the desire to go back there. But he had things to do.

50—A DEPLORABLE TRAGEDY—1898

Monday morning Mitchell rose and went about his usual ablutions preparing for work. He kissed May, who did not stir. "Tonight, dearest."

Downstairs he kissed his girls. "Would you like me to walk you to school this morning, my little ducklings?" Edie giggled and Frances nodded. "Eva, are you all right with Anna until Aunt Mary gets here? She gets here at eleven on Mondays, right?"

"Oh, yes," said Eva, smiling happily. "Yes, sir. This child and I gets along just fine, don't we baby?" Anna gurgled.

After leaving his girls at the school, Mitchell made a detour on his way to the bank. He had to take care of something first. If he was early enough, Gerald should be able to fit him in quickly. It should not take long.

"You're lucky, Mitchell," said Gerald M. Luce, Esq. He was surprised to see Mitchell there. The last time he saw him was on that hunting trip they had taken at Bison, the one where they bagged all those turkeys. Mitchell looked terrible. Whatever he wanted to talk about must not be good. He'd find out soon enough; lawyers always did. "I always get to the office an hour before opening. Tell me what you need."

"Thank you, Gerald. I need you to draw up my will. Today. May, as you may have heard, has been quite ill with *the consumption*. Dr. Kell has ordered her to enter a sanatorium. He said it's the only thing that might save her and was able to get her into the Brexton Boarding House in Asheville. That area, as you know, is highly regarded in the treatment of the disease. She and I must leave tomorrow. However, she is terrified she might die at any moment, and that terror includes my death also. She wants the girls protected, as of course do I. She won't leave unless I make out a will first." Mitchell looked at Gerald expectantly. "Can you do it? Now?"

"Well, Mitchell, it is unusually fast, but it sounds simple enough. My secretary gets here in twenty minutes. She can type it out then and witness it. If you don't mind waiting outside in the waiting room, I'll call you when it's ready. Or if you want, go to Valverde's. Best breakfast in town if you ask me. My first appointment isn't until ten."

After finishing his business with Gerald, which he paid for on the spot with a check, he went to the bank. It was ten o'clock, and he was an hour late. He walked inside, put his hat and jacket on the hook as always, and said hello to Ira, his friend. He ignored Easton, the sycophant, already behind Mitchell's old window. Without a pause, Mitchell went to his new window, the one with the nameplate H. M. Plummer—Assistant Cashier. Except for a few raised eyebrows at the changes in cashier real estate, the morning was uneventful.

At lunchtime, Mitchell set out to meet Edgar at the hotel where they had a long, leisurely lunch, with several drinks for Mitchell. "I don't know if I told you, Edgar. But I ran into Gerald Luce a month ago, which reminded me that May and I still hadn't drawn up a will. As a bachelor, you don't have to worry about wills, but as a husband and father I must. He took care of it for us in a very timely way. With all the other difficulties going on in my life right now, it's one less thing I have to worry about."

Edgar did read to Mitchell from last Friday's *Pascagoula Democrat-Star*, the two-line mention of his demotion. "For reasons unknown to Wade, H. M. Plummer, the cashier of the Scranton State Bank, has been demoted to assistant cashier. The erstwhile assistant cashier, the always pleasant P. E. Jane, has been promoted to head cashier."

Mitchell's response to the column was a snort of laughter and a gulp of his drink. Edgar was surprised at Mitchell's heavy consumption of alcohol but nonetheless was pleased to see Mitchell adapting so well to his change in status.

After work, Mitchell went straight home. He went into the kitchen and gave Eva a big hug. "Just because, Eva. Because you're the best dang cook in Scranton. Oh, now, Eva, stop your blushing."

He then went upstairs to the bedroom. May was sitting up in bed waiting for him. "I saw your note," she said peevishly. "What is so important that you only left me one dose to get through the day? I almost got angry, but you said you had good news."

"I do. Tonight, we're going to solve all our problems. I'll tell you later. I need you to be awake tonight and dressed for dinner. I'll help you. I know you're weakened from your stay in bed. We'll go down for drinks in the parlor, just as we always do, or maybe on the porch. It's so beautiful out, if a bit chilly on this April day. Then we'll dine with all our girls, even little Anna. After they go to bed, we can talk about what we will do."

Dinner was almost festive. Eva had baked a special dessert as soon as she knew May would be eating at the table. Anna sat in her highchair chortling at her dinner companions, picking at morsels of food. The girls were thrilled to finally have their mother with them. Edie, particularly, couldn't stop jabbering, trying to squeeze into one night all the things she had been saving to tell her mother. Frances was quiet, though, participatory. She was suspicious of the jocularity of her parents yet grateful for their presence together at the table.

After dinner, the girls went upstairs to get ready for bed. May and Mitchell went to the parlor. They sat quietly together on the sofa, holding hands and drinking a fine brandy Edgar had brought them.

"I wish we could be like this always," said May. "I do love you and our little family."

"Oh, May, me also," Mitchell said. "But the way things are now, I wonder how we can keep going. I think I may have a way to make life better for the girls and for us. Let's retire upstairs and we can continue talking in our room."

May went upstairs while Mitchell stopped in the kitchen to say a word to Eva. "Tomorrow morning, you rest and sleep in. I already told Aunt Mary to take all the girls next door for breakfast before they go to school." After seeing Eva's incredulous face, Mitchell added, "Mrs. Veillons invited them. Sort of a picnic for them. They begged to go."

Eva barely nodded and slowly turned back to the sink as she tried to keep her mind from going to frightening places.

The girls were already in bed—in Aunt Mary's bed. When she had first started working for them, back when the Plummers were still living in the Blanchard house, the girls had been sleeping in the same bed due to nightmares from the fire. Sometimes they were inconsolable, their fears assuaged only when Aunt Mary crawled into bed with them. Later, when they moved into the new house, Edie was still scared, and the practice continued. Even though Frances was older, their mother's frighteningly odd behavior hung over the children, making them cling to old habits and each other and their kind old nurse.

May and Mitchell went in together and kissed them all good night. Frances could not remember the last time they both had done that. She shivered and pulled the blankets close.

May and Mitchell dressed for bed. He remembered he had forgotten to wind the clocks, one of his nightly duties. He started to go downstairs then thought, what for?

May got into bed, commenting on the nice evening. She reached over and poured a dose of the morphine.

"No thanks," Mitchell said, in response to her offer. "Once was enough for me. Don't take too much now, May. I want us to stay awake and be with each other until the last minute."

Mitchell talked companionably as he told her of his plan. "I know you'll think I'm crazy. And maybe I am. The only time I have ever really fit in, been comfortable with who I am, has been with you. It is you who has given me courage. It is you who made it clear we had to leave Bangor. It is you who made it possible to gain friends and socialize so comfortably. You're the one who gave us three beautiful babies. And helped me survive the loss of Sweet Alice."

At this, his voice cracked. He found he had tears running down his face. "It was all so fulfilling. I was so grateful to you for showing me how to live such a life."

May hardly heard the words, Mitchell's monologue was so lulling. She aroused enough to slur out, "Not just me, dear. We gave it to ourselves."

"And that's the crux of it all, isn't it? We can't give it to each other anymore. I can't go on anymore. And I certainly can't go on without you. There's no more fight left in me."

He stood up, shook his shoulders. "It's as if I've been planning this my whole life. You've already found a way to end it for yourself. But I can't do it your way. I can only do it one way. I think I always knew I would go this way. Guns have always been in my life. A hobby I've enjoyed and excelled at. But there is dark side to that hobby, one I have always been afraid of. And now it's calling me. The ultimate test..."

She looked at him. "Mitchell, what are you talking about? We can't do that to our children."

"May, we already have. You have left them— all of us. It has been too cruel to watch you die a little each day. And now I won't be able to provide for the girls anymore. They will be embarrassed by my failures and by your illness. And then by their motherless state when you've succumbed."

She looked at him, raising one hand off the bed, then letting it drop. It was all she had energy for. Awareness dawned, but she did not stop him. An end to this place of misery she occupied would be a relief.

"It will be fine, May. Soon you'll never have any more pain," he said. His eyes teared up and he paused to compose himself in order to continue. "I wrote to Edith and Edward on Friday. The girls will be better off with them. They can give them the future they deserve." He put his hand in hers, rubbing his thumb gently on her skin. "I wrote a small note to Ira. Just asking him to keep the news as quiet as possible. Do you want to leave a note for anyone?" asked Mitchell, his tone very matter of fact.

May, whose mind was slowly grasping what he was talking about, did not resist his hypnotic words. "Yes, I think I'll write one to Amelia, telling her to do as she wishes with the cookbook. And I'll leave her that rhinestone choker and the earrings you gave me on our first anniversary here in Scranton. She always loved them."

After she wrote the note, they shared a glass of brandy. May fell back gratefully into her pillows, the dull haze she so loved taking over. The whistle of the 4:00 a.m. train aroused her enough that she had a sudden urge to see the children. For the last time, she thought. Aborting this path she and Mitchell were now on did not cross her mind. She went into their room, crawled over Aunt Mary, kissed each one of the girls, and then stumbled back into her bed.

Mitchell sat beside her. "It's time now, May. You can take another dose now. I can tell you're in pain again, and it will help you to sleep. Here, let's toast each other with Edgar's brandy. He'll understand."

They lay side by side, May in her haze and Mitchell sipping brandy and continuing with his soliloquy. "We'll do it together. I'll watch you until it's over for you and you're finally at peace. Then I'll do the same in my way. We will be happy together, forever."

"That's sweet, Mitchell. You've always watched over me, haven't you?" She stirred and opened her eyes. "Make another note, Mitchell. Tell them we want to be together in one grave. In the same one, beside our Sweet Alice. Together always."

Mitchell sat in the chair beside May, holding her hand, staring at her and out the window. At the first sign of dawn, he stood in the open door of Aunt Mary's room to check on the girls, all still sleeping. He stood there silently, not wanting to disturb them.

May was restless and moaning when he returned to the room. He went to her, raised her head, and slipped another dose into her mouth.

There was a tap at the door. Mitchell jumped. "Yes?"

"Mista Mitchell?" Aunt Mary's tremulous voice came through the door. "Is Miz May sick again? Should I get some hot water?"

"Yes, Aunt Mary. Thank you. She is sick. Get the water if you want to."

Aunt Mary returned and called through the door again. Mitchell said, "Put it down. She will be better in a few minutes."

He heard the girls rising and getting ready for school, Edie's voice ringing out as she excitedly talked about breakfast next door. How Mrs. Veillons made the best French toast ever and allowed them to have as much syrup as they wanted. He heard them clomping down the stairs.

He breathed a sigh of relief, washed up, and dressed in his business clothes minus the jacket. He resumed his vigil, waiting to hear when the children left the house. He dozed off for a few minutes then woke with a start. He shook May's shoulders but got only a small groan for a response.

"God, May, what if I've made a mistake? A terrible mistake? The girls can go on without me but surely not without you. Oh, Lord. What have I done? I've got to get the doctor for you."

Mitchell ran downstairs and told Eva, looking forlorn in her quiet kitchen, to go for Dr. Kell. "For May, Eva. She's in a bad way."

Aunt Mary was at the top of the stairs when he returned. "The girls. They've been sent away, as I asked?"

"Yes, Mista Mitchell," she said, looking at him with alarm.

"Good. Don't leave this spot. Stay right here."

Mitchell then went into his room, locking the door behind him. May was breathing, barely. "I hope it's not too late for you, May. But I must do my part now."

He stood at the foot of their bed, stepped before the mirror, put his cigarette in his mouth, took his old Smith & Wesson .38 caliber revolver, spun the cylinder, placed it against his temple, and pulled the trigger. It clicked...it clicked...it clicked...it went off.

NOTICES

Friday, April 29, 1898 *Pascagoula Democrat-Star* Jackson, Mississippi Page 3
Deplorable Tragedy
Cashier H. M. Plummer Commits Suicide. His wife Dies from Effects of Poison.

Last Tuesday morning about 9 o'clock the community Scranton and surrounding country were startled by the report that Mr. H. M. Plummer, the well-known cashier of the Scranton State Bank, had committed suicide—and an additional shock was felt when the community learned his wife, Mrs. May Plummer, had sought death by another means than had taken Mr. Plummer from our midst.

It appears that the lamentable tragedy was caused through domestic trouble. We are not in a position to state why or how the tragedy was caused, we only, with the many friends of the unfortunate couple, can and do say that our sympathies are sincerely and honestly tendered to those who may be interested in what has taken place.

Before the unfortunate tragedy, which culminated in the death of Mr. Plummer, it seems from reliable testimony that Mrs. Plummer had taken a dose of morphine, which eventually caused her death at 2 p. m. In the meantime, while Mrs. Plummer was under the influence of the opiate, Mr. Plummer deliberately stepped before a looking glass, and, with a cigarette in his mouth, places [sic] a Smith & Wesson .38 caliber revolver to his right temple and pulled the trigger—the ball passing from the right [sic] temple to the left [sic], causing instantaneous death. For some time after the tragedy the body of the unhappy deceased lay in the pool of blood, which poured from the wound in the temple.

Dr. Kell, Bedingfield and Cowan were immediately summoned after the fearful deed had been told on the street, too late, however to render assistance to Mr. Plummer, whose death, as we stated afore, was instantaneous, but used their medical skill upon Mrs. Plummer which availed nothing.

Crowds of people, under the influence of curiosity, gathered at the house, but upon Sheriff Moore taking charge the crowd was dispersed, and only those permitted, were allowed to enter the residence, which was the scene of death.

The unfortunates, Mr. and Mrs. Hazen Mitchell Plummer leave three children, namely, Frances, 9 years, Elith,[sic] 6 years and Anna, 18 months old.

Mr. Plummer was about 32 years of age and a native of Bangor Maine, from whence he came in 1891, locating in Mobile, where he remained a few days until he took charge of the British American Trust Co.'s [sic] of this place, afterwards becoming Cashier of the Scranton State Bank, in which position he won legions of friends by his uniform courtesy, and they sadly acknowledge his untimely taking off.

The bodies of the deceased couple were embalmed by a New Orleans undertaker preparatory to removal by their relatives. On Wednesday Mr. Harry W. Plummer from Asheville, N. C., brother of the deceased Cashier, accompanied by his friend, Mr. Edward Stetson, of Bangor, brother-in-law of Mrs. Plummer, who will reach here on Friday Morning.

Friday, April 29, 1898 *The Pascagoula Democrat-Star* **(Jackson, Mississippi) Page 2**

Hazen Mitchell Plummer "A Genial, Whole-Souled, Generous Man..."

While no words of condemnation can be too open or severe for the evil tongues whose accursed gossip struck down an over-proud and sensitive nature, let us cast, as far as possible, the mantle of oblivion over the immediate cause that led to the deplorable tragedy, which has touched and stirred the hearts of this community as they have never been touched and stirred before. Let us think of him as he was—as we knew him—the genial whole-souled, generous man, whose debonair and winning ways, whose sympathetic social character, free from affectation, won the lasting affection of many, the deserved confidence and esteem of all; and whose untimely and – it must be said – unmerited fate has cast the shadow of sorrow over so many hearts, that knew him and appreciated the bright and loving side of one whose career, under other conditions, was destined by nature to be that of usefulness to his fellow-beings, of length and happiness for himself. OH! YE TONGUES THAT GATHER AND SPREAD THE VENOM OF SUSPICION, THAT KINDLE AND FAN THE FLAMES OF JEALOUSY, THAT ENOENDER [*SIC*] THE SPIRIT OF MARTIAL [*SIC*] DISCORD, BE YE NOW SATISFIED AND SILENT IN THE PRESENCE OF THE WRECK YE HAVE DONE SO MUCH TO CREATE!

And now that the bitterness of death hath o'erpowered the bitterness of life, it may be that some justice will not be withheld from the man whose qualities of head and heart will leave no uncertain impress upon the memories of those whose privilege it was to know him best.

E H

April 28, 1898 *The Weekly Corinthian* **(Corinth, Miss.)**

Scranton Banker Suicides – He Shoots Himself Dead and Wife Follows Him by the Morphine Route

Special Dispatch to the Daily Corinthian

Scranton, Miss. April 27 – H.M. Plummer, carbier [sic] of the Scranton State Bank, and a prominent man here for years, fatally shot himself through the head yesterday, at the foot of his wife's bed. A few hours later his wife died of morphine poisoning, self-administered. Both were very prominent in society. Domestic trouble is supposed to be the cause. The banks [sic] affairs are in correct shape.

April 30, 1898 *Sea Coast Echo* Bay Saint Louis, Miss.

Double Suicide At Scranton Tuesday Of H.M. Plummer And Wife, Leaving Three Children.

The Evidence Shows That the Deed Was Carefully Planned- -No Cause Assigned.

Scranton, Miss., April 26 [*sic*]

This morning, about 8:30 o'clock, your reporter was informed by a little boy that Mrs. H.M. Plummer, wife of the cashier of the Scranton State Bank, was dangerously sick and would probably die. The reporter hastened to Mr. Plummer's residence, where he found two of the neighbors, who stated that the bedroom door was locked and someone was groaning inside. Dr. Kell forced open the door, and found Plummer lying of [*sic*] the foot of his wife's bed in [*sic*] a bullet through his brain, the ball entering the left [*sic*] temple, coming out at the right [*sic*].

Mrs. Plummer was in the bed in a dying condition; probably suffering from an overdose of morphine. Seeing that Mr. Plummer was dead, Dr. Kell and Dr. Pedingfield [*sic*] turned their attention to Mrs. Plummer, but without success, as she died at 2: p.m., having never recovered consciousness.

Aunt Mary Beck, an aged and respected negress, is the only person living who was near when the awful tragedy occurred. Her story, briefly is:

"I came here yesterday at 11 o'clock. Yesterday evening Mr. and Mrs. Plummer gave orders that breakfast was not to be got until 10 o'clock this morning, and that the children were to be sent away in the morning to Mrs. Veillon's. I afterwards noticed that all the clocks in the house had been stopped, Mr. and Mrs. Plummer did not seem to have gone to bed, as I could hear them during the night walking [sic] to each other in a civil manner. This morning at 4 o'clock – I know it was 4, as I heard the 4 o'clock train whistling – Mrs. Plummer, came into the room where I was in bed with the children, and crowled [sic] over me and kissed each of the children and then went back to bed.

About 7 or 8'oclock I noticed someone breathing heavily in the room I inquired at the door if Mrs. Plummer was sick and if I should get hot water. He answered. "Yes she is sick; get the water,

433

if you want to." When I brought the water to the door he called out, "Put it down; she will be better in a few minutes." A little time afterwards he came and told the cook to go for Dr. Kell for his wife. He then asked me if the children had been sent away, I answered yes. He then told me not to leave the place but stay where I was. He went into the room and I heard the pistol snap three times. [*sic*] the fourth time it went off and I jumped and ran for the doctor."

Mr. Plummer was about 30 years of age and he and his wife have been the recognized leaders of society ever since they came here, about six or eight years ago. They were both exceedingly popular, numbering their friends by the score, and no cause can be assigned for the awful deed. Mr. Plummer wrote on a small visiting card the following message to Mr. J.I. Ford, vice president of the bank:

"Dear Ford: Keep as much of this out of the papers as you can. For God's sake do not let any sensational story be published. H.M. Plummer, April 26."

Mrs. Plummer wrote on a card a short note to a lady friend, thanking her for her kindness and leaving her a few presents.

May 6, 1898 *The Pascagoula Democrat Star*
Jackson, Mississippi
Funeral of Mr. and Mrs. H.M. Plummer

On Friday last between the hours of 2 and 3 p.m. the obsequies of the two unfortunates were conducted by Rev. H. Bennett, Baptist minister of Moss Point, and the Knights of Pythias, in the presence of a large concourse of people, amongst whom were many whose open sorrow testified to the love and affection which they held for the deceased.

The interment took place in Machpelah cemetery, where one grave received all that was mortal of man and wife, who refused to be separated even in death.

The religious ceremonies at the grave on the part of Mr. Bennett were followed by the imposing ritual of the Pythians, conducted by Mr. R. I. Bullard.

The pall bearers for Mr. Plummer were Messrs. W. P. Ramsay, Fred L. Lindinger, J. W. Allman, J.D. Clark, J. P. Fox and V. Brown. For Mr. Plummer: Messrs. J. A. Miller, W. M. Canty, I. P. DeJean, G. M. Luce, L. D. Herrick and J. W. Stewart.

Requeiscat in pace.

EPILOGUE

Tuesday afternoon, the girls and Aunt Mary stayed next door through dinner, such as it was, with the Veillonses. After the bodies had been removed and the bedroom scrubbed and put to order by Roosevelt and Eva, the children and their nurse returned home to a bedtime snack of cookies and hot cocoa laced with Dover's Powder; Eva's, Aunt Mary's, and Roosevelt's laced with rum. Roosevelt placed the cushions from the sofa in the vestibule and laid himself down for the night, a self-appointed sentry against any further misfortune. The three adults were bereft but gratified to be the ones caring for their babies.

Anna was more querulous than usual but unaware of the catastrophic event. Edie was quiet and weepy, clinging to the two women so dear to her. Frances knew that the recent behavior of her parents was abnormal and held herself accountable for their demise, withdrawing into herself. But that night, she was in that same bed with her sisters and Aunt Mary, on the edge of the mattress, a bit apart, her thoughts going to what had happened behind the closed door across the hallway.

Edgar notified Harry Plummer, Mitchell's brother, who called Edward and Edith Stetson. Edgar offered to begin the funeral arrangements. He told Harry about his conversation with Mitchell about a will and would he like him to contact the lawyer, to which Harry agreed.

When Edgar met with Gerald on Wednesday, he was shocked to learn it was only Monday that the will had been drawn up, leaving everything to the three girls. Mitchell had told him it was months ago. Good God, Edgar thought. It was the day before yesterday. He wanted to berate Gerald. How could he have written someone's will the day before he kills himself? But one look at Gerald's face told him he was just as distressed. Edgar was dumbfounded. Mitchell and May, his best friends, that he loved. Who were they really? He thought he knew them as well as he knew himself. When he read their notes, in particular about them wanting to be buried in the same grave, he nearly fainted.

When Harry arrived on Wednesday afternoon, he checked into the Scranton Hotel, reserving a room for Edward who would be arriving on Friday from Bangor. On Thursday he and Edgar attended to the funereal issues. The burial was to be on Friday. Despite an appeal from their dear friend, William Mead, the Presbyterian Church, his and the Plummers' own church, refused to do the services, as did the other churches in town. Gerald knew a minister who was quite liberal in his thinking: the Reverend Bennett, a Baptist minister from Moss Point who agreed to do the obsequy at the cemetery. Harry and Edgar were moved by the offers of friends to be pallbearers.

The service was held at Machpeleh Cemetery. The two were buried in one grave, as they had requested, on one side of their baby daughter. No stone or marker was placed on their final resting place; only the stone of Sweet Alice marked the plot. After the service, the Cantys invited Edgar, Amelia, Harry, the Meads, the Veillonses, Gerald, and some others to meet in the back of Canty's Store for a few stories and reminisces. Edward arrived in time to join them at the gathering.

Edward and Harry, two old acquaintances from college, now, because of a horrible event, were reunited and united in doing the best for the girls and getting them back to Bangor. One a banker and one a lawyer, they were able to make quick work of what needed to be done for the estate.

Two days later, the family prepared to leave. Edgar had come to the house early to see the girls off. Through his anguish, he somehow was able to tell the girls a Limerick story. More than one, in fact, that told the story of three little girls going to a new place—Bangor, Maine—where, in the summer they could pick blueberries and raspberries right outside their house and in the winter play in snow that would reach to their knees. In fact, Bangor was so close to the North Pole, Santa stayed there when he wasn't delivering his toys. Others, too, in the house listened to the sad man with three little girls sitting on and around him on the sofa in the parlor.

Edgar, Amelia, Eva, and Aunt Mary escorted the girls to the station in a Hansom. Harry and Edward had gone ahead to the station with the luggage. Edgar and Amelia had gathered what they thought the girls might want of their parents' personal effects and let them each choose one to carry on the train. The rest was given in care to Edward, now the head of their family. Someday, hopefully, the girls would cherish these mementos of their parents.

***

Aunt Edith met them in Bangor at the station, her memories of leaving them at the station in Scranton after Alice's birth heavy in her heart. Her sense of foreboding had come true. Her dear sister had not been able to resist her demons, and Mitchell had chosen not to live without her.

Edith fell to her knees when the girls descended from the train. They looked so forlorn— Frances holding Anna with one arm and Edie clinging on-to her other hand. Edward rushed to Edith, helping her up, and moved them all to a bench, where Edith hugged them all tightly. Her familiarity and likeness to their mother eased their tensions, particularly Frances's. She had held herself together somehow, but seeing her aunt, who had been so caring to their mother, sent her into tears. Tears of relief that this role as mother she had assumed for herself might be shared.

***

Alice had never gotten over her dislike of May. Her quickness in becoming pregnant—*so common*—her mental aberrations after Frances's birth—*such weakness in character*—her severe morning sickness with Edith—*surely a sign of a poor constitution.* In time all those deficiencies offended Alice such that they overcame whatever her initial feelings of goodwill toward May had been. When they had moved to Scranton, her relief was palpable.

Except for a check to Mitchell each Christmas—half for him (no mention of May) and the other half to be divided in thirds for the girls' savings accounts—she had severed all contact. She fully believed that May was the cause of all things bad that had happened to her son, and now, their family.

Their deaths—she refused to use the word suicide—unnerved her. Unwanted thoughts about her dire warnings voiced so long ago (could it only be eight years?) scurried through her head. Could her own behavior and treatment of her son and his wife possibly have been the cause of their downfall? This created turmoil in her usually guiltless brain. And now the girls were coming back to Bangor, a reminder to her and everyone else in the city of her own failure. But she had a duty to those girls, as unpleasant as it was; a duty she knew others would expect her to assume. Those children had been raised, who knew how, in the South with a crazy mother; they could all be wild hellions. Only Anna, the baby, might be untainted by the mother.

Alice and Thomas met with the Stetsons the day after Edward had returned with the children. They discussed possible scenarios of caring for the girls. Edith and Edward were prepared to take all three, especially having received the letter Mitchell had written requesting them to take the three girls. Edith knew them, and Edward was the executor of the estate. It only made sense that the girls stay together.

Alice disagreed and firmly declared that *she* would take the baby. Anna, the infant, would be the most labor intensive, and Alice had the means, the room, and the help to raise her. Three extra children, one an infant, was too much for one family to absorb, especially when there was the grandmother in town perfectly able to share the load. Marion was fourteen and would be happy to be a companion for the child. The Stetsons could take the two other girls. Being older, they could help around the house. "It will save you from having to keep a maid." It was all Edith could do to not slap Alice's sanctimonious face.

Thomas, who was mourning his brother and trying to hide his anger at his mother, saw the look on Edith's face. Though he thought his mother's idea ridiculous, he knew how determined she was once she was set on a path. He was not going to publicly oppose his mother. But this might be the perfect time to finally set her straight, in his own way. He interrupted before Edith could reply and reinterpreted his mother's request.

"This way, the girls will still be together in the same town, going to the same schools, and celebrating holidays together," he said. He knew the estate was probably not large. Maybe finally, he could atone for what he had done to Mitchell. "Perhaps trusts for each girl." He avoided looking at Alice who was twitching beside him. Serves her right, he thought. The least she can do for sending her son to his death is to take responsibility financially.

Alice's unrealistic plan of separating Anna from her sisters, thus allowing her to raise the child herself (and erase any hint of May) was a fantasy. One that became patently obvious within the first months. It had been a preposterous idea to begin with, a fact even Alice had to admit to herself. What in heaven had she been thinking? Alice wasn't interested in spending time with an infant; she hadn't even liked her own children when they were babies. Luckily, Marion did a fine job of playing big sister.

Marion and Anna, though, had become inseparable. The girls slept in the same bed, something Alice and the nurse were unable to put a stop to. They allowed it the first month; after all the poor child had just lost her parents. But every time the nurse attempted to separate them, Anna became hysterically distraught, her panic passing to Marion. It was a frightening reminder of May to Alice.

***

Five years later, Marion was nineteen with a busy social life that Alice was enthusiastically managing. It was long past the time for the two girls to be separated. She should have let the Stetsons have her, but how to explain that to others. No, best the child just leave town.

In 1904, when Anna was six, Alice decided that the child should get a real education—at a boarding school—far away. She knew she had to get the Stetsons' support. Despite her own feelings on

Catholicism, she chose the Convent of the Sacred Heart in New York City, thinking it would appeal to the Catholic Stetsons. Sacred Heart was a well-known and respected school for girls, some of whom were boarders.

The Stetsons did not approve of the idea, Catholic or otherwise. The Bangor schools were fine, they said, and the girls were close, despite living in separate houses. They did not need to be separated again. Alice insisted. Anna was incredibly intelligent and deserved this chance. "If Anna is so smart," Edith snapped, "why don't you hire a tutor or a governess?"

Despite her tone, Edith's mind was not closed to the proposal. The past five years had been a trial to her. She had developed arthritis, making it increasingly difficult to get around, and she had heart problems. Two extra small bodies in the house had exhausted her, although both girls, especially Frances, were a great help. The Stetsons left the meeting saying they would get back to the Plummers the next day.

They told Frances, who at fourteen continued to be mature beyond her age and had remained an important person in Anna's life.

Frances had no intention of abandoning her baby sister nor of letting either sister forget their parents and the good memories she told them of repeatedly. Frances was not surprised that Alice would do such a thing. When she and Edie visited their grandmother, ritual quarterly teas that they suffered through, she had formed her own opinion of Alice. Frances knew the woman would not brook any outcome other than what she wanted. If the families decided to let Anna go, she would go with Anna, so she would not be alone. She also insisted on being at the meeting with Alice.

Edith and Edward, with Frances sitting between them, met with Alice and Thomas. Still the estate's executor, Edward told Alice the only way Anna could go was if Frances, at fourteen, went with her. Frances could finish her schooling at the convent then get a job nearby. She would be Anna's guardian, not legally of course, but her companion. Frances boldly faced Alice during this part of the meeting, resulting in Alice looking away.

Edward informed Alice that even though the girls weren't Catholic, because of their situations— being orphaned (he had not divulged the reasons for that state)—and because he was a Catholic in good standing, Sacred Heart had allowed for subsidized tuition rates and multi-child discounts. Edward made it clear in the contract he had drawn up that Alice would pay the tuition for both girls and a place for Frances to live when she graduated.

Frances worried that she and Anna would never see Edward and Edith again. They both reassured her they were still family, that this was Frances's and now Anna's home, and this was where the girls would return on school breaks. Many families sent their children away to school. Why, their own father had gone to boarding school, as did Uncle Harry and Uncle Thomas (though not at six, they couldn't help but think).

And so it was. Anna and Frances left in September with Uncle Edward escorting them. He couldn't help but remember when he had married his Edith, that May had been the same age as Frances was now. In some fashion since, he and Edith had been caring for and worrying over May and her family. He could only hope these three girls could overcome their pasts and thrive.

AUTHOR'S NOTE

Often, while growing up, my cousins and I would wonder about our grandmother, Mammy— Anna Holland Plummer Hoagland. We knew only that she and her two older sisters had been orphaned when they were little children, and we somehow understood (erroneously) that the two older girls had been adopted, but no one had adopted our grandmother until later.

This was a *tragedy*. She was just an *infant*. Why didn't someone adopt the *baby*? How *lonely* she must have been and when she was so *tiny*. Obviously, we grandchildren identified with the injustices done to our grandmother and added our own imaginative frights: She went to a convent...I heard it was horrible there...she did get adopted...finally, when she was older and not a baby anymore...she was alone all that time...did the sisters ever see each other again?

When we asked our parents how our grandmother's parents had died, we each got differing answers, none of which remotely came close to quenching our curiosity (nor to the truth, as it turned out). Our questions were brushed off in hushed tones, so we made up our own stories about their deaths. We took what tidbits of information we had gleaned (or made up) and told stories of their demises. Both parents were killed in a car accident...A train smashed into their car on railroad tracks...It was a murder suicide...It was a double suicide...

In 1974, after Anna had died, my grandfather, Hudson Hoagland, wrote a book about his life, *Road to Yesterday*. He was quite a famous scientist, but I skimmed through the science. I read the first chapter about his life and devoured the chapter about his wife.

"Both parents of my wife, Anna Plummer, died when she was only a year old. She was born in 1896, the youngest of three sisters and was taken care of by her grandmother until she was six. At that time her grandmother died [the only living grandmother was Alice, who died in 1912], and she and the oldest sister, Frances, then fourteen, were sent to the Convent of the Sacred Heart in New York City. Her other sister, Edith, was adopted by an aunt in Bangor, Maine, from whence her family had come...After her grandmother's death the convent, which had the reputation of being a good school, seemed an answer to the question of what to do with the two little orphans...[Later] at the age of thirteen, Anna was adopted by Professor and Mrs. Wendell T. Bush of Columbia University and was their only child. Mrs. Bush [née Mary Potter, mentioned in chapter three] was her late father's first cousin. Her oldest sister [Frances] visited about with the Bush family and her relatives in Bangor, but she was never formally adopted, as were the younger two."

Now, with my new knowledge obtained through my research and especially after I learned through ancestry sites, that the only living grandmother, Alice, did not die until 1912, when Anna would have been 16, it seems that even Anna's husband did not know all the facts about her childhood. Who knows what Anna knew?

I was twenty-seven when I received this book from my grandfather. In January 2008, a cousin emailed a copy of the two shocking articles in the *Pascagoula Democrat-Star*. The deeds were horrifying in themselves, but the lament and emotion in the second article astounded me even more. It was signed by E H. Who was he? Or she? Why such naked, fervid despair? Who was he to them? Were these bad people, sad people, good people, cruel people? Why?

These questions stayed with me, and ten years later, in 2018, after I retired, I started writing this book. I began with the information and dates in the articles from the *Pascagoula Democrat-Star*. Between genealogy sites, family, census records, and newspapers, I was able to put together a true timeline. Though Mitchell and May's timelines and their basic personal information are factual, this story of their lives is not. It is mine.

Most of the characters are real—their names, their births and deaths, their children. All the family characters of Mitchell and May are real except for Thomas and Louise Plummer, John Mahoney, and his parents, Lucy and Sean. Ivan Festair, Mr. English (the detective), Harlan and Winifred Johnson, Amelia, and Mr. Burnsby are also fictional. Aunt Mary Beck is real. All the other servants are fictional, even Eva, though, she is a personification of a friend—a real Eva Ransom, as well as a real Roosevelt.

I assume E H was real, because of his initials at the end of his article in the paper but found nothing about him anywhere. Thus, I used those initials and created Edgar Hamlin, giving him Sweet Alice's true middle name for his last name.

In April of 2019, my husband and I took a trip to Pascagoula. Scranton is no more; in 1904, Scranton and East Pascagoula consolidated into the city of Pascagoula. I stood on Canty Street, on the spot where I supposed their house was. The second Presbyterian Church had also burned down and was rebuilt in a different part of town. Some of the old houses from the 1800s are still standing and there are many signs on other lots, with pictures of the houses that once stood there, which I used to help imagine and describe their home. I walked past where Scranton State Bank, Canty's General Store, and Noy's Hotel would have been on Krebs Avenue. On Delmas Avenue, there is a restaurant named Scranton's, where we had dinner.

We found Machpeleh Cemetery, and with guidance from a kind clerk in the city, finally found Sweet Alice's stone, but no stones for Mitchell or May. I called back the clerk who assured me they were indeed buried there, in the same grave as they had requested, but that in those days it was not uncommon to omit headstones on the graves of suicides. There was a large obelisk-shaped monument near them with the name of John Phillip Smith, the insurance man who helped Mitchell by sharing the cost of the plot with them when Sweet Alice died. I placed an Easter Lily above the lone stone, wondering if we were the first family members to visit the site.

Did Anna do *big things* as Eva had predicted? She married a man who certainly did; he was a famous scientist in the field of neurophysiology. All four of her children were successful, with one son also becoming a well-known scientist. There are sixteen of us grandchildren: teachers, nurses, businesspeople, a boat builder, a shop owner, retailers, and an editor/writer. Some of us are also artists, who now in retirement can spend all their time on their passions, as am I. There are sixteen great-grandchildren forging their own paths and four great-great-grandchildren.

But Anna herself, as Eva predicted, did do big things. In the 1950s, when she was in her late fifties, she took a correspondence course in braille and began transcribing books for the blind. She obtained a brailler and in short time was typing braille with impressive speed and accuracy. She concentrated on college textbooks, and over the next twenty years, transcribed books on history, philosophy, music, math, physics, chemistry, and biology for which she received numerous civic and industry awards.

Did the sisters ever see each other again? They did, and I think more than any of us knew. I remember Anna excitedly telling me once that "Auntie Fran and Aunt Eewee" were coming for a visit (Eewee being the name Anna had called Edith when she was a baby).

Did they talk about the tragedy that so affected them? How much did they remember? What were their feelings about their parents? Did they ever go back to Scranton? To the cemetery? Maybe they had moved beyond it all and just enjoyed themselves as sisters, telling each other stories about their children and husbands and recipes, and books, and... just life.

All three had long and good lives. Frances Bennoch Plummer Seybold had one son and lived to be eighty-seven. Edith Stetson Plummer Hansen had three children and lived to be ninety. And Anna Holland Plummer Hoagland had four children and lived to be seventy-seven.

Once, we grandchildren *did* see the three sisters together. At the wedding of my aunt Joan. A photo shows all three smiling and gracefully aged—Frances, Anna and Edith. The Survivors.

ANCESTRY NOTES

PLUMMERS:

Watson Emery Plummer	1838-1880
m	
Alice Bradford Mitchell	1838-1912
children	
Harry Walter Plummer	1865-?
Hazen Mitchell Plummer	06/09/1867 - 04/27/1898

LOBDELLS:

Ebenezer Thomas Lobdell	1814-1870
m	
Agnes Susan Bennoch	1825-1875
↓	
James Francis Lobdell	1847-1926
John Lobdell born & died	1849
Clarence Lobdell	1852-1899
Edith Holland Lobdell	1857 - 1933
Arthur Lobdell	1859-1861
Mary 'May' Agnes Lobdell	07/24/1864-04/27/1898

Hazen Mitchell Plummer
m 10/12/1887
Mary 'May' Agnes Lobdell
↓

Frances Bennoch Plummer	11/25/1888-1/26/1978
Edith Stetson Plummer	06/06/1890-06/08/1980
"Sweet' Alice Hamlin Plummer	07/20/1894-08/18/1895
Anna Holland Plummer	10/18/1896-05/01/1973

Mitchell's father, Watson, banker, died 1880, Mitchell was 14.

Alice Plummer, married Charles Pond Wiggin in 1882, Mitchell was 16 [ancestry said 1878, but I say 1882, after Watson died in 1880].

Marion Mitchell Wiggin, Alice's and Charles' daughter born 7/22/83, Mitchell was 16.

Charles died 7/9/1889, Mitchell was 23.

Alice died 5/7/1912, in Ashville. [Went to live with Harry?]

Alice's father's first name was Mitchell.

Harry had no children and never married, per ancestry.

Agnes Lobdell, May's mother, only child, originally from Orono, Maine.

Ebenezer, May's father, was from CT. All their children were born in CT, except James, in Boston, MA.

The father, Ebenezer died in 1870, May was 7. I say they stayed in Hartford until 1874, when Agnes took the 2 girls to Augusta to live with Agnes' sister (fictional) Lucy, (named after Agnes' mother Lucretia, real) and her husband (fictional) Sean Mahoney.

Agnes died in 1875, May was 12.

Edith married Edward Stetson in 1879. May moved with Edith to Bangor, May was 16.

In *The Road To Yesterday*, my grandfather says Anna was taken care of by her grandmother until she was six [1904] when her grandmother died. [Alice, the only living grandmother, did not die until 1912, so how could "her grandmother's death" be the

reason she was sent to the convent?] The children's move to Bangor is documented. Once, when Ed

460

Stetson is noted as executor of H.M. Plummer estate of 'Frances Plummer et al' per Pascagoula Democrat Star in 1900. And again, by census data: 1900 Anna, 3, 1910 Anna 13, 1915 Anna 18 living with Alice and Marion. [I question that one]. 1920 census has Anna, 21, living with the Bushes. Edie is documented in the census as living with the Stetsons. Edie's relation category reads 'niece of head' while Anna's says, 'granddaughter of head.' There is no mention of Frances anywhere in the censuses.

Mitchell, May and Sweet Alice are all buried in Machpelah Cemetery in Pascagoula, MS. There are no markers for Mitchell or May, only Alice, which reads Sweet Alice (no last name) 07/20/94-—08/16/95. The burial plot (I-13) was owned jointly with John Phillip Smith (11/13/1850-01/26/1900) who has a tall, obelisk type marker. Per obit, May and Mitchell are buried in the same (unmarked) grave; "who refused to be separated even in death," per the Pascagoula Democrat Star obit on 05/06/1898.

Frances married Robert Francis Seybolt. They had one son, Robert Sherwood Seybolt. Frances died in 1978 at the age of 89. She is buried in Durham, NC.

Edie married Hugo Hansen in 1919. They had three children, Edith Holland Hanson Coors, John H. Hanson and Hugh B. Hanson. She died in 1980 at the age of 90. She is buried in Denver, CO.

Anna married Hudson Hoagland in 1920. They had four children, Mahlon Bush Hoagland, Ann Holland Hoagland Crawford, Peter Hoagland and Joan Hoagland Humphrey. Anna died in 1973 at the age of 77. She is buried in Gloucester (Annisquam) MA.

ACKNOWLEDGMENTS

As this is my first novel, I think it is impossible to ever thank all the people who helped me write this book. But I shall try.

First, I thank my husband Steve Carney, who's talent of sleeping late in the mornings coincides perfectly with my favorite time to write. He patiently supported me throughout this long process, offered suggestions, re-read the many iterations and subtly led me away from the many rabbit holes I tried to go down.

My writers' group, "Writers' Ink" helped me learn to write well. Ellen Mims, former teacher extraordinaire, did two full readings of the manuscript. Other members, Dave Axelson, Deb Anderson, Susan Mallgrave and Jean Callison also offered insightful comments and suggestions.

My sister, Genii Cockshutt, read and edited the full manuscript, offering wise advice. Jonathan Humphrey, my cousin, and his wife Patty were the first to hear me read chapters out loud. Patty, ancestry maven, started the whole process when she sent out the email with the obituaries and introduced Ancestry.com to me. Ethan Humphrey

463

sent me the two photos; all anyone could find. Judy Hauck, my editor cousin, took a stab at what I had thought was my final version, only to send me back, again, to the manuscript.

Johanna Moran, author and good friend, shared her hard-earned knowledge of publishing hell and gave the book a lovely endorsement. Our longtime friend Susan Park, also a manuscript reader, went with us to Pascagoula.

Many people in Pascagoula helped me. Karen Kennedy, City Clerk, gave us a map of the cemetery and verified that Mitchell and May were indeed buried there, without headstones. Tommy Wixson, local town historian and researcher, was particularly helpful, as were Amanda Brooks and Reba Brown at the Singing River Genealogy Local History Library. Stephanie Williams and Linda Cooper, clerks at the Jackson County Archives gave me old photos of the town in the late 1890s (one of which was The Hanging Tree) and let me go through back issues of the *Pascagoula Democrat Star*.

At the Convent of the Sacred Heart, Susan Burke-O'Neal, Victoria Allen and Mary-Elizabeth Schaub all communicated with me, surprised that someone so young had been there. They sent a copy of a page from the school's ledger from 1907, with Miss Anna Plummer written on the top.

Finally, I'd like to thank my son, Jonathan. Despite being uprooted from Miami and plopped down in the woods of South Carolina, he has been a support to me, especially in the early morning hours when he wanders in to sit with a cat and chat a   bit.

ABOUT THE AUTHOR

Alix Crawford Carney has written short stories, on and off, for the last thirty years. *Deplorable Tragedy: A Family's Mystery Answered,* about the mysterious deaths of her great-grandparents, is her first novel.

Originally from Massachusetts, born in Gloucester and raised in Worcester, Alix moved to Miami, Florida where she lived for some forty years. In between her job as an operating room nurse, she traveled to Europe, cruised the Bahamas on a sailboat, renovated an old farmhouse in France and wrote stories.

Now retired, she, with her husband and son and two cats, are enjoying living in the Upstate of South Carolina. And she is finally spending most of her time writing.

Made in the USA
Columbia, SC
14 December 2020